# The Treasure of the Chisos

BOOKS BY JOHN H. CULP

The Treasure of the Chisos
Timothy Baines
A Whistle in the Wind
The Bright Feathers

# The Treasure
# of the Chisos

‹‹‹‹‹‹‹‹‹‹‹‹‹‹‹‹‹‹‹‹‹‹‹‹‹‹‹‹‹‹‹‹‹‹‹‹‹‹‹‹‹‹‹‹‹‹‹

A NOVEL BY

## John H. Culp

*HOLT, RINEHART AND WINSTON*
*New York   Chicago   San Francisco*

TO *Hy*

# The Treasure of the Chisos

# 1

<<<<<<<<<<<<<<<<<<<<

After getting off the steamboat at the wharf in St. Louis from my voyage down the Ohio, I walked up the cobblestones with Father Dore, who wore a heavy cassock. The wide Mississippi with its lighted barges was left behind, then we turned into a poorly lighted alley.

I wore a close-billed cap and knee-length trousers, the way many students of seventeen or so did during the mid-eighties, and I carried my valise. I had straight-up ears and red hair, and in my valise was the telegram the padre had sent.

"I will take that," Father Dore had said, reaching for the valise when first I met him.

"I can carry it," I said. Besides, with my hurried preparations in leaving school, the valise was nearly empty.

By the steamboat and waterfront lights I saw that Father Dore was a short, plump man, with gold-rimmed spectacles; his round face and head, bulging back in the middle, looked like an old moon rising over the water.

"As you say, Colin."

"It was nice of you to meet me."

"Your grandfather is dying. He will not last the night."

The riverfront was perhaps Father Dore's parish, for to save wear and tear on his shoes, he wore iron cleats on his heels; he clicked and threw sparks with every step we took up the rounded cobblestones.

Odd, I thought, a man of God throwing sparks at the devil. Then I put such thoughts aside, for my mission was a serious one.

We entered a shanty, and inside an old man as yellow as parchment lay on a sparse bed. Beside the bed stood a doctor dressed in black, a stethoscope around his neck. The room was almost bare of furniture; there was only a chair and a box or two.

The old man in the bed would have attracted attention anywhere. Even though he was dying, there was something noble about his head and face—the thin high forehead, the aquiline nose. His eyes were closed.

As Father Dore and I moved closer, he opened them.

"Is it Colin?" he whispered to the doctor.

"Yes, with Father Dore."

I had never seen anyone dying this way before, and it startled me. I had not even seen my grandfather for many years.

"You must come nearer," said the doctor. "He cannot see you."

Father Dore took my bag.

As I approached the bed, the old man whispered, "Colin?"

"Yes, grandfather."

"I am glad you are here. I have waited so long."

"I remember before—a long time ago—we sat all day beside the river."

My grandfather, Don Ruiz Herrera, tried to turn his head. "Come closer, Colin, to the side of the bed. I am dying tonight,

2

and there is much I must tell you. But first, come kiss my hand."

And what a hand of fingers it was! As if I held a bundle of dried sticks and kissed it.

Father Dore placed a straight-backed chair near the head of the bed, and the doctor helped turn the old man's head toward me. Already, the blue eyes were dimming.

"Colin, I have never told you about your father. Now I must tell you, and of your family."

The doctor placed his stethoscope over my grandfather's heart and felt his pulse. He turned his head toward me; then spoke to my grandfather.

"You must hurry," he said.

His eyes and those of the priest met; I took my cap off and sat down in the chair.

"I can tell this only once," the worn face said, "and you must listen well. You are the last of the House of Herrera. But your last name is O'Reiley."

"O'Reiley! I am Colin O'Reiley, and not Herrera?"

"It was Coley O'Reiley who stole my daughter from me. You are her son."

Yes, how much I had wondered at school with my red hair what my name really was, and how and why the old man in the shanty had kept me there.

"But grandfather . . ."

"I must talk," he said. "You know now that you are half Spanish. The Herreras were an old family, and came here soon after Cortez. We were granted lands in what was later to become Texas. You may have learned in your studies how it was then —a grant covering the distance a cow could wander during the day, and still come back to water by nightfall. It was so with the boundaries of the Herrera rancho."

My father coughed and a froth came to his lips. The priest wiped it away.

"There were the Sostelos, an arrogant family, but powerful with the crown. They owned a grant adjoining ours. Don Sostelo and I had once been friends, but in our search for gold we had

3

learned to hate, although we still ran cows on the barren land. Gold, and after three centuries!"

I could feel the red hair prickle my scalp. What was I to be called upon to do?

"It was a strange land, Colin. The mountains of the Chisos and the desert wastes north of the Rio Grande had blunted the northern drive of the conquistadores; they staggered and died of thirst. Later, Mexicans moved on one side of the mountains to the pastoral lands of New Mexico, and others moved eastward to become *tejanos.*

"There was our spring—Los Alamos, for which our rancho was named—surrounded by cottonwoods. The Herreras and Sostelos both claimed it; I went into court, but the original grant had been stolen, and I had no proof that I owned the waterhole. Later, after our hacienda had been destroyed by the Sostelos, a faithful servant recovered the grant. Since then I have kept it hidden. But even before the hacienda was lost, there was always gunfire between the Herreras and the Sostelos. And then your father came.

"I remember the day he rode in; he was casual and agreeable, but he wore two guns. He stopped his horse and asked, 'Do you need a hand?' Already he had seen your mother, Violetta, who was in the garden of roses. She was the only reason he wanted a job."

"And he was red-headed?"

"Yes, and your mother was beautiful, and olive like you. I told your father that I needed no help, that the fight for Los Alamos was between the Herreras and the Sostelos. The young man grinned and thumbed his hat back. 'No,' he said. 'The O'Reileys are in the scrap, too. Where,' he asked, glancing at your mother, 'do I stay?'

" 'I will ask that you ride from my hacienda.'

" 'That is your daughter in the rose garden,' he said, swinging his big bay horse. 'Within a month she will be my wife.'

"And within a month it was so. He managed to meet Vio-

4

letta secretly, and by hiding out by day near Los Alamos, he shot down two Sostelo rustlers. Then he and Violetta disappeared. Two weeks later they returned. They had been married, and the first thing your father said to me was, 'I am going to live here. I want my first job.' "

As I listened beside the bed, I would swear a twinkle came to the don's fading eyes.

"Your father cleaned stables for a month and looked after the horses, the useless guns I could have used at his sides, but he always came back for the next job, smiling. I failed to beat him by the work I gave him. He and Violetta lived in a stone hut, but their heads were always up. Then you were born, and soon after that the Sostelos struck. Your father had learned of the approaching raid, and rode to a group of jacals, or huts, to meet Quandaris, their gunman. But he was fatally wounded, and was hidden beneath a pile of straw by other peons. Meanwhile the hacienda was destroyed and your mother killed. Quandaris still sought revenge, but your wounded father rode from the peon hut into the cactus and was never seen again.

"But Don Sostelo still held his power in the courts; I was sick and lifeless from my folly, and took the recovered grant and what little gold remained and came here. I hid you in school and have lived only for this day—this night I die, that you might regain the land of the Herreras."

"But grandfather . . ." I said.

"Bring the chart," he said to the priest. His breathing was heavier now, then suddenly lighter—almost shallow.

"Forgive me what I did to your father, but an old man can grow jealous."

I had often wondered why he had kept me in expensive eastern schools along the Ohio while he lived here in this shanty; I knew now—I was the last of the Herreras, even though in name and hair I was Colin O'Reiley.

The don said as the priest brought the waterproof tube of the parchment, "Come closer, son. I can barely see you."

5

I stood up and leaned over the bed. "What happened to Quandaris?"

"He became a lost man, driven by some fate. No one ever saw him. It is said he hides in Mexico."

Down by the wharf the whistle of a steamboat screeched.

"Don Herrera," the doctor said, after placing the stethoscope over the heart, "you must hurry."

"Hurry," the don whispered. "Yes, I must hurry."

With the parchment brought by the priest—a rolled scroll as yellow as my grandfather's face—he said to me, "This is the grant, signed by a king and queen, and all it surveys is yours. Many things will seem strange to you in the future, but you must face them. Padre," he whispered, "unroll the parchment."

It was a large rectangular sheet with a border of red and black. Under a golden crown there was close exquisite writing in Old Spanish. I was certain of this, for my grandfather had always insisted that I study this language in school. There were old seals and faded ribbons set in wax, and signatures of witnesses.

"The parchment," Don Herrera whispered. "You must keep it forever, and you must prepare for all eventualities."

The thin hand groped for mine, then the tired eyes closed forever.

The next day we buried Don Ruiz Herrera. The padre had brought a coffin in, and it was carried by the good and poor friends my grandfather had made on the waterfront and in the alleys. It was carried to a rise overlooking St. Louis—the Gateway to the West, it was called.

The padre would not consent to my talk of a hearse. "No," he said, "there is little enough money left for you as it is. We will carry the coffin."

After the funeral, as we walked back down the dusty path, we were joined by the King and the Countess, and a more mismatched couple I had never seen. The two had been at the wake the night before with other riverfront dwellers. I had learned then that the King had gained his title because he was a master

6

of the pool and dice tables, although there was never any certainty as to how the Countess had gained hers.

The King was short, rotund and ruddy, of a size with the padre; he wore a plump top hat and a gold watchfob, although more likely than not the watch at the opposite end of the chain might remain in some pawnshop.

The Countess was equally striking; she was six-and-a-half feet tall, gaunt as a rail, with sharp blue eyes and a one-whiskered mole on her chin. She wore an upright feathered hat, as if by her height and hat to appear to be taller than she was and so further ridicule the King's shortness. Her robes were long and flowing, and might have come from a trash can in some better alley elsewhere in town; she was something of a shill, and well-known to the waterfront and police.

Yet despite their dubious characters, the King and Countess had sat faithfully beside my grandfather's body all night.

The Maderas family followed us down the hill, also. The senor and senora, soberly dressed, were dark and part Mexican. They had a pale, shy daughter who was slight and straight, with a slip of light hair which hung covering one eye.

Father Dore and I reached our alley, and those who had followed us went on to other alleys or to their shanties. We entered our own and I sat in the straight-backed chair again. The padre sat at the foot of the bed. I glanced at the pillow; it seemed the old don should still be there.

Father Dore sighed as if the weight of the world lay on his shoulders, then he removed his spectacles, which had become sweaty on the climb, and wiped them with a handkerchief. He patted his round face.

"Colin, do you have money?"

"Only three or four dollars, padre."

"I left the parchment with a priest at the church. Let us go there," he said rising.

We left the shanty and walked up the cobblestones among fierce-whiskered, hide-wearing trappers, late coming buffalo-bone hunters, and newcomers from the East. A log cross sur-

7

mounted the church. Father Dore genuflected. Beyond the wide door, a young priest knelt before the altar. He heard us enter, finished his prayer, and turned his head. Then he stood up.

He was lean, with something almost laughing in his eyes. "Another waif, Father?"

"The parchment I gave you—where is it?"

The young priest produced the tube from the folds of his cassock.

Father Dore said, "The lad here and I must talk. If you have confessionals, we are not to be disturbed. I will be in my cell."

The cell was only an appendage built against the church, its logs chinked with clay. It held a cot, a chair and desk, and a small metal safe. The walls were adorned with pictures of the Savior and saints. A folded checkerboard lay on the safe.

While I watched, the little man went to the safe and unlocked it; he took out a small bag of coins, sprinkling them on the cot.

"This," he said, "is all that is left of your grandfather's money. You must guard it well, for it must pay your way to Texas. But I confess," he said, his plump face worried, "that I do not know how you can carry the scroll. There is much thievery abroad, and your valise could be stolen."

"Let me have the scroll," I said, and unrolled it. It was just as before—the red and black border, the golden crown. Even tightly rolled, it was too long to put into a valise.

I noticed a spool of thin wire on the padre's desk—wire he used to hang the pictures of his saints. The spool reminded me of how we at the school had slipped forbidden candies into our rooms.

"I have it!" I said. "Let me have a piece of wire, and I know I will get the scroll to Texas."

I rolled the scroll carefully, and placed it in its tube; with my pocket knife, I reamed two small holes at the top, opposite each other. I ran the wire through the two holes, then cut it.

While the padre watched, I let my trousers down and stuck the scroll along the side of my leg; when I was hooked up again, I

8

fastened the loose ends of the wire over my belt to a strap of my trousers.

"You see," I told the padre, "the scroll will always be with me. Someone may take my money, but not my scroll or trousers, for I will always sleep in them. By day, my coat or jacket will hide the ends of the wire."

The padre scraped up the scattered gold from the cot. "This is all you have to reach Los Alamos. Do not keep it in the carpet-bag, or all in one pocket. I know the waterfront too well and the long path you must take to your destination. When you see the Chisos—the Misty Mountains—and reach Tornillo Creek, you will be on the old Herrera grant. But place the coins in different pockets, so you will not be robbed all at once."

The next morning, after I had slept on a pew of the church while drunken derelicts from the riverfront came in and out for confessionals, Father Dore said at our scanty breakfast in his cell, "It is strange, but I learned early this morning that the Maderas family and the King and Countess are going south on the same steamboat as you—the *Mississippi Queen.*"

"I did not pay much attention to the Maderases, but I do not understand the King and the Countess."

"Neither do I know much about the Maderases. They have been here only about two months—since the don's illness began." The padre laughed and continued. "The King and Countess have many tricks. Some are very ridiculous. When they lose at gaming, they go out into the smaller towns and sell silver polish. They take their small bottles, buy a box of soda, mix it with water, and peddle the bottles from house to house. The housewife has soda in her own home, but she always buys the silver polish. Sometimes the King may tour as a preacher, or as a salesman of farm items, or hold collections and conversions. Yet even so, he and his wife were faithful to your grandfather."

We heard the hooting of the *Mississippi Queen,* and I rose from the kitchen table.

"Padre," I said, "I thank you."

9

Still sitting, he found his handkerchief and wiped his spectacles. "It is all the will of God, my son."

The last I saw of him from the deck of the *Mississippi Queen* was when he waved farewell from the wharf; then his round face became smaller and smaller until it was nothing.

I did not know, with my grandfather buried, how I could do the task he had set for me. I had a parchment, and I knew only the name of a creek and a range of mountains. I was no gunman, and I had no great knowledge of the West; I could not go to Los Alamos, shoot everyone in sight, and become the master of the old Herrera grant, even though it had been given by a king and a queen.

So on the first day downriver, I stood close beside one of the sidewheels, watching the foaming water and thinking. No matter what I must do later, I knew first that I must free myself of these ridiculous short pants they had made us wear at school. There was a Negro cabin boy about my age aboard who cleaned my stateroom, and I traded him my trousers for his. He said he was too hot in long pants anyway. I kept my coat and jacket, and so had a two-way outfit and looked older.

That afternoon the Countess found me beside the wheel. "Why," she said, fingering her mole and its long whisker, "How surprising! We are on the same steamboat!"

"Yes. I thank you for going to my grandfather's funeral."

"The Lord giveth, and the Lord taketh," she said, her eyes glittering, a purple scarf from her neck billowing all over me. "Did your grandfather leave a good poke?"

"No, ma'am. Only enough gold for passage, and a little over."

"Now don't you worry," she said, her eyes like sudden agate. "The King and I will see you through. Where are you going?"

"To Texas—Los Alamos," I said.

"How surprising—that is where we are going! We will see more of you, young sir."

Then after some small talk about how her soul was always on

the deep waters about us, she trailed away with her scarf billowing, and I began to wonder.

What had she wanted anyway? How large a place was Los Alamos? I had understood it to be only a waterhole with a few jacals, or huts, about it.

Meanwhile, the King had selected his cronies—cardsharpers all—and they had gone up to the Texas for a game. I had not seen Effie Maderas or her parents since coming aboard. Effie was a shy girl and would not want to be alone on deck.

I was tired from my trip to St. Louis and from sitting up all night. Watching the meandering banks of the river slide by didn't help either, so I went to my stateroom for a nap.

As I approached the door, the Negro boy with whom I had traded trousers came out. He was black as ebony and his face and white teeth were a solid smile. "I left you a pitcher of ice water," he said. "It's hot today."

He was neat as a pin in his white jacket and short trousers.

"Did you have a key to my door?"

He laughed, showing his big teeth. "Oh, yes, sir. I have keys to all the rooms. I've been with the *Queen* for years."

When he had gone, I went inside the room and closed the door, leaving my own key in the lock. Then I sat on the bed, thinking. I believed the boy to be honest, but I wanted to be certain.

Before we exchanged trousers, I had said, thinking of not revealing the scroll, "Let me go to the closet. I need a fresh shirt."

In a corner where he could not see me, I slipped the scroll loose and placed it on the floor with the money from my trouser pockets. Then I took a shirt from a hanger and went back holding the trousers.

When we were dressed he said, pulling a hand from my old pocket, "Here's a gold piece you left."

"Thanks," I said. In leaving the closet I had forgotten some of the gold coin, having so many pockets to reach into hurriedly, for I had placed the money as Father Dore suggested. I had left most of the coins on the floor beside the scroll, then had recovered them after the boy left. I had reason to trust him, and later I might need a helper or a confidant of some sort. No, I thought, sitting on the bed and looking at the beaded pitcher of water, the boy would be honest; he came only to bring the ice water.

I poured a glass, drank it, and lay down to sleep.

When I awoke it was with the feeling that someone stood outside my door. I heard movement, then someone moved away. But a scent of delicate perfume continued to flow through the open transom. Perhaps it wasn't important, but with the parchment I was on guard against everything.

Perfume meant a woman, but who could the woman be? Why had she stood at my door?

The only three women I knew on board were the Countess and Senora Maderas and her daughter. It was not likely that any strange woman would have been at the door, and Effie had hardly spoken to me. Besides, she didn't wear perfume.

As soon as I got my wits together, I tiptoed to the door, hoping to see the person. But I was still so groggy from sleep that when I grasped the key I turned it the wrong way; then as I turned it back it clicked and caught in the lock. I stood there completely frustrated, clicking and clicking. I made myself be calm, and knelt and lifted the end of the key, wiggling it back and forth until at last I opened the door.

Nothing was in sight, nor was the scent of perfume in evidence.

I began to wonder if I was more upset about Don Herrera's death than I had thought—if that was why I had become nervous and suspicious.

I returned to the room and straightened my tie in the mirror, then went down on deck. I saw Effie standing against the rail, but before I could go to her I met the King and Countess promenading the deck.

Judging by the King's affability, he had done well at the tables. "Good afternoon," he greeted, lifting his low top hat while

I raised my cap, courtesies which should be performed when two gentlemen meet in the presence of a lady.

"I have done well today," the King said, his eyes bright. "I have done well, thanks to the help of my beloved mate."

"Oh, Mr. Jarvis," the Countess said, raising her high head proudly as if to let her scarf billow farther. "You flatter me."

"Later, we will examine the pocketbooks," the King said. "Good day, young man."

I suspected that the Countess had filched the pocketbooks of some of the gentlemen at the gaming tables, but I went on to the rail and Effie. I stopped beside her.

"I haven't really talked with you on board."

She half turned her head, the light hair blowing across one side of her face. She wore a poor checkered gingham dress, even though she was on one of the most ornate steamboats on the Mississippi.

"No," she said, "I don't talk much."

"Would you go to the salon for an ice?"

For the first time she faced me fully, but the hair still hung over one eye. "Go like this, in a gingham dress?" Tears leaped into her blue eyes, and her face seemed even thinner.

"Then I will bring them here," I said.

But when I came back carrying the ices, she was no longer at the rail. I flung both ices into the river.

But we were to have a gala evening after all. The King and Countess, flushed with victory from another round at the gaming tables, invited the Maderas family and me to dinner in the grand salon.

Never in my life had I see such beautiful lights and crystal chandeliers and mirrors set in solid mahogany frames, or such thick and rich carpeting and bowing waiters.

Mr. Maderas wore a black coat which was not too old or threadbare, and the Countess had so perfumed and decorated Mrs. Maderas and Effie with an excess of veils and scarfs that their poor dresses were quite unnoticeable.

For the first time, seated at the large table and waiting for a

13

course of oysters to be brought up, I studied Mr. Maderas, or Senor Maderas, should he prefer to be called that. I had not seen much of him, and was curious.

In the first place, he was rather short, only a few inches above the height of the King, but his face was dark and broad with more character. He could look at you with veiled eyes, or sometimes with a twinkle. He was not embarrassed by poverty, in spite of the condescension the King showed, or the gold watchfob and diamond stud which the King wore in his tie, or the glass diamond on his fingers.

But poor Senora Maderas! She was not a beautiful woman, but rather stolid and proud; she showed poverty, but she was thoroughly humiliated by the veils and scarfs she was forced to wear. She was an excellent match for her husband, good and reliable, but how did she have a daughter like Effie?

At table, Effie had been placed next to me, and although we conversed at times, never once did she look at me as completely as she had done at the rail.

The King, flushed with wine, nudged his elbow into the stomach of a black-clad waiter.

"My man, do you know how to keep your credit good?"

The impassive waiter said, "No, sir, I suppose not."

The King laughed uproariously, seconded by the Countess.

"When you go into a strange town, borrow five dollars from someone, and say you will pay it back Saturday. Keep the bill in your pocket, and on Saturday go back and repay the same five; thereby you establish credit. The next week you can borrow ten or fifteen dollars, or even twenty-five from the unsuspecting man. You may in time borrow even fifty or a hundred. Soon you can work a dozen people at once, because your credit is good."

The Countess, feeling her whisker, raised her wine glass to her lips and sniggered. "Then after a month you can suddenly leave town, richer by a thousand."

"Pretty good, isn't it?" The King gloated.

The waiter raised his brows and said stiffly. "I see, sir. Yes, it is a very good plan."

14

The King waved an arm graciously. "No charge at all, sir. No charge at all."

I had noticed the quick flicker in Mr. Maderas's eyes, and seen the disgust on the face of his wife.

Effie, who had listened closely, said suddenly, "It is too warm here. I don't feel well."

"Euphemia!" her mother cried, alarmed.

"I will take you outside," I said to Effie, and led her through the tables to the deck.

It was a different world at the prow. The moon was skuddy in its clabber of clouds, and stars twinkled in vacant places. The river loomed like a serpent before the red and green running lights of the *Queen* and the oncoming barges, and steamboats came and went.

Effie said, "You are very quiet."

"I suppose from all that has happened, and meeting you. But you are so aloof."

I didn't think Effie wanted to talk, so we stood at the prow, subdued by the illusion that all the waters of time were rushing toward us. But while we waited, or while I waited if for only a sound from her, a name leaped into my mind—Euphemia.

In the old language her name would have been Euphemia. There were light-complexioned Spaniards, but why would she be called Effie here if her name was Euphemia?

After my remark, her thin face stared straight ahead.

Suddenly she turned, that wisp of hair blowing across her face. "Colin," she said, "it is all very strange to me, too. But I do like you."

Then her lips brushed my cheek; she turned and ran to the upper deck to her stateroom.

I stood there at the prow, my head swimming like an idiot's, with river lights coming and going everywhere. It was like being lost in a world of dizziness; at last I went up to my cabin.

# 2

‹‹‹‹‹‹‹‹‹‹‹‹‹‹‹‹

I was awakened during the night by a scuffle outside my door. I had slept deeply, still fatigued from travel, and the disturbance could have lasted for some time before I was aware of it.

But what made me waken was the banging of flailing bodies against the door, and then a scream of agony.

I leaped from bed and lit the lamp on the table; I turned the wick high, knowing that by the time I had the door opened, the flame would be bright enough for me to see well.

But as I neared the door, what surprised me most was to see my own key on the floor. It had been shoved from the keyhole, and someone had undoubtedly entered my room by manipulating another key, and had been caught on the way out.

The first thing I instinctively felt for was the parchment, since I had fastened it to the belt which I had worn beneath my nightshirt. It was still there, and my coat and trousers were still piled on a chair, but I could see the shirts in the closet scattered about the floor. When I had gone to bed, I had been so excited over Effie's kiss that I had tossed my coat and trousers over the chair, not folding them under the sheet as I had intended, to protect my money.

I pulled the outside door open, and a body lay in the hall. The first thing I noticed was the grimace on the face of the Negro cabin boy. He was as dead as the doorknob above him, with a knife stuck under his heart. About him people were gathering—all I saw while I knelt beside him were many bare feet, or feet in bedroom slippers, and then a stronger light and the long tails of nightshirts. I looked up and saw the faces which had been brought from their staterooms by the commotion.

The captain of the *Queen*, standing in his bathrobe, said, "Son, did you do this?"

"No, sir. I heard a fight. I just came out."

Captain Ferguson was a tall man, with swaths of black whiskers on either side of his face, although his upper lip and chin were clean-shaven.

"He is right," Mr. Wyche, the mate, said. "I was already in the hall when I saw him open the door."

Mr. Wyche also presented his peculiarities. As tall as the captain, he wore a mustache which drooped from the corners of his mouth, but otherwise his face was clean-shaven. I had the odd feeling that his and the captain's heads should be rubbed together, so that only one face would emerge, either whiskered or hairless.

The captain said, glancing at the key on the floor. "Do you have any idea who did this?"

While I was rising from the body and shaking my head, the King appeared in his nightshirt, the Countess in a nightrobe behind him.

"Captain," the King said, "you are beginning a very poor

method of investigation. You should get down to facts." He asked me, glancing past my shoulder, "Did you have any money in your coat and trouser pockets?"

"I had some—to get me to Texas."

The King stepped over the body of the Negro as indifferently as he would have stepped over a dead rodent. Brusquely, he went to the chair where my coat and trousers were thrown. Surrounded by the men in nightshirts, he reached into all my pockets. "No money here," he said.

He passed the coat and trousers around for inspection. He told me, "The black boy stole your money."

"But why?" I asked. "And what was the fight about?"

The King said, "I intend to find out."

"Mr. Jarvis," Captain Ferguson snapped, "you are not in charge of this ship."

"Very well," the King snapped back, "suppose you tell who had the Negro boy rob the young gentleman, and who killed him, and why."

"Mr. Jarvis," the Countess said, floating her veils about, "you are wonderful in your analysis."

"You presume, sir," the captain said to the King.

The King said, "I suggest you search the black boy's pockets, and see what gold he has."

An elegant lady in a nightrobe said, "Can you please remove the poor Negro's body?"

The captain searched the boy's pockets; he found only a single goldpiece. "I gave him that last night," the mate said. "The boy had caught someone in the act of theft and had sought to prevent it. Now he has a knife in his heart."

While the mate and several crewmen removed the body, I flung a coat over my nightshirt, for the wind was up and it became cooler, and I followed the captain forward to the pilot house.

In the distance a gleam of lights shone from the right bank.

"Helena," the captain said. "Upstream from the mouth of the Arkansas. We'll leave the body there to be embalmed and have

18

it taken back to the North—the boy's home—on the next steamer." He told the pilot behind the large wheel, "Dock at Helena."

I went back to my stateroom and sat on the bed and thought. I was completely adrift now, penniless, with only my passage and board paid until I reached Napoleon, the transfer point at the mouth of the Arkansas. After the transfer, what? Or would there even be a transfer? Would I stand in Napoleon and watch the sternwheeler I should have boarded splash its way West without me?

Suddenly I thought of what had happened, and in a new light. There was only one answer—someone, looking for the chart had also picked my coat and trousers, and the Negro boy had come upon him. The lifeless body had proved that.

Did I have a friend anywhere? Could I even tell or trust the King and Countess, or Senor and Senora Maderas and Effie?

The perfume I remembered. When I had been awakened from my afternoon nap, the perfume had been tell-tale through the transom, but before dinner in the salon last evening the Countess had so doused herself and Senora Maderas and Effie from some other bottle that there was no resemblance to that I had smelled before.

I went back to bed and spent a miserable night—or what was left of it—haunted by sudden nightmares; Effie drinking whole vats of perfume, the Negro swimming backstroke up the river and laughing with a knife sticking from his stomach—yes, the knife stuck from his stomach, not his heart. Then I was being caught in a paddlewheel and whirled around and around.

Despite the furies of the night, I climbed out of bed at daybreak, quite sane and with a good appetite. I knew I had something to do, and wherever the Chisos Mountains were, I would find them, no matter how long it took or what else might happen.

Perhaps it was the resilience of youth and the task at hand which made me feel well, in spite of the obstacles.

As I walked through the plush drapes of the salon doorway

for breakfast—for I still had two meals coming from the *Queen* before I reached Napoleon—I was grabbed by the Countess and the King.

"My poor boy," the Countess said, holding me all over, "what a tragedy last night!"

The King extended his fat hand. "My boy, you have our sympathy. We will discuss your future at the breakfast table."

I saw Senor and Senora Maderas and Effie at a table; I would have preferred to eat with them had I been invited, but now it was too late.

We took our table and the King ordered ham and eggs and chilled watermelon cubes and coffee. While he ate ravenously— and the Countess with great affectation—he said, "There is nothing now but for us to put our fortunes together. We are all going to Los Alamos—the Countess and I will see that you arrive safely."

"You forget," I said, "that I do not have a fortune—in fact, I do not have a penny."

The King smiled jovially, while the Countess beamed her approval. "Forget it," the King said. "What are a few dollars between friends? But if you wish, you may pay me back at leisure."

It was then that one of the odd moments of my life occurred. Two waiters had jumped ship at Helena; a deputy had assured the captain that a search would begin at daybreak with the hounds to seek and investigate them for the black boy's murder.

Perhaps the ship-jumping waiters were the cause of the captain's adding a red-headed cabin boy to the staff for such duties as refilling the coffee cups, bringing extra silverware, and upsetting things in general. I had seen the boy at a distance, but had paid no particular attention to him.

I have told you something of my personal appearance—that I am olive-complexioned with a crop of red hair—but I have not overly stressed my ears, which are large and rise to an extremely elongated point. Sometimes I call them my ass's ears.

Imagine my surprise when, without knowing that the boy with his steaming coffee pot was near me, he suddenly and awkwardly stumbled against my chair, the hot coffee pouring from the spout upon my trousers.

I half rose, grasping my wet trousers and holding them from my leg, meanwhile gazing down at the face which was half on the table before me. Never had I seen anyone so like myself. There were the ears, and the same hair, but while my complexion was olive, his was paler and heavily freckled, as if it had received a bucket of stars tossed into the night.

But those ears!

It was as if two donkeys, walking in opposite directions around a haystack, had suddenly come upon each other, and each saw for the first time what a donkey looked like.

"You sure made a mess of me," I said, looking at the sprawled figure and still holding my wet trousers away from my leg.

Then the second surprise came. While the boy remained in the same position—half prone upon the table—his back to the King and Countess, his left, or lower eye, closed in the most prodigious and excruciating wink I had ever seen. The right opened wider, and in it was what I can only describe as a message, the freckled face all screwed up in the agony to express itself.

It was a message first of understanding, then caution and alliance.

The redhead shoved himself from the table, his expression seen by no one but me. His elbow had been in my eggs, and he looked as bad as I.

Somehow he had held on to the coffee pot. Now he placed it on the table, seized a napkin, and began to wipe and dry my leg, meanwhile saying what was obvious to all, "I tripped, sir. After your breakfast, I will take your trousers and have them cleaned."

"I'll be in my stateroom," I said shortly.

As the boy backed away from the table, he continued to look at my ears and hair, and I at his.

"How catastrophic," the King said. "You should have hided him then and there. But you are enough alike to be twins."

Another waiter brought me a second full plate, and I enjoyed a good breakfast.

"We were saying," the Countess spoke, gazing at the King

and then at me, "that you must make the rest of your trip with us. You cannot be alone, hungry on some river or lost in a desert. Perhaps the Lord has put us here for a purpose."

It was about nine o'clock before that red-headed jackass came for my trousers. I had already put on my bathrobe and the scroll was in place.

I heard the knock on the door, and called "Come in."

As soon as that apparition entered, I got up and looked at myself in the mirror. There was no doubt about it—I was the other donkey coming around the haystack.

I turned, and motioned him to a chair. He sat, freckled and grinning.

"What is your name?" I said.

"Meander O'Reiley."

"O'Reiley?"

"You don't think you're the only O'Reiley on earth, do you?"

"Not as long as I see your ears."

Meander grinned. "I'm your cousin."

"You'd have to be," I said, "but I need a dozen. Where did you get that name, Meander?"

"It's like this," he said. "When I began coming along, Ma looked in the family Bible for a family name. She found one she liked, but Pa said the old writing was smudged and it should be Leander. I was late getting here, so they named me Meander."

"That was a good act you put on in the salon. Why?"

Meander grinned again. "My dad moved into the Chisos country two years after the old Los Alamos hacienda was burned. He's always been at odds with the Sostelos, and when he learned that your old don was dying, he sent me here to see you back to Texas. Something might have happened to you."

"But where have you been hiding? I didn't think you knew any of these people going to Los Alamos."

"I didn't hide, but Pa—he's your Uncle Michael—said to keep away from the don, or from anyone who might suspect something. The don must have sent word of something. Anyway, Father Dore got me a job on the *Queen,* since he knew your grandfather had arranged passage for you, and he said when you came aboard I'd know you. I've been watching you like a cowhand watches a hydrophobia skunk, only you didn't know it."

I didn't care to be likened to a skunk, but I'd let myself be called anything if it would save my hide, since the matter of the scroll was getting larger and larger.

"How did you get that snaggletooth?"

"The mate was teaching me how to pilot, but the dang wheel got loose and one of them spokes hit me in the mouth."

"This Quandaris," I said, "the man who killed my father. Where is he?"

"Lord knows. Always running from something down in Mexico. He'll take a jacal in some village, stay a month, then he's off again."

"Do you know the Maderas family?"

"You mean the ones with the daughter? No. Remember, I've been working up and down the river on the *Queen* until you came along."

"What are you really looking for?"

Again, that freckled grin. "Just getting you home. Well, give me those trousers. I'll have them back in no time. I'll have a stoker dry them after washing." At the door his face screwed up in an ironic grin. "Good-bye, cousin."

So after Meander's visit I knew two things—I did have a friend I could trust and an uncle I hadn't known of, even though he was a thousand miles away. Yet my uncle must have had some good reason to send Meander here, and I thought it odd that both the Maderas family and he had arrived in St. Louis at the same time—about two months ago.

In mid-afternoon, before we reached Napoleon, Effie came to me at the rail. This time she talked.

"What will you do now, Colin?"

"The King and Countess want me to go on with them, and Meander, the cabin boy, says the captain of the *Queen* will put in a good word for us when we reach the sternwheeler at Napoleon. Maybe we can work our way up the Arkansas to Fort Smith, then strike south or southwest on one of the old military roads."

She turned her head, that hank of hair blowing. "I don't want you to do that." Her skin was almost translucent.

"Why?"

"Something—a feeling—has made me afraid. I want you to be with us. My father and mother wish it, too. They don't trust the King."

"But I haven't a penny in the world."

"I have no money, Colin, or I would give you some. Senor Maderas has it all."

So here was another thing for my disturbed mind. A moment ago, Effie had called the Maderas couple mother and father—now, had she lapsed back into some Old World formality, or was the first or second naming a mistake, a slip of some sort?

"I couldn't take your money, anyway," I said.

She turned to leave, saying, "I must go upstairs to pack for the transfer."

She was so small and slight that a good wind might have blown her across the deck.

It had become my suspicion that Father Dore had told the captain of the *Queen* far more about Meander and other circumstances than Meander himself knew, and remembering the old don's last words, that many things on my journey would seem strange to me and I must prepare for all eventualities, I accepted my fate with patience and waited for the landing at Napoleon. Once a busy town had been there, but it had been washed away by flood. Now a temporary supply shack stood on the point, and a few floating docks were tied together.

When we reached the place, the King and Countess set out immediately for the grog shop and gaming tables which were set up on one dock—a thing something like a large raft. The King preceded the Countess across the narrow plank.

My earlier thought was proved correct when the *Queen*'s captain took Meander and me to meet the captain of the little sternwheeler which was to take us up the Arkansas.

As we boarded the craft, I noticed a slender, nonchalant young man who leaned against the superstructure with his captain's cap at a raffish angle, a coil of rope at his feet. He wore a pistol in his belt. When we reached our position before him, he still had not moved, and it was then that I first saw his eyes.

They were pale blue and almost veiled, as if a curtain hung before them to hide his thoughts. No one could mistake their penetrating shrewdness; I felt they knew my every thought, and Meander's, too. What struck me next were the humorous creases at the sides of his mouth, and there was a suggestion—I repeat, a suggestion—of recklessness about him, but also one of honesty.

"Captain Ferguson," he said at last, still leaning against the superstructure as he extended his hand to the *Queen's* commander.

"My compliments, Captain Vale," said Captain Ferguson, extending his own hand.

"I suppose," Captain Vale said, still not moving from his indifferent position, "you have brought me two lads to work passage to Fort Smith."

"I will vouch for them, sir." Captain Ferguson's eyes twinkled. "Where is the *Dewdrop?* Do you carry a cargo for her?"

Captain Vale said, the corners of his mouth whimsical, "A partial cargo, sir. The *Dewdrop* waits at Fort Smith. Whiskey wagons will meet us above Fort Smith, then after the loading at the old Choctaw Ferry on the Poteau, I'll run the *Dewdrop* into Indian Territory and the mouth of the Illinois. The Cherokee bootleggers will meet me there."

So that was it—we were to go up the Arkansas to Fort Smith aboard a whiskey-runner.

Captain Ferguson said, as he must have said many times before, "Why do you persist in this traffic, Captain?"

The young man laughed aloud. "As I've told you before, for the sheer joy of it. I like excitement."

"You could in time become a mate or a captain on the *Queen's* line."

"But where would my pleasure be?"

Still without moving, Captain Vale assigned our duties. We were to throw wood or coal into the furnace, keep the fire stirred, keep the machinery oiled, wash dishes, scrub the deck, make beds, empty slops, and do a few other things. "Eight-hour shifts, staggered," Captain Vale added. "I don't want you boys too much together. When I say work, work. Agreed?"

We nodded.

"You are my witness, sir," Captain Vale told the *Queen's* captain.

"You will visit me on the *Queen?*"

"Immediately."

As Meander and I walked to the side with Captain Ferguson, he said, glancing where Captain Vale still leaned, "Do not try to jump ship or do anything to doublecross that man. He is gentle, and faultless to a point, but one unfaithful act on your part, and he will follow you forever for revenge. He'll ride you down like the hounds of hell. I have known him to do it to others, although it might take months or years."

We had also been given another task—in our spare time we were to catch fish for the captain's table. Since we had not been given anything to do for the present, and since fishing was least objectionable, the first duty we took was that, sitting on the deck cross-legged with our hooks hanging over the side, although in the hubbub of the transfer and the raucous sounds from the floating grog-shop, no fish would stay within a mile of the place.

I was still interested in Captain Vale and the *Dewdrop*. "What is this *Dewdrop?*" I asked Meander.

"A little shallow-draft scoot that draws about a foot of water. Captain Vale says she will float on a heavy dew. That's why she's good for hiding in creeks at the bootleg camps."

When our hooks were good and wet after an hour with no luck, the Countess came across the plank to the sternwheeler. She went at once up to her stateroom, if the cubbyholes of the sternwheeler deserved the name. Within a few moments a dozen empty wallets flew over our heads into the water.

26

"Oh, oh," said Meander. "She must have done some good behind the tables."

For a moment the wallets bobbed like corks in the water, nodding at each other as if becoming acquainted, then they all slithered downward zigzag and sank.

When the King returned, he was ebullient and in good spirits. He came to where we sat with our poles. "My cup runneth over," he said, even his coat pockets bulging with gold coin. "Never have I had such luck, a veritable string of luck."

Yet when the passengers and crew came aboard, there was much animosity expressed toward the King. Almost every man had a scowling face.

A determined little man in a string tie confronted the King. "Sir, you have won my wedding band. I do not say that it was not won squarely, but I want it back. What can I do to get it?"

The King, cognizant of the muttering crowd, emerged from the difficulty adroitly.

"Do?" He laughed heartily. "Do? Why, absolutely nothing." He reached into his vast pocket. "Here is your ring, sir. Your company was a pleasure." He wagged his finger wisely. "But I suggest you do not tell your wife what you did."

The King felt in an opposite pocket. "I declare," he said, "another wedding band. Now, gentlemen, which of you lost this one?"

A tipsy crewman came forward. The King laughed. "My friend, you have not learned the holy state of matrimony. Until you do, I would never gamble again."

The King's gesture of magnanimity put another face on the matter; the crowd was still sullen after its loss, but the scowls disappeared, and a few of those who had fallen to the King's wiles nodded approval at his gesture.

The Countess had joined the King. "My dear, giving the wedding bands back was wonderful."

The King said solemnly, "There is nothing from the Lord like the gift of a good wife. As a lad, I led a sheltered life. I did not

27

leave home until I was thirty-one. Then I stepped into a passenger car and tripped on a brass cuspidor, falling into the arms of the woman who was to become my own wife. I have never regretted it, my dear." He patted her hand. "What," he asked Captain Vale, who had returned from a visit to the *Queen,* "is our menu for the evening?"

The captain grinned. "Sowbelly, cold boiled potatoes, cabbage and sourdough."

"Not at all," the King said. He selected a crewman, giving him some gold coins. "My man, bring back all the delicacies from yonder shack, which I believe is a store; bring good meats and a case of whiskey for all the gentlemen present."

The crewman struck out for the supply shack. It took two other crewmen to bring the King's food and drink back; that evening there was a sumptuous repast at the tables which were set under the superstructure.

But Meander and I were not to share the meal; we had been jerked summarily from our fishing poles to serve as waiters under our ass's ears. The wines and whiskeys flowed; the gamblers, their past animosity forgotten, filled themselves full and started games of their own in the glare of lanterns and flaming pine knots.

The King, I noticed, wisely decided not to participate. Next morning the gamblers were angry with each other, but seemed to have forgotten the King.

But during the dinner at the captain's table, I had not waited on Effie a single time. I left that for Meander to do, for Effie had come to the table with one of the Countess's scarfs about her throat, and had hardly glanced at me. Perhaps this was not one of her speaking evenings.

She had sat through the meal silent and thoughtful; on the Mississippi she had wanted to lend me money; now I was a complete stranger. When the dinner was over, it was almost with relief that I saw her go up to her cubbyhole beside the Maderas's.

Meander and I had slept that night rolled in tarpaulins under the superstructure; at daybreak we awoke yawning and chilled.

Then we had another rude awakening—Captain Vale came toward us. He stood over us and said, "We put out in an hour. Begin your regular shifts now. You'll see a little of each other, depending on how the clock changes."

So it was like that all the way up the Arkansas to Fort Smith —whining steam sawmills under the trees, small towns along the banks, and people on cotton farmlands stopping their picking to wave as we passed. We saw Little Rock and Dardenelle Rock and Mount Magazine and stopped at the mouth of Piney River, with its sawmills and lumber barges. Then the big bend as we neared the mountain at Van Buren, and a few miles later we touched Fort Smith.

Meander and I hadn't minded our work. Our staggered shifts did mean that we saw something of each other day or night, and it would be hard to say which was prettier to be in.

By day there were all the autumn colors on the warm hills, red and orange and yellow, but always touched somewhere by distant greens of pines or cedars.

At night frosty stars hung in a cold sky, and we listened to the solitary clunking of the paddlewheel. There were dawns, gauzy and misty, with rolling fog, wide glints of sand, or a thin ribbon of river, its banks now close, now vanishing.

Black-clouded, clabbered nights, no light at all but our red and green running lights and the flaming pine knots in the iron cage at the bow—our own small circle of light—but by day always other people in the changing fields waving us onward.

And whiskey stills up every shimmering creek, where we loaded cargo in gallon fruit jars and shoved them under the deck flooring.

And Effie on my mind every minute, day or night, and in everything I looked at.

# 3

‹‹‹‹‹‹‹‹‹‹‹‹‹‹‹‹‹‹‹

In Fort Smith we located at a place near the Rogers Hotel on Washington, or Second, Street a couple of blocks from the river; we put up on the King's gold, of course. The log hotel had a wide hall and a stone fireplace at each end, and a railed-in office.

But among the passengers and crew which we had left behind still remained the matter of the King's big winnings at Napoleon.

The King had been astute in not playing his card games on the sternwheeler. Only once had he done so, and that after a professional gambler had boarded the sternwheeler at Little Rock. The sternwheeler's gamblers had quickly lost what little remained to them; now they had looked to the King for succor and revenge.

Only then had the King said, bobbing his head to the gambler, "May I sit in, sir?"

He had taken a dozen hands in succession; his former opponents had clapped his back roaring in triumph for his upholding the honor of the ship, but still, in some minds, a nagging uncertainty prevailed. A few die-hards had decided to test the King against the Fort Smith gamblers, some of whom had come from the luxury sidewheelers of the Mississippi after the days of the great river clean-up.

Meander had told me of this decision, which he had overheard while scrubbing the deck near a dice game.

Although it was inevitable that the King must face his showdown, Meander and I faced our own problem. We were perhaps one-third of the way to the Chisos, and it remained to be seen how we would get there.

We got along well, and we had debated whether to strike out shanks mare or take the next means which came our way. We might at least leave Fort Smith with some wagon train moving south or west. Either direction would be fine; the mountains lay almost due southwest.

Yet we had not conceded that we were certain of going so far a distance—almost to the Rio Grande and Mexico—with two such questionable characters as the King and Countess.

In a conversation with quiet and imperturbable Senor Maderas, he had suggested to us that the entire party continue onward together for greater safety in the wild lands we would enter. This would not be bad, provided the King and Countess could be trusted.

However, Meander and I considered our own decision best, and next morning before breakfast we walked the cobblestones of Second Street and turned up the rise toward the corner—Texas Corner, it was called—where for decades wagon trains had made up.

The street had once been the drill ground for soldiers; it was wide, and now flanked by store fronts and saloons.

But times had changed. Only a few wagons were in the plaza,

not the hundreds which might have been there twenty or thirty years ago in the days of the forty-niners and homesteaders, all pushing west.

Among the hitched wagons was a rope corral which held a dozen horses. An old man in boots and a slouch hat sat under a sign, chewing tobacco and whittling on a stick. The sign read UNCLE HANK—FINE HORSES. Now and then Uncle Hank drank from a bottle he took from his boot.

Meander gave his freckled grin. "If we could steal one of those horses, we'd sure get to Texas. That bay looks like good bottom, and that sorrel over there could travel."

"Sure, we'd get to Texas, if the rope on the tree would swing that far."

Meander grinned again. "You don't want a horse, and you don't want a wagon. What's really on your mind is going on with Effie."

"Maybe you're right."

A sideswipe of a norther hit the town while Meander and I looked at Uncle Hank and the horses. The animals turned their rumps to the wind; the air chilled; a few spits of snow came down, enclosing the corral. During the nights on the stern-wheeler we had learned how much cooler the weather had become; nightly the November rise of the Little Dipper and Orion was higher, and above them, like a sprawling old woman stuck in her corset, Cassiopea waited.

With the norther whipping sand and dust in our faces, and now snow, Meander and I walked back down the street, helped by the wind.

"You know," Meander said, pulling his head into his shoulders and shivering, "I've known cows to freeze to death in twenty-six degrees—they just weren't used to cold."

When we reached the hotel, the King had just finished his breakfast; he was surrounded by a delegation which had come from one of the uptown hotels to suggest a few card games during the day.

The King was greatly flattered. So was the Countess, who gave him the last penny from her handbag, and went out into the blow with him, the winking delegation following.

We had our own breakfast, then joined Senora Maderas and Effie where they sat before the spluttering fireplace, Effie impatiently tossing that little mane of hair from her eye when we joined them.

"It looks to me," Meander said, propping a boot upon the andiron, "that the King is ready to be took."

"It is not surprising," Senora Maderas said. "Sooner or later, someone would find him out."

While we sat comfortably, listening to the wind, we wondered more and more what was happening at the King's game. Then the heavy front door flew open, and in gusted the Countess. She went immediately up to her room. No one wondered why she went there. It would be another matter of wallets.

At last the Countess came down the stairs, her veils and scarfs listless. She said, "I am afraid for the King. Each wallet I took at the Le Flore held only cut-up newspaper; I wonder if we are suspected. And to think, I gave the King all my money!"

She sat pensively, her nose as angular as ever, picking her whisker.

While I watched her, I determined that Meander, while not as well educated as I, did know the country we were going into. It was then that I made up my mind to be ready to follow his lead in case of something unforeseen, for so far everything had been this way.

We had a bountiful lunch on the King's account at the hotel, all but the Countess, who ate sparingly, then I left alone and walked the streets of the waterfront. I was curious for information. I talked with Choctaw Indians and Cherokees, gathering all the information I could of the country to the south and west. I learned the location of the Choctaw Ferry at the mouth of the Poteau, of the paths which led there, and the roads which would take us into Indian Territory, and the best way south down the Arkansas line to Texarkana and into Texas.

If we followed this line we would head for San Antonio and the land south of the big plateau and the hill country of Texas; if we crossed the Territory and went through the reservations of the Civilized and Plains Indians, we would, after turning south, pass to the right of the plateau and then be in the cactus and desert lands of the old Comanche trails, from waterhole to waterhole into Mexico.

Anyway, it looked as if we wouldn't have wild Indians trailing us, although we might be followed by a few angry white citizens.

But there was no use now to worry too much which route we took unless we could get safely out of Fort Smith, and I confess that I thought of the possibility of the King, and even Senor Maderas, being ridden out of town on a rail, after first being tarred and feathered.

I returned in the wind to the hotel.

The King had not yet appeared; the Countess tried to be courageous, wearing a new set of scarfs and veils. I could not help but be sorry for her. Poor soul, how she needed comfort!

At last she said to Senor Maderas, "I know it now—the worst has happened. Since I am without money, may I borrow twenty-five cents from you to buy some of Dr. Hostetter's Stomach Bitters? I am sure my husband will be upset when he returns."

She went out for the bitters, then borrowed a spoon from a waiter. She took her seat by the fire again, and sat waiting, holding the bottle. She went upstairs, then came down again.

It was mid-afternoon before the King returned. We were sitting in the lobby, listening to the wind. Effie had just whispered to her mother, "The Countess has packed her carpetbag, and the King's," when the door of the lobby opened.

The King stood there, like the ghost of a dead man. His eyes stared dully, his jowls sagged in creases. The gold watchchain across his chest was gone, and so, I suppose, was the watch. The glass diamonds on his fingers were also missing.

Whatever her dubious character might have been, I could not but admire the greatness of the Countess. She rose, taking the King by the hand as she might a child, led him to a seat beside the fireplace, then knelt beside him.

"How did it happen?" she asked.

The King, speaking from a stupor, said, "After I had lost almost everything, I tried to palm a card. But they were too shrewd—they all knew it."

"Yes," the Countess said. "Their wallets were all filled with paper. The gamblers suspected us from the beginning. Let me give you some of Dr. Hostetter's bitters, my dear, and you must have tea."

Then the Countess hesitated. We all knew now that neither she nor the King had a cent of money—not even for tea.

The King muttered, his head in his hands. "There is talk of a necktie party tonight."

Senor Maderas said, rising, "You, sir, have befriended me and my family. I will look after the tea and other matters at the desk, but our twenty-four hours will be up at six o'clock. Order the tea as usual, Senora."

The Countess summoned a waiter; the King sat as if stricken with ague, his teeth chattering like the tea cup in its saucer. He spilled tea on his coat, and the Countess wiped it away. I thought the King was having a stroke.

While the King slowly recovered under the ministrations of the Countess, a piping shriek rode the wind.

"Captain Vale's *Dewdrop!*" Meander said. "Listen to her whistle!"

"That little whiskey-runner," I said.

Meander said, "Let's go."

He knew I wanted to talk as well as he, but perhaps for different reasons. We threw on our jackets and walked the lower street to the river. Snow was still whipping, and clouds were darker.

Meander said, reading my thoughts, "If there is a necktie party tonight, or a tar-and-feathering, we ain't got much time. How come you think the burden of saving them is on us?"

"How came you to think of it?"

Meander grinned in the spitting snow. "Effie."

At the river, we saw the *Dewdrop* pulled near the stern-wheeler. She was slim and light, clean-lined and shallow on the water, drawing not more than the foot they said she drew. Captain Vale was walking about the deck, clad in a buffalo coat. We hesitated at the plank.

"Come aboard," Captain Vale shouted.

"He looks like a grizzly with the hair left on," Meander said. "You ain't got this whiskey-runner wired with dynamite?" he asked, stepping up the plank. At almost the same moment the sternwheeler we knew so well pulled from the bank into the channel, looking like a ghost ship in the snow.

Captain Vale said, the crinkles at the corners of his mouth alive, "Why should I have the ship wired? Come back to the superstructure and we'll be out of the blow."

Meander said, "I thought you'd wire it to destroy the evidence."

Captain Vale said, "The Indians at the mouths of the rivers will destroy the evidence."

I asked, "Where is the sternwheeler off to?"

The captain leaned back against the superstructure. "Since we are old shipmates, I'll tell you. It goes to the Choctaw Ferry, and my whiskey wagons will be on the bluffs at dark. I'll take the *Dewdrop* up a little earlier and have the liquor transferred from the wagons and the sternwheeler. Then I'll be off into the night. I didn't want any suspicions aroused here by unloading from the sternwheeler. I've heard the King is in another great game."

"Some of the town gamblers are at the Le Flore."

"Yes, I saw the party leave. If you intend to travel with the King, watch him closely."

I wanted to ask Captain Vale if there was any way our entire party could board the *Dewdrop,* but I knew he would not want us seen on board, especially if the trouble we feared might develop. Meander and I left the *Dewdrop* and went back to the hotel.

When we entered the lobby we found the King almost recovered; he was trying to learn from Senor Maderas how much money he had, but was making scant headway. Yet occasionally he licked his plump lips and looked at the clock.

The way Meander and I felt after we talked things over at the opposite fireplace, there wasn't anything for us to do but get everyone out of the hotel before six o'clock, hoping the lateness of the year and the snow would help make us invisible. Even with the bad weather some hardheaded bunch might still come for the King; we didn't want ourselves or the Maderas family involved.

We might meet the captain at the Choctaw Ferry, where it wouldn't matter who saw us board the *Dewdrop*. But escape, at best, might not be easy. If we followed the Arkansas line to Texas, some Arkansas or Texas deputy might be waiting for us at Texarkana. That left only the Territory for certain—or at least much more certain than going south through Arkansas.

While Meander and I sat by the fire we saw the desk clerk talking with a flashy gambler. The King and the others had gone to their rooms.

"No," the clerk was saying, "they are in their rooms now. They are paid for until six o'clock, and I can't put them out until then. I do enough for you gamblers, so don't come down here breaking my furniture up."

The gambler grinned. "We'll make it right after six."

Meander was squirming in his seat. The clock over the fireplace said five. Meander stood up. "Think I'll go outside and walk around a bit."

"Good," I said. "That will let me think."

As soon as Meander left, I went upstairs. I knocked on two doors, and found the rooms empty; in the third room I found the King and Countess and the Maderas family in serious conversation.

Poor Effie seemed frightened to death. It was the only time since I had known her that she seemed genuinely glad to see me. The King had returned to his half-stupor.

"Listen," I told him, "they're coming for you at six o'clock, snow or no snow, as soon as our time runs out. Put all you've got in your carpetbags and be ready to move. There's that old rattletrap fire escape down the back where no one can see you leave. At about fifteen till six come down the escape and I'll have horses for the women. I'll tell you the rest later."

The King's lower lip puckered as if he would weep; the Countess caressed him, and I left the room.

It was a cold walk back to Uncle Hank's horse corral, and as

I shouldered into the snow I was surprised at how quickly I had absorbed certain characteristics of the West—I was to become a horse thief.

At last I stood at the edge of the plaza and sized things up, backing against a covered wagon to keep the wind broken. Inside the wagon a baby cried, and I heard its mother singing.

I could barely see the church spire up the rise; in the November darkness only one fire blazed on the opposite side of the plaza within a ring of wagons and tents.

The sparks of the fire kept blowing, but I saw no one around it. I didn't see Uncle Hank at the corral, but his fine horses still stood, their rumps to the wind.

How did you steal a horse?

I lay down flat on my belly beneath a wagon and thought. I'd ridden at school, and knew a little about them, but stealing was different. Steal them Indian style, creeping toward them on hands and knees, cutting the ropes and driving the whole outfit with a war whoop?

"You durn fool," a voice said. "Get on your feet. Uncle Hank ain't here. We'll walk to the corral like we owned the place. We'll get what we need."

I stood and that snaggle-toothed grin faced me. "How'd you get the same idea?" I said.

"We're cousins, ain't we?" Meander said. "We know things."

"Then where would you take them?"

"Me? Just like you—up to the mouth of the Poteau and to the Choctaw Ferry. Then we make reservations on the *Dewdrop.*"

So we walked boldly up to the corral as if we owned the place or had been sent there, and I learned that Meander knew far more about wild horses, or just horses, than I.

He climbed through the ropes slowly, then stood up and patted the sorrel and bay, and did a little scratching behind their ears. He turned and grinned. "I've been thinking of one for Effie. I think that little pinto will do, but if we take more than three it will be noticed too soon."

So it happened just as simply as that—me just standing there,

38

and Meander making every horse in the corral want to come with us. "This ain't theft," he said. "It's just making friends." I could hear the bell ringing up at the church.

I supposed that Meander, being a Texan, had been born on the back of a horse; now in the excited corral it became a question of not how few horses we could steal, but how many we must not steal. The horses were all excited; they wanted out of the corral for some good activity.

"Untie the ropes from the end post, and stand close," Meander said. "I'll drive these three past you."

We fastened the ropes back to the post and swung up bareback on the sorrel and bay; with the pinto between us, eager and ready to run, we cut over to a side street to make our way to the rooming house. There would be less likelihood of someone seeing us if we avoided the avenue.

When we reached the back of the hotel, we could barely see our shadowy snowbirds framed in the doorway above the ladder. They lost no time coming down, the King in the lead.

The first thing he said as Meander and I climbed off our horses was, "Which one is mine?"

"You walk with the rest of the boots," I said. "The horses are for the ladies."

He chattered, "Have pity on me."

Then I explained the plan. The women were to mount the horses and make their way on down the side street Meander and I had followed, then they were to turn and cross the lower avenue and make their way up the old river road which led to the Poteau and the Choctaw Ferry. There they would find Captain Vale and be safe until the rest of us appeared.

We men were to cross the avenue on Second Street, trying to get across before the vigilantes came down from the Le Flore. I had been told that morning of the various paths which led to the Ferry landing; we would take one of these, and not be as conspicuous as we would have been all together with the women.

Meander and I helped the women mount the horses straddleways, and they set out in the snow. As they disappeared, I felt

39

now that they would be safe, but it still remained for the rest of us to learn our own fate.

We did not wait long to get our first inkling. As we shouldered our ways toward the avenue, we heard a great chorus of shouting up to our left.

"Quick," Senor Maderas said. "We must get across the avenue before they come near enough to see us."

We ran at breakneck speed—or what would have been breakneck speed had it not been for our slipping and sliding, and from the middle of the intersection of Second Street and the avenue we glanced up the slope.

What we saw through the snow was not encouraging. There was the dim glow of lanterns and flaring pine knots, drunken and joyous shouts, snatches of song, everything coming down to us arm in arm at once. Standing there, the King began to shake with his ague. Soon the vigilantes would be close enough to see us.

" 'Pears like they're carrying a long rail," Meander said. "And I bet there's tar in those buckets they carry." I could imagine Meander's grin.

The King cried, "A rail? Oh merciful God, oh merciful God!"

I couldn't keep from grinning myself at that long-eared cousin of mine. He was doing all he could to determine the King's future, for Meander at that distance couldn't tell whether the men carried a rail or a matchstick.

But there was nothing funny about the snow now. It was coming down in blinding sheets, long rags of snow that twisted and curled about us with the wind. The voices of the vigilantes came and went.

"Oh, Lord! Oh, Lord!" the King cried. He bolted on to the other side of Second Street.

We began to run now, as best we could, hoping to keep the same distance between us and the vigilantes.

Senor Maderas panted. "At the end of the block, turn up toward the old fort. They would hardly look for us to go back toward town; when they find we have escaped, they will search the waterfront."

Senor Maderas's good judgment was vindicated, for after we turned the next corner, we had a whole block of shacks and other buildings between us, and could slow our pace for a moment. The King groaned and moaned, the sounds coming in jumps as we trotted.

Then we stopped for a moment to listen for the other sounds. They still came now and then, but they were beyond us and on down closer to Second Street. Perhaps we were safe, if we could find our way to the landing, for the paths would be covered and lost in snow. We cut closer to the old fort, then angled toward the Poteau.

The branches of trees and bushes hung low with snow, and it was this which helped us most, for along the slightly used trails the closer and lower branches had been cut back so a man on a horse could pass without being brushed. The overhead branches still drooped, and it was as if we walked through a tunnel of snow.

At last the exhausted King slumped down and sat in the snow with his back against a tree. Strangely, his spirits had revived. He gibbered over and over, "Do you think we are safe now? Do you think we are safe?"

Senor Maderas was also a little the worse for wear, but he answered the King with his usual forethought. "I think we are safe. It is not likely they would look for us here." Then he added, "I think you boys laid your plans well."

"It all depends on Captain Vale," I said. "If he will take us aboard the *Dewdrop,* we'll be safe from anything."

Meander said confidently, "He'll take us. We got along pretty well on the sternwheeler."

Of course, not a single one of us would ever forget the flicker of lights which came down the slope toward Second Street; we would never forget the welcome sight of other lights when we reached the old ferry at the mouth of the Poteau, and saw the

*Dewdrop* dimly and our women waiting on the snow-covered deck, a few lanterns glowing here and there.

There were lights, too, on the flat barge-like ferry of the Choctaws, and lights of wagons and men who waited on the higher ground near the bluffs with their loads of liquor. Our three horses were tied near the ferry.

"That's a good sign," I whispered to Meander. "I bet Captain Vale tied those horses."

"It's all set," Meander said.

The King waddled across the stage plank and embraced the Countess. "My dear, my dear," he said, "we have eluded them all. And something tells me that our good fortune will return. Sir," he said to Captain Vale, "you are to be congratulated. You have a wonderful ship here."

Captain Vale, wrapped in his buffalo coat, looked the King up and down sardonically. "I think, sir, that any ship would look good to you at the present moment—even a rowboat."

Captain Vale took the women to his small cabin at the rear of the superstructure, where they huddled about an oil stove.

Meanwhile, on deck and in the surrounding trees there was other activity. The *Dewdrop* was nosed against the ferry, and from every nook and cranny of the snow came bearded or unshaven ruffians, whites and Indians with short or long hair, the masters of the border trade, each with his liquor load.

Captain Vale, a heavy rifle slung over his shoulder, the barrel pointing upward, checked his manifests by the light of lanterns and pine flares with a wide-shouldered, gray-bearded and shabby-coated man. As the cases and kegs were carried to the ferry and then aboard the *Dewdrop*, I noticed how carefully the captain had the kegs placed along the open sides of the superstructure, leaving only a small open space on either side to walk through.

Once while Captain Vale waited for the gray-bearded man and his help to return, I asked, "Why do you arrange the kegs that way?"

He smiled thinly. "Rifle fire from the banks. It gives us protection. Sometime I may be bushwhacked."

"You haven't said anything about our going with you."

Again, that whimsical smile. "I thought you and Meander had decided that."

"Meander and I will work for passage."

"I had expected you to say that. Senor Maderas has already offered to pay, but I refused him."

"Why?"

"Because perhaps I look beyond the mouth of the Illinois. Perhaps he and the King can help me later."

"Will you start out in this snow?"

"In less than an hour. The snow will help me."

The gray-bearded man came back, and he and the captain again began to check manifests by the light of a swinging lantern. The manifests consisted of the names of the men who had brought liquor, the quantities, the price, and what the captain would pay each on his return downriver.

When another pause in the activity came, I said, "Let me ask you a question—do you drink?"

"I never touch it. As I said at Napoleon, I like the excitement."

"What will Meander and I do with those horses?"

"I know Uncle Hank. He has told me to borrow horses whenever I wish. I'll get them back."

I kept watching the horses.

"You want one of them, don't you?" Captain Vale said.

"Sure I do."

Captain Vale gave a devil-may-care laugh.

"Then get the pinto aboard. I'll settle with Uncle Hank, and send you a statement to Los Alamos."

"That won't mean I'll have the money ready."

I led the pinto across the stageplank, and now all the fires in their buckets were being kicked off the ferry, and the logs from the shore fires were being kicked into the water. Then there was only blackness where moments before dozens of men had moved. The whiskey ruffians had vanished.

Before we backed from the ferry, Captain Vale led me and

Meander to the engine and boiler room. He said, "My fireman was bopped over the head in Fort Smith today." Vale showed us the gauges of the boilers and the speaking tube. "You two will man the firebox, and keep it roaring. Call the pressure up to me every five minutes. Once into the Arkansas, we'll light the pine knots in the cage at the bow, and with our passing lights on, we'll begin the run. We've plenty of pine knots—keep the cage full. I'll need good light in this snow."

From being horse thieves we had become whiskey runners. As the *Dewdrop* sped through the snow to the Illinois, with Captain Vale piloting, Los Alamos seemed very, very far away.

How would we ever get there?

# 4

When the *Dewdrop* reached the mouth of the Illinois, the late day was crisp and clear and tinkling. The snowfall had ceased; there was only the sparkling of sun on a million bent branches.

After Captain Vale had edged the sternwheeler to the whiskey camp, and Meander and I had stopped the engines, he came down from the pilothouse in his buffalo robe slowly, like a very, very tired old man. The whimsical lines at the corners of his mouth were gone; in their place, after his arduous job of piloting, and especially on the night run, were only taut lines of weariness; his eyes were bloodshot from strain.

We had come up the Arkansas like a disembodied ghost; a ghost, but not completely unguided, for now there stood before us the man whose unfailing sight had led us through an almost impenetrable night. Senora Maderas handed him a cup of scalding coffee.

The mouth of the Illinois was a few miles downstream from Webber's Falls, where a rock ridge ran across the Arkansas, and where in low water even the shallow draft sternwheelers might have to be pulled over by horses or mules. North of the Arkansas lived the Cherokees, and to the south the Creeks, Choctaws, Seminoles, and Chickasaws.

The *Dewdrop* had put in amid the cheers and huzzahs of the expectant customers; expecting her arrival, they had driven their teams and wagons through the snowstorm, or come by horse or foot to be present to buy early. In the snowy trees stood ragged lean-tos or tents or shacks or supply dumps, and from them still other whites and Indians came to the river.

Captain Vale seated himself on one of the kegs piled along the superstructure; he drew his pistol and held it for the benefit of those who clustered too near the ship.

He shouted to the mob, "There will be no liquor sold until Chief Tomley is here."

There was a trace of the whimsical mouth again when he told me and Meander, "The chief manages my business when I am gone, and keeps things in order. Go down the rutted road— his cabin has a wide hickory tree in the yard—and tell him I am here. And bring Chujo back."

The King and Countess and the Maderas family watched the crowd from behind the whiskey kegs. It was not a prepossessing group—there were entirely too many pistols and beards and rifles present; some Indians carried stubby bows and their quivers of arrows.

Meander and I had no desire to become heroes, but we flung the plank across and pushed our way through the crowd toward Chief Tomley's cabin. We learned later that this was called the Old Whiskey Road, for it was through these ruts that liquor was also brought from Fort Smith.

I don't want to give the impression that a town or settlement was at the mouth of the Illinois, but as Meander and I walked through the snow we saw more and more scattered shacks and lean-tos; there was even a big thatched Wichita tipi of the Indians farther west, which looked like a beehive.

The huts and lean-tos were set back from the road, and half-hidden by trees and brush. No one, viewing the trees from the Arkansas, would be likely to see them. The only permanent thing at the site was whiskey.

As we approached the hickory tree in Chief Tomley's yard, we gave a loud haloa before the cabin, and a slender Cherokee boy of our own age stepped from the doorway.

He was dressed in a fringed jacket and buckskin pants; he was topped off by a wide-brimmed, flat-topped black sombrero.

I said, "We are from Captain Vale. He wants to talk with Chief Tomley. And is Chujo here?"

"I am Chujo." He stepped aside to admit us.

He wore his hair long, curled down to his shoulders. His eyes were black as obsidian.

"Come in," he said.

If we had been surprised at the sight of Chujo, we were even more surprised when we stood before Chief Tomley.

He sat like a supreme Buddha on a flat bench in the center of a fireless room, a man of such proportions that I can only hint them to you. His head was wide and prominent; he was obese to extremity; the girth of his belly should be measured in length of yards rather than feet.

In spite of the cold, he was bare from the waist up; his navel was hidden between two rolls of fat. He sat, his eyes wide, and smoked a calm pipe.

"Chief Tomley," I said, having read something of Indian ceremony, "Captain Vale of the *Dewdrop* invites your presence at the river."

There was an immediate flare from Chujo, who stood beside us. "You mean he orders him to be there." As he glared at me, his eyes snapped in hatred.

He said to his father, "You will not go there again."

A large hand moved impatiently. "If you speak once more, I will have you lashed."

"You have had me lashed before, and what good has it done?"

Meander and I thought we had said enough; we did not know what quarrel we had stepped into, so we turned to go back to the *Dewdrop.*

"Wait," Chujo said, stepping from his father's side, "I will go with you."

As we walked down the lane to the river, Chujo sneered. "A chief! My father is no more a chief than I am. It is only a name used by Captain Vale to flatter him. If my mother still lived, she would not let him be in this business."

I was surprised at this revelation of Captain Vale's character. He certainly was not what I had supposed him to be, or had he simply recognized the type he dealt with, and flattered him accordingly?

Chujo was silent for a moment, then he said, "Someday I will run away from this."

Meander's head jerked with a terrific sneeze. We had both developed a case of the sniffles during the afternoon; it had been brought on by caring for the fire boxes the night before, then staying too close to the pine knot cage in the cold weather on deck. Now we paid for it. I answered Meander with a sound like a whickering horse; it nearly jerked my cap off, and we walked on to the *Dewdrop.*

When we boarded ship, Chujo marched past Captain Vale, who still sat on a whiskey keg with his rifle and pistol. Chujo didn't even speak. He went to the engine room and brought out half a dozen large cans which he placed about a whiskey keg. Then he, too, sat and waited, while the crowd cheered.

The King and Senor Maderas had been pressed into service by the captain; they stood near the cans and the keg, armed, flanking Chujo and Captain Vale. We didn't know if anything had happened in our absence or not, but the captain took no chances.

Then, as if in concession to those who waited beside the

river, Chief Tomley was carried up the snow-crusted road on a sapling litter held by four jacketed Cherokees.

There was a unique quality to the litter.

At top and bottom it was woven over with vine growth, but a hole had been left in the middle. This was to facilitate the mounting of the chief; the litter was placed on the ground, the chief stepped into the hole, and the litter was raised. When it reached the height of his buttocks, he sat, facing the direction he wanted to go, his legs and feet dangling through the hole.

The chief had put on a jacket, but had left it open, as if the more easily to follow his ponderous belly to the river. The unruly crowd cheered louder.

But Chief Tomley's ride to the *Dewdrop* was to be delayed.

There appeared from the trees three mule-drawn wagons with high sideboards, loaded with unshucked ears of corn. Each wagon was followed by a horse on a rope; the captain moved toward the plank. By the way they handled the wagons, the drivers were rough but competent men.

"It's like I thought," Chujo muttered. "I knew those men would be here."

"Who are they?" Meander said.

"Part of the McAuliffe gang—some of Captain Vale's men. It means trouble somewhere."

The drivers of the wagons leaped to the snow, crusting their way to Chief Tomley's litter. Vale watched, a thin smile on his lips.

"What kind of trouble do you mean?" I asked Chujo.

"Anything Vale thinks of. He puts somebody out on his dirty work, then he has them watched by McAuliffe."

"Which is he?"

"The tall red-bearded one."

Red McAuliffe was shaking hands with Chief Tomley. Both men looked at the corn-covered wagons and laughed.

Captain Vale called impatiently and the gathering broke up.

The chief, as he was carried nearer, puffed serenely on his pipe; it was a stub corn-cob, and not the longer Indian type.

49

We watched as he was lowered to the deck. The bearers let him down gently; his feet touched, then he was left standing, the litter about him.

As the evening waned and the liquor was dispensed, there was little difference in this camp and that at the Choctaw Ferry the night before, except that tonight the whiskey was being taken off the *Dewdro*p instead of being loaded.

Chief Tomley sat on a keg at the end of the plank; he allowed only one customer at a time to be on deck. These persons, whites who had married into the tribes, or half-breeds, or Indians, were questioned by the chief, who wanted no liquor sold to some federal marshal's secret agent; if the questioning was satisfactory, the customer bought his liquor by the keg or bottle, stopping at the circle of cans to pay Chujo, who dropped the bills or gold pieces into his containers.

Red McAuliffe and his men danced in the snow with renegade Indian girls. Early fires blazed. A knife fight broke out on the bank; a body was dumped into the river.

In addition to rolling keg after keg down the plank and helping to load them in waiting wagons, Meander and I were sneezing and sniffling and becoming woozy.

At last Meander leaned over a keg near Captain Vale and panted.

The captain said, taking his eyes off Chujo's counting for a moment, "What is the matter with you?"

Meander said, straightening, but with his hands still supporting him on the keg, "It's a cold struck me, or something else. Me and Colin both got it, maybe from getting too hot at the fire boxes last night."

The Countess stood beside the King and his rifle. "Why, you poor boys," she said. "Captain, it is inhuman for you to work them this way."

"Madam," Captain Vale snapped, "this is the first I have known of it. Of course, I will not work them. Chief Tomley," he called, "bring two boys aboard to roll kegs."

The Countess said, "Captain, do you have sugar?"

"In the little galley, madam."

"You poor boys," the Countess said seizing our hands, "come with me."

She led us to the cabin where Effie sat silently brooding on a keg, and after checking the King's carpetbag for a moment, came up with a small bottle and an even smaller box.

"Turpentine and calomel," she said brightly.

She led us to the galley and filled a spoon with turpentine and sugar, then gave us the calomel tablets.

"I ain't hoping," Meander said. "I've took this calomel before."

The Countess said, "What you need now is a good poultice on your chests."

Now that she had begun this errand of mercy, even as she had earlier worked with the distraught King in Fort Smith, there was to be no stopping her. If one dose was good for a cold, ten would be better.

Out in the open again, Meander and I stood dizzily, sneezing and hee-hawing at each other, wishing we were dead.

During the afternoon an industrious squaw had worked about the Wichita beehive, now and then playing with her many children.

"Oh," said the Countess, while Senora Maderas watched our suffering with compassion, "there is that Indian woman. With so many children, she must have many native remedies with her."

The squaw did have, and when the Countess flitted back up the plank she held a clay bowl in her long fingers. "Come to the cabin," she said. "Now you can have your poultice."

In the cabin, she began to strip our shirts open. Effie stood up and left.

"That looks like axle grease to me," Meander said, watching the gooey fingers come toward him.

The elated Countess cried, "It is! The squaw said that the grease is only the base for the other ingredients—peppers and the ground leaves and roots of native herbs."

Then she put the fire ball to us. She rubbed Meander's chest and throat first, leaving a slimy goo, and with her long finger massaged within his nostrils. She ran a streak under each eye for sinus, then pinned a cloth under his shirt.

Then she turned to me. And while she worked, her hands always moving over me, I remembered something curious—the way she had run her hands over my chest and shoulders when she had tried to console me on the *Mississippi Queen* after my grandfather's death and the loss of my money. Had she in some way learned of the parchment I carried? Her oozy hands drew closer to my belt.

All that saved me, I suppose, was a wild shriek from Meander, upon whom the potion was just now beginning to show its strength.

He kicked his heels together like a pony going off in four directions, and screamed as no scalped settler had ever screamed. Above the two streaks beneath his eyes, streams of tears poured.

He screamed to the Countess, "Are you trying to kill us? I'd rather be dead than this."

I was still thinking of what the Countess might really have wanted when the power struck me. I had thought that Meander in his leap had gone halfway to the ceiling, but I felt that I was going right through it; I had never felt such eternal fire burning me in my life.

The Countess said, wiping her hands on a towel while Meander and I chased each other around the room, "Now you must wrap up and sleep until morning. Keep the cover on all night. I will see that you sleep in the pilothouse and I will get blankets from Captain Vale."

Maybe the Wichita medicine woman did do her work well, after all; when we awoke and looked across the pilothouse at each other all of the irritating sniffling and sneezing was gone, but our heads felt very solid and remote.

Meander said, "That was the longest night I ever spent at the gates of hell."

"Not gates—it was the back end."

52

"You know," Meander said, "we've got to come clean with each other. We've been good friends, but you haven't told me everything. I've noticed how that woman always wants her hands on you. And the reason ain't hard to guess."

"You mean you know about the parchment?"

"That was what I was sent up here to help guard."

"Then you know why I didn't tell you."

"Sure, but that time's over. With this crew we travel with—nobody you can trust—you really need a friend. Even when I was hurting worse with that burning, I saw how you flinched when she was rubbing you. Where do you keep the parchment?"

"In my britches."

"Pretty smart," Meander said.

"I guess worrying about it for so long helped bring me down with this cold."

"No, it ain't all worry. We worked hard coming up the Arkansas with that good captain, but we earned every mile we made. And we ran around Fort Smith in these thin clothes trying to save a bunch of crooks, you with that cap and me with no hat at all. We worked ourselves to death that night on the river, but now is the time for us to look after me and thee."

"It's not that easy—there's Effie."

"I wish I knew who she is," said Meander, "Or what. I'd bet she don't belong to the Maderases; she's too considerate for them to be her parents. Kids don't care how mean they are to their folks. Now about that parchment. From now on we switch it everyday. Once in a while you can let the King or Senor Maderas see you with your pants down. That will eliminate that. Now rub your ears back and we'll get up and eat."


If I have appeared not to be a hero in this story, it is because I am not a hero.

Having had my life laid out for me by Don Herrera, and all with the best intentions, I had never before had the need for heroic decisions. Yet in spite of my deficiencies, I had always

53

possessed watchfulness and a certain caution. It was not that I did not want to march into something strange or dangerous, but that I simply wanted to know what I was moving into. There were better men in the world than I—Meander, for instance, who would battle a tub of wildcats.

At my school, where we had a military class, we all knew what the objective was, and I never hesitated to plan for it. I knew how many men were on this side or that, and where they were located.

But since leaving St. Louis, I had known nothing of what faced me. I had, therefore, relied on caution, rather than action, except on a few occasions, and fortunately these had all come off well. I had guessed my way rightly in everything but Effie, but I had tried there, too. But sometimes I brooded as much as she.

When Meander and I came down from the pilothouse the morning after the treatment from the Countess, everything assumed its old place. Effie got up and left the table the moment we entered the galley.

After a breakfast of venison and hot cakes which Senora Maderas cooked, we went out on deck. Since we had retired early the night before because of our colds, we were surprised to see over two dozen whiskey kegs which stood behind the superstructure. Captain Vale had not sold everything after all. He stood on the bank with the King and Senor Maderas.

Chujo came up the plank. "Do you see Red McAuliffe and his men talking with Captain Vale? Have you heard"—he gestured—"that you will take those whiskey kegs in the corn wagons down to the Canadian River to the Edwards Trading Post near Little River? And you will go even beyond, to a grog shop set on stilts in the middle of the river at the tip of the Chickasaw land."

"It's news to us," I said. Perhaps that was why Effie left; she may not have approved of what had been planned.

As soon as Captain Vale saw us he left McAuliffe and moved up the gangplank. "I suppose you know my decision?"

"You do want to make characters of us," Meander said.

"I have an obligation to even up," Captain Vale said, the whimsical corners of his mouth twisting. "After all, by making the trip, it will take you closer to Texas."

"I'm not sure we're in for that," I said.

"Why not? Haven't I helped you in every way I could? After all, you do owe me for a horse."

"That was a separate deal. We were talking this morning—we earned every mile we made with you."

Captain Vale laughed good-humoredly. "The King and Senor Maderas have agreed to go. You wouldn't want to be separated from the young lady, would you?"

"Then what do we do?"

"The men are already throwing the unshucked corn from the wagons. We will place the kegs, then cover them with the corn. If anyone suspects you, you are simply taking three wagons of corn to the trading post. The King and Countess will have one wagon, the Maderas family the other, and you and Meander the third. You will not sell the whiskey at the post, but will wait near it until you are approached. The King will collect, and I have means to get the money forwarded. The third wagon goes on down to the grog shop on stilts in the river. It's in the river to keep it out of the Chickasaw land. Do you understand everything?"

"I guess we do."

"From here you will go upstream and cross the Arkansas on the rock ledge at Webber's Falls. McAuliffe and his men will guard you until you are out of the settlement and well into the opposite woods. I have already told the King and Senor Maderas the trail from there."

"One other thing," I said. "If we do this, we will need clothes and blankets. In another norther we'd freeze to death. And our having colds wouldn't get your whiskey moved."

"Chujo," the captain said, "get buckskins and boots and blankets and hats. Get some tarps. Put them in the wagons

55

when the corn is loaded, together with food. Or," he said to me and Meander, "you might want to wear your new clothes to start with."

"That's what we'll do."

In spite of the fact that we were pretty disgusted with Captain Vale, when we left in the whiskey-laden wagons we couldn't keep from waving him a high farewell.

Either way you looked at it—from the standpoint of morality —it was because of him that we were this far on our journey.

# 5

The three men who had ridden through Webber's Falls stopped us and their horses just beyond the headstones of the old military cemetery.

Red McAuliffe said to the King, "We'll leave you now. Do as the captain told you, and don't try to steal the money."

"My dear sir," the King said, "such an idea is ridiculous."

As we struck for the trail Captain Vale had told us of, the outlaw band sat watching, then turned its horses and rode back toward the shelf.

Now we were off again, all of us on four wheels except Effie, and she walked her pony beside one wagon or another, or trotted down the trail to gallop back, her hair flying.

The King and the Countess drove the first wagon, Senor and Senora Maderas the second, and Meander and I brought up the rear. Meander and I felt pretty good because we looked pretty good in our new clothes, wearing our fringed buckskins and black sombreros. And there were more clothes and jackets in the back on top of the corn shucks.

For the first time we looked and felt respectable.

We had not gone more than three or four miles from Webber's Falls, the mules shying at overhanging branches and bouncing the wheels over every rock, when a figure leaped from the brush into the back of the wagon behind me and Meander.

He lay flat in the corn where the ears slanted down to the side boards, a rifle beside him, panting. It was Chujo.

"Why are you here?" I said.

Chujo said, raising his head, "I told my father I would run off, and now I have."

"You mean you will not go back?"

"It is a hard thing to say, but I will never go back to my people."

"But why come with us?" Meander said. "You won't bring anything but trouble. Chief Tomley and Captain Vale will have the whole country watched."

"Do you think you are not watched now? McAuliffe and his men only pretended to go back to the Illinois. I know, because when I waded the ledge, I did not see them. Captain Vale would not send them on with the wagons because they are criminals, and too well known. Instead, they will watch you all the way to the trading post, then they themselves will collect for the whiskey you sell. They have a letter to the King from Vale."

"Smart thinking," I said, realizing that Captain Vale was as much with us now as he ever had been. It came as a shock that he would continue to use us like this, even though he had used us before.

"What will you do if you are caught in Texas?" Meander asked. "Down that way, they don't like Indians."

58

"I can pass for a Mexican, because my mother taught me Mexican words, and I will bathe all over on San Juan's day. If you and Senor Maderas will teach me more words, I should have no trouble."

In the wagon seat, Meander and I looked at each other. "You can go with us," Meander agreed, "but it's your own funeral."

A rocky hill was before us, and as I turned from looking at Meander I saw the head of a man and then a horse come over the top.

I told Chujo, "Keep low and out of sight, but slide your rifle forward."

The man, I knew, was McAuliffe.

One thing I had learned well at school was to shoot. I threw a quick shot toward McAuliffe, where it splattered on a boulder, sending up its fragmented cloud.

Then all we saw was the rump of the horse heading down the opposite side of the crest.

"Doggone," said Meander, slapping his leg and laughing uproariously, "I'm going to like this trip."

But the sudden sound of the shot had bolted the King's mules down the trail, and Senor Maderas's into the brush. By heaving and sawing at the lines, we got our own mules under control.

By that time the florid King had walked back to join us. "Who fired that shot?" Then he looked at me. "Who gave you a gun? The captain gave me and Senor Maderas pistols, so we could appear as honest men protecting our families, but no one else was to have a firearm."

Chujo sat up. The King looked surprised.

I said to the King, "Chujo says that McAuliffe and his men are still following us, that they, and not you, will collect the whiskey money at the trading post. That's why I used Chujo's rifle to shoot toward McAuliffe."

The King seemed to have blanched. "How do you know they will collect?" he asked Chujo.

"Because they have a letter to you from Captain Vale."

The King moaned. "My God, how I have been duped!"

"Time to eat," Meander said.

So Senor Maderas moved his wagon up to the King's, and we moved ours up behind Senor Maderas's. Then Effie came in and got off her pinto, and we sat down and built a fire.

Then for no reason at all, Effie and I and Chujo and Meander were all standing, looking at each other in a suddenly woven bond that would last forever.

There is no reason to describe the path we took to the trading post; it wasn't as easy as it might have been, had we traveled south of the Canadian River along the old military trail and the remains of the California Road. The river was sandy; we avoided crossing it.

But everything on the brown and blowing earth—its scrub oaks and prairies—had compensation. I remember one morning when I awoke from my tarpaulin where I had placed it under the wagon in case a snow came.

Effie was kneeling over me, a tin cup of coffee in her hand. "Colin, would you like coffee before you get up?"

But by noon we were back again where we had started, the same old distance between Effie and me.

One thing, though, was most amusing. That was the Countess when she went to the bushes. Had she gone naturally, as we all did, no one would have thought about it.

Instead, thirty minutes before she would go, she climbed out of the King's wagon and walked beside it. Then when we were all tired from watching and waiting and had turned our attention elsewhere, we would notice that she had disappeared.

Now we all stopped the wagons to wait, and I could no more write exactly how she reappeared than I could write the book of Genesis. Suddenly there would emerge from the trees and brambles a zephyrish and gaunt thing floating her veils and scarfs, tripping lightly, fantastically, as if the whole world lived in her toes which barely touched the earth.

As the Countess flitted closer, she would say, her arms waving the air, "Have you seen the bluebirds in the woods today? I simply had to go see the happy bluebirds."

All she did was to make things worse than ever, and we in the back wagon began to have our own joke about the bluebirds.

But as the wagons went on, a strange thing was happening—I was learning to love this brown land. Going from wood to wood or from prairie to prairie, I felt I was a wide wanderer, and found new cities wherever I looked, something I knew but had never known.

It was really like that, too, for each hill or prairie held its own personality, as towns or cities do, and there were always the would-be homesteaders who traveled to the Unassigned Lands to the west, or whites who had come to lease land and live among the Indians, and Indians from reservations visiting other tribes. Sometimes we stopped at a Kickapoo wickiup made of hide and bark, or at a Shawnee or Pottawatomie cabin. Indians often begged us to lease land, so we could stay with them.

It was all one thing—a new history moving over the old. In those short days on the way to the trading post, I began to feel a strange peace, even with unpredictable Effie.

And Chujo had proved his worth, for on foot in prairie gulleys or among trees, he could pick the easier path for us, and tell us at any time where our three-man escort lingered.

He had changed also. In spite of my more sophisticated Castilian, he had learned a few phrases of native Mexican from Senor Maderas and Meander which would have branded him as a native of Los Alamos. And meanwhile he was intent upon discovering and learning each of us.

Meander told him, "If you run into trouble talking with someone, just shrug your shoulders. And always complain about the weather being too much *caliento* or *frio.*"

To bind our bargain with Chujo even further, we agreed that in our wagon we would use only the Mexican language; this would help Chujo and also me. He had learned quickly how to dominate a conversation with some homesteader we met on the trail, or on a cold day to speak to a wagon of whites, *"Buenos dias, senors. Mucho frio."* Then he would fold his arms, laugh inwardly at those who knew less language than he, and stare somberly somewhere into space.

But having opened the conversation, he always would let me or Meander continue it.

On the day before we were to reach Little River, we had a sudden warning.

A rifle shot ripped into Old Dun, one of the King's mules, injuring but not killing it. I fired back with the rifle, and saw a familiar horse disappearing into the trees.

That night about the fire we were rather miserable.

His chance for a fortune gone, the King said, "That shot was simply to let us know that the liquor will be transferred tomorrow. Then McAuliffe and his men will collect from us."

Next day from a timbered ridge we saw the trading post. Smoke rose from the clean chimneys of the main buildings and the outlying cabins, and wagons and horsemen and solitary Indians made their way toward it. When we started down to Little River Chujo said, "I will take my rifle and follow on foot. We do not know what the liquor men will try to do."

But we did not even make it to the river. McAuliffe and his men met us on a wide prairie, and four roughly dressed strangers rode from the surrounding brush.

McAuliffe, his beard aflame, jerked his horse close to the King's wagon, and shouted, "Unload your possessions from the first two wagons and throw them in the last."

It was odd, but the four strangers paid McAuliffe immediately, and we could only conclude that the price included the wagons and the four mules. As an afterthought, and while the King stood fuming, McAuliffe handed him the letter from Captain Vale. The King pretended to read it. "Yes," he said, "I am glad you took the payment. It relieves me of the responsibility. Simply put your name on the letter to show I am clear."

McAuliffe laboriously marked the letter with an X from the King's pencil. "We will meet you on the Canadian," he said.

62

"Watch your step." He and his men swung their horses and disappeared into the brush after the liquor buyers.

Now we were off again with the last wagon to the grog shop at the edge of the Chickasaw country. We let the ladies share the wagon with the King, and Senor Maderas walked with me and Meander and Chujo.

"Why do we have to take this wagon to that houseboat on stilts?" Meander asked.

I said, "Because every mile westward means an extra dollar for Captain Vale."

It happened to be warmer that evening, and we sat around the fire talking, but the King was depressed. He rose and paced the ground.

"Why," he said, "did Captain Vale not trust me?"

The Countess, in from counting her evening bluebirds and sipping her coffee, laughed merrily. "Perhaps he knew you too well, my darling."

We had camped on a hill in the late light, and in the distance lay the dusky line of the sandy Canadian. I sat beside Senora Maderas on a flat ledge. Some feeling of impending tragedy made me talk to her as I did, feeling that we were all taking the wrong way in the life we led, instead of taking the right and harder one.

About the senora hovered a delicate odor of perfume. I knew now who had stood outside my door on the *Mississippi Queen,* for the scent was identical, but to have asked why she had stood there might have aroused her or brought forth too many complications.

So I talked of Effie, hoping by a more devious means to learn what I wanted. I asked, "Why doesn't Effie like me?"

The broad face and its dark eyes showed surprise. "My son, she does like you. I know there is much you are not aware of, but you must believe that the Senor and I are your friends. And in time Euphemia will love you—I think she does now—but she is only a young girl and does not understand her feelings.

63

You must believe what I tell you, but be very, very careful in whom you place trust."

"What you say makes me know why Senor Maderas always watches his pistol." She had mentioned no names, but I knew well what she meant.

"You wear perfume this evening. It is the same I smelled through my transom on the *Mississippi Queen*—you were standing outside my door."

"I would have told you then what I have hinted at, but I was afraid."

Senora Maderas had called Effie, Euphemia, and with great respect, as if she were someone apart from her. "But Euphemia? Why is she here at all?"

"I cannot tell you why. But I have a feeling that all will be well; do not worry."

So above the distant river with its pink sunset the world had taken on another hue, and it was then that the King and Senor Maderas began to argue violently.

Senora Maderas clutched my arm. "The King has been very curious about what little money we have. He seems to think that with his bad luck part of it belongs to him."

The quarrel soon ended, and nothing happened next day except the onward pull of the mules, and the increasing value of the cargo in the wagon. But it became increasingly evident by the King's renewed quarrelsomeness that having been forced to let the gold of the first two wagons slip through his fingers, he had no intention of letting this happen with the third, no matter how much he might be watched from afar.

I tried to put myself into the King's shoes and decide the course he would take. Chujo still made his solitary excursions of observation into the timbers, returning always with the same information. McAuliffe and his men were still with us, always alert.

For the life of me, I could see no way by which the King could manage the coup I knew he planned. I think the King also despaired at times, and took his frustration out on Senor and

Senora Maderas. I was convinced that as soon as the King saw the complete futility of escaping with the whiskey money, the harder he would try to get that of Senor Maderas.

As we went on up the Canadian, we plunged deeper among hills and ridges of blackjacks, which made it more difficult to keep the wagon moving, for in some places the thickness of the scrub was almost impenetrable. An axe or hatchet or machete would clear our way; then, unless finding some easier path, we would clear our way to the next stop.

Since leaving Webber's Falls, we had crossed the lands of the Creeks and Seminoles unmolested, saying to any who questioned us that we were homesteading families who hoped to lease land to plant a corn crop next spring; we had passed through the Pottawatomie and Shawnee and Kickapoo country, and neared the tip of the lands not yet assigned.

At last we reached our destination, a red bluff on the Canadian's north side, and we looked across it into the Chickasaw lands, and down at the houseboat on stilts, as Meander had called it. The river was wide, but held little water. On the farther bank stood a fringe of cottonwoods and salt cedars.

To shave a fine point of law, Captain Vale or his agents had run a pole bridge from the liquor-prohibited Chickasaw land to the grog shop they considered to be beyond the boundary. The bridge crossed more sand than water, for we could see from the height of the bluff that the water sparkled only in a winding and shallow channel.

The grog shop rose like a patched-up hen house over the water.

"I see, I see," the King said as we studied the place. Then he glanced toward the northwest where dark clouds had gathered. "It looks as if the moon will be hidden tonight."

We made camp out of sight of the grog shop, behind some protecting cottonwoods, and Chujo left on his usual scout. The King would allow us only the smallest of fire, and so determined was he in his actions that no one dared insist upon a larger.

Chujo came back with his report. "McAuliffe and his men are

all drunk with some boomer gang. They will probably sleep late in the morning."

When it was dark, the King ordered the corn to be thrown from the tops of the whiskey kegs and the kegs unloaded. Then he threw into the wagon tarpaulins, blankets, food, and unsuspecting Chujo's rifle. Without speaking, he seized the lines and drove into the darkness, which began to be broken by sheet lightning from the distant clouds. I suppose he thought there was little likelihood that we would be found by McAuliffe's men tonight.

While we waited near the fire, or some of us sitting on top of the whiskey barrels, we tried to fathom the King's plan. The Countess, flipping her whisker now and then, protested that she did not know. Senor and Senora Maderas sat together silently.

Within two hours, the King returned on foot. He was wet from the knees down from wading the shallow river.

"Ah," he said in satisfaction, taking a cup of coffee the Countess prepared, "our first step is accomplished."

Then we learned his plan.

As soon as daylight came, he would go to the grog shop and seek a buyer for the whiskey. He would claim to operate independently from the Unassigned Lands, and that he was not a member of any other bootleg gang. He would say that the barrels were hidden in a secluded place, and would allow a witness to be sent to inspect them while we waited, then collect his money. All very early, of course, before McAuliffe and his men were about.

But if McAuliffe should find him before the whiskey was sold and he had collected, he would tell him that the mules had bolted soon after we had stopped for the night, spilling the barrels out of the wagon in their breakneck run back up the bluff. The mules had disappeared, dragging the wagon behind them. But the kegs were still on the bank, and in seeking a buyer he had tried to do what was best for Captain Vale.

"As a matter of fact," the King said to us, well pleased with himself, "I have already taken the mules and wagon and hidden

66

them across the river. That is why I am wet tonight. They will be ready for our escape tomorrow."

Senor Maderas said bluntly, "You are a fool. One slip and you could be shot."

The King snapped, "I have not asked your opinion, sir. But you will go along with my plan, or you and your family could face unpleasant consequences."

At daybreak we were surprised to see that there was more water in the river. It flowed almost to the low floor of the grog shop, and coursed beneath the pole bridge to the Chickasaw bank. On that side the channel was deeper; on ours there was more sand, yet a shorter bridge had been built on this side also.

The King said, glancing uneasily at the water and the boiling sky, "There has been a heavy rain upstream. We must leave here quickly."

With our tarpaulins and blankets and what food we had left loaded on our backs, it was hard pulling to get across the sand.

"My dear," Senora Maderas said to Effie, glancing worriedly upstream, "ride your pony straight across the river and wait for us at the opposite bank. We should not be too long behind you."

Meander said, "That damn grog shop will cave in before we get there. It will be washed away like splinters."

Then the thunder and lightning began.

We could see headrolls of foam across the entire river, a further sign of the rising water. Much of the sand was covered now—a shallow covering, but covered.

When we reached the beginning of the nearer bridge, we were knee-deep in water. In the deepest part of the channel, Effie was swimming her pony.

It would serve no purpose to describe the interior of the grog shop, for after we entered, it was there hardly long enough for us to have an impression of it. Already water was creeping over the plank flooring.

Then Meander, who was the last to enter, took a look up-river. "Good God," he screamed, "look what's coming!"

67

I stepped back to look; a solid wall of water, in height I should think between three and four feet, swept toward us. The occupants of the shop—hung-over whites and Indians—saw the rise through the open siding. There was a stampede to the door which led to the farther bridge.

I saw a confusion of flying bottles as the liquor shelves came down, and tangles of arms and legs. The floor of the shack began to float like a raft.

The King had no chance to talk business or money at all.

When the crash came, Senor and Senora Maderas were swept into the water. There were screams of women and shouts of men, themselves being washed away. The Countess had reached the opposite bridge; she ran for her life before it collapsed.

I must in honesty give credit to the King for his courage. Chujo had plunged into the water and was attempting to swim his way to poor struggling Senora Maderas; the King had also swum after her.

The plank flooring of the grog shop tore from its last piling and broke apart; Meander was struck on the head by a falling scantling. As the flooring plunged downstream, Meander and I both were shoved under. I think he was unconscious, for he made no effort to swim, even the poorest effort, for Senora Maderas had at least tried. I could not see her now, but Chujo was raising his head from the water and looking for her.

While I supported Meander, hoping to swim with the current and perhaps be carried into the more shallow water after the river curved, I saw a thing which you will doubt, and which at the time was beyond belief.

In the midst of the flood, the King was trying to strangle Senor Maderas. It was a weird thing to see him strike and choke the bulging-eyed man he tried so desperately to hold above water.

At last Senor Maderas went down; I saw him no more. Only the King was left, and apparently he had the same idea as I—to be swept into shallow water after the bend.

As I dragged Meander from the river, I saw the hatless King

standing before me, the gold watch and chain of Senor Maderas in his hand. He was placing a wallet into a coat pocket with the watch.

There remained lost only Senora Maderas, and this dear soul was never seen again. Disconsolately, Chujo climbed from the water. "I think she was tangled in her skirts," he said, "but she never came up."

And the courage I thought I had detected in the King had turned to this; thwarted on all sides, even by God and the weather, to get the gold he wanted from the sale of the illicit kegs, he had deliberately drowned and murdered a man to gain what little he possessed.

There was no purpose now in fearing McAuliffe and his men who might be on the opposite bank—no one, in the still rising water, would attempt to cross the river.

Effie rode up on the pinto.

"Where is my mother?" she asked. "And father?"

I told her. She looked oddly at the King and began to weep softly, then rode the horse some distance away and sat alone.

The Countess came toward us, just as two bodies from the bridge floated by.

"Ah, you are safe, my dear," the King said, embracing her.

"But the senor and senora?"

"Foolishly, they have let themselves be drowned."

The rain which had done so much havoc upstream was falling in torrents now, but that did not keep Meander and Chujo and me from doing what we thought was our duty.

All day we searched the lower river bank, seeking the bodies of Senor and Senora Maderas. It was useless in such a flood; the bodies could be miles away by now. At last we returned and sought out the wagon.

Fortunately, there were the tarpaulins and blankets and food the King had brought across the night before, so we had a measure of comfort from the rain and lightning. And the King had taken a battered sombrero from his bag.

In the morning, just before we left for the old Chisholm Cattle Trail, some thirty-five or forty miles to the west, Effie asked me, "Colin, will you put up a small cross beside the river?"

Across from the red bluff I put up a marker, and it was good stout oak.

Then we rode or walked on, for I would not ride in the wagon with the King.

# 6

It was the night after our departure from the Canadian that we decided our course into Texas.

I say we, but the King made the decision. We would continue our present plan, but striking more to the southwest to a junction with the trail over which so many millions of Texas longhorns had been driven north to the cowtowns of Kansas—the Chisholm Trail.

Since its great days following the war, traffic on the trail had changed. As the railroads cut new paths across the plains, cows had been shunted to the newer Western Trail and to Dodge City; what drives were made to the southernmost railheads on the Kansas border—Caldwell, Kiowa, and Hunnewell—were closely watched by soldiers on Indian duty who required that the cows not be thrown off the trail for grazing, and that they bed down not more than a few hundred yards from it.

The King considered this depleted use of the trail as fortunate. Also there would be less chance of our being detected at a time of year when no cattle drives would be made; the remains of the worn trail would make the wagon-going easier without so much brush to contend with, and if McAuliffe and his men still sought us they would hardly think we would go so far west before turning south.

One night Meander said to the King, "You talk like you know this old trail."

The King replied, "I never saw this trail in my life."

Meander smirked. "I know how a cowhand sits. And you've got other characteristics, too, like that old cowhand hat."

The King doubted that we would be pursued at all. With the dead which could have been seen along the river, McAuliffe might think that we, too, had been washed away; that the same fate had overtaken the wagon and mules; even the whiskey kegs, if found downstream, might have been carried there by the flood.

For the next several days, as the wagon and mules pressed forward through the usual scrub and across swollen creeks, the King appeared even more confident of escape, congratulating himself at the night fires for his forethought in having taken the wagon across the river before the flood struck.

We still had machetes, hatchets and axes, coils of rope and food for ourselves, and even a smattering of the unshucked corn for the mules. When we turned into the ruts of the old cattle trail, its sides marked by the bones of horses and cows, every mile which ran beneath the wagon wheels buoyed up the King's spirits, and only occasionally did he take precautions against pursuit.

The Countess had taken complete charge of Effie, who had become more enigmatic. She apparently had accepted the deaths of Senor and Senora Maderas with the same grief as we, yet

72

with Effie it did not appear to be the depth of grief one her age would have felt for a father or mother.

Yet Effie was aloof at night, and rarely spoke. At the same time there was the greater affection with which she regarded her pony, as if it had some special meaning to her.

One day on the trail the Countess snapped, "Effie, stop running your horse ahead of us. From now on, stay behind the wagon."

"But the pony must have exercise."

"Then it can get it by walking." The agate eyes gleamed. "From now on, never leave my sight."

I became more suspicious than ever.

When we put up one evening at Monument Hill, an old camp ground of cowhands, Meander and Chujo and I sat on some of the boulders at the base of the hill and talked. The brown grass and swells and the distant blue hills of Texas stood far away. About us were old initials cut in the weathered stone.

Chujo had been told about the parchment; its sealed tube had held against the waters of the Canadian, and only one outer corner had become stained.

"If what you say about the King drowning Senor Maderas is true," Meander said to me, "there could be a murder charge filed against him."

"Yes, but only if someone had money and power and position to file a suit. Take the first Texas town we come to—what if I went to some sheriff or Ranger and told the story. Do you think it would carry weight against the King's glibness? He could convince anyone that he was trying to save Senor Maderas. I'm sure Effie saw what happened, too, from the other side of the river. She could be a witness. I've tried to spare her and not talk about it, but we'll have to wait until we get the right chance, whenever that is."

"The King ain't got any intention of giving up the mules and the wagon," Meander said. "He says that they are a mark of respect and position, that we can impress people and work wonders

73

when we get to Texas. He's got a dozen schemes boiling, and one is the route we'll take. We'll go to Bowie first, then strike down between the caprock and the plateau. The country will be dry, and it's hell on women and men, but mules might make it. I think he's going that way to keep away from towns like San Antonio because of Rangers. I bet he's got a record in Texas."

"There will be the springs of the old Plains Indians," Chujo said somberly. "At least, we'd have water between jumps. We might even fill the wagon with barrels."

"Who's taking jumps in that country?" Meander asked. "Farther down, it ain't nothing but sand and mesquite and cactus."

In a showdown, we knew that we could get away from the one-wagon caravan, but there was the problem of Effie, who was watched closely day and night. I felt that the King and the Countess never slept at the same time, that one or the other of them was always alert and vigilant and watching her and us.

Chujo was most positive about this. "I have seen them wake each other and change places many nights. And it would be wrong to leave Effie. We do not know what they might do with her."

"They're saving her for something," Meander said, "only I ain't smart enough to figure it out."

"They knew something about the Maderases, too," I said. "Senora Maderas almost told me something once, but didn't. She was afraid to."

Yet I still remembered she had told me that Effie was a young girl, and not certain of her emotions, these being new and strange to her. Yet there was no doubting that in the last few days Effie had come to place more and more dependence upon me.

What broke the longhorn's back came when the Countess made Effie go without supper one evening. During the day, despite the angry shouts of the King, Effie had galloped her pony ahead of the wagon. Upon her return, the Countess had castigated her, then pronounced her punishment.

But it was no trick at all for me, and then Meander, to wrap a heavier than usual roll of sourdough about our sticks at the fire, or Chujo to cut a few extra and thicker slices of bacon, meanwhile stealing his rifle from the wagon. We with Effie did the cooking anyway, since the King and Countess abhorred the task. The Countess was with him now, sitting on the ground near the mules and pulling her whisker while she conspired with the King about the future.

We slipped a cup of coffee to the back of the wagon where Effie sat, and I suppose that Effie ate better than we that night.

At times the King turned his back and raised a hand to his vest; he was looking at Senor Maderas's watch.

On the last day north of Red River, the boundary of Texas, I leaped behind Effie on the pinto and we galloped full speed ahead of the wagon. We heard the irate shouts of the King and the screams of the Countess.

"Effie, I have wanted to talk with you for days, but we are never alone. You have wanted to tell me something—what is it?"

"Colin, I can't tell you. Not now, perhaps never."

"The King and Countess know something about you. What is it?"

"I can never tell you. And there are other things, too, but you must know I would like to tell you."

There was the whine of a bullet from the King's pistol; Effie stopped the pinto and we trotted back to the wagon.

"Don't worry about the King," I said. "Chujo has taken his rifle back, and Meander and I will watch you."

Back at the wagon it was the same all over again—Effie without supper.

At the cooking fire the King told me, "Another stunt like that one today, and I'll kill that pony."

"Not with that rifle pointed at your back."

The King turned, and stared at dark Chujo. He said to both of us, "Then this means war between us."

"Yes, and I am glad we know where we stand. From now on, watch us, because we will watch you. When we cross Red River, don't try to drown us. We are three, and will be ready. You might

be the one to sink. Think of that while you watch Effie tonight."
I got up and left him.

Well, we swam the Red to old Red River Station of the cowhands days without difficulty, logs on the sides of the wagon, the
mules with their lips drawn back over their teeth, and as a pre-
caution Chujo in the rear of the wagon with his rifle on the
King's back.

Yes, we all understood each other perfectly now.

Meander and I held to the backs of the logs, perhaps helping
by kicking our way across, and Effie's pinto took her to the far
bank in fine shape. The little devil—Effie, I mean—did have
nerve; no cowhand ever crossed water better.

Once across the river and after dumping the logs, we set out
into Texas with our homes on our backs. We cut off the trail as
soon as we reached land to avoid Red River Station, just so no
one would see us so close to the border, then we cut back again
and reached the trail again.

As we rode and walked on toward Bowie, the first town of
consequence, Effie appeared to be happier and more confident.
Perhaps it was the knowledge that she was in Texas again which
made her so.

Yet it was in Bowie that we were to know the full depth of
the King's chicanery. It was now that to obtain money above
Senor Maderas's pittance he plunged into the activities good
Father Dore at St. Louis had told me of—his sale of watered
silver polish, and his pretense to evangelism.

As I have said before, I could have reported Senor Maderas's
murder to a sheriff or Ranger, but who would have taken my
word against the King's? And who could pinpoint the location of
the murder—whether it was in the Chickasaw domain or in the
Unassigned Lands, with all the complications these points would
raise as to jurisdiction?

I have mentioned the King's glibness, and I was soon to know
its full extent.

We had pitched camp that night amidst a group of wry little

76

mesas which tortured themselves near a creek, and next morning the King asked me to ride into town. He rode the pinto, I a mule.

Bowie was a busy settlement, hitchracks and cowhands and blue-clad farmers and big-bonneted women in all the streets, and we rode immediately to a drug store. We left our horse and mule at a hitchrack and entered. The King walked confidently to a prescription clerk, whose skull-like head and dull parchment face indicated perhaps a too great love for his own narcotics. His eyes were dull, and there was a rabbit twitch to his lips.

"My man," said the King, removing his hat and bowing, "I am Dr. Elias Hostetter, the inventor of Dr. Hostetter's Stomach Bitters. I am also a sometime evangelist."

To establish his identity, the King reached into his inner coat pocket and brought out the labeled bottle of bitters the Countess had bought for him at Fort Smith. He looked about the shelves.

"Ah, I see that you have a bottle of my medicine. And I dare say it is patent number 28314. Will you look at the bottle, sir, and see if I am not correct?"

His lips twisting as if he wanted a carrot, the clerk reached for the bottle. "You are correct, sir. That is the exact number. We have sold down to this one."

"That is why I am here," the King said, "with my son Colin. I understood in the countryside that there is a great effluvia among the populace, and in the spirit of humanity I came to you. I have enough ingredients to prepare some few hundred bottles, but I have no bottles. How many could you spare me, and is there another drugstore in town?"

The clerk, who desperately wanted his needle, looked beneath the counter.

"Maybe two hundred," he said.

"And what will the charge be? We must stop this epidemic."

"Three cents a bottle."

"Then give me all. I must get to work at once, and I must see the other drugstore. By the way, what is the price of my bitters here?"

"With transportation what it is, three-fifty a bottle."

77

The King said, "I would think that. Ah, I see you have a typing machine on yonder desk. I have no labels with me, but I suppose we could type some. And as a favor to you, you may have one hundred bottles at two dollars each."

The lips said, "Fair enough. When will you be back?"

"As soon as I go to the other drugstore for bottles. But I promise you, sir, I will sell the store no bitters. You have proved to be my friend, and only you shall benefit. Now, could you begin typing the labels—just as on the bottle you have?"

"In a few moments," said the lips.

"Then I shall be off," said the King. "I shall return this afternoon."

So with an extra one hundred fifty bottles purchased from the other drugstore, the King assuring the druggist that he alone would handle the emergency bitters, and with the first clerk typing furiously on the labels to be used at his store, we rode back to camp with four gunny sacks loaded with empty bottles and corks.

But first, the King would make his silver polish. He had picked up a few pasteboard boxes of soda, and a pink and a brown coloring. At the creek among the mesas he took off his coat and hat and began to work furiously. He filled a hundred bottles with creek water, then dropped a pinch of soda into each along with a drop or two of the coloring, plugging the corks as he went.

Then he called me and Meander. "This," he said, holding a bottle before his sweating face, "is Dr. Hostetter's Silver Polish. Two dollars a bottle. Take the mules and ride into town and sell the polish to every housewife. Don't be afraid to demonstrate—ask for an old spoon. I guarantee it will work. Also spread word of the stomach epidemic. Say that Dr. Hostetter has been called here for the emergency, and his bitters will be on sale at the drugstore before nightfall."

Yes, Meander and I sold the silver polish to staring housewives who watched our demonstrations, even though they had soda in their own kitchens.

After we returned to camp, we loaded up again with the bitters, and with the King riding the pinto we returned to the first drugstore, Meander going on to alert the next.

The prescription clerk, who had unusually bright eyes now, asked the King, "Can't I buy all your bottles? There has been a rush all afternoon. I will pay fifty cents above our agreed price for all of them."

"Since you have been my friend and have typed my labels, I will do that," the King said.

When we had collected our money, we rode to meet Meander. At the second drugstore, it was the same all over again. The King collected, all on the little money he had taken from Senor Maderas.

The King left town well satisfied with himself, but a quarter of a mile out on the road we heard galloping hoofbeats; we turned to look back. Such was the rider's speed that almost by the time we stopped, he pulled his horse up in a cloud of dust. "Stop," he shouted, waving his hat, "stop!" We saw a deputy's star on the man's shirt.

The King muttered, "Someone, perhaps a doctor, has killed the golden goose." He lifted his hat to the deputy. "My good man, what can I do for you?"

The deputy scratched his head. "Now that I think of it, I don't know. The druggist at this end of town came running out with a crowd of people and asked if I had seen a man and two boys leave town. I said yes, and he yelled, 'Stop them, stop them!' and I took off like a rocket without asking why."

"Oh," said the King, "I know what the druggist wanted. I am Dr. Elias Hostetter, the inventor of Dr. Hostetter's Stomach Bitters. You have heard of the epidemic?"

"Oh, God. It's all over the county."

"I have just delivered a quota of my medicine to the two druggists in town. The last asked me to make a double-strength compound for his wife, who is always susceptible to the epidemic." The King reached into his coat pocket. "I apologize, sir, for my forgetfulness." He gave the deputy the same bottle he had shown to the first druggist. "This double-strength bottle

79

will be six dollars. You will see that I took one dose myself to test its efficacy. In the midst of our business, I simply forgot to leave the bottle. Shall I take it back to the druggist, or shall you?"

The deputy pulled from his pocket a small roll of currency. "Here's your six. I'll take the bottle back. But I'm walking my horse. I ain't galloping off on a wild goose chase like I came on. Well, Doc, the people of the county thank you. When I get back, I'll buy a bottle myself. It won't hurt to ward off that epidemic. And if I disturbed you, I'm sorry."

"Not at all, my good man. I am a servant of the public, also."

The deputy turned his horse and walked it slowly down the road. He turned and waved, "Adios, gents."

As soon as a bend in the road hid us, we broke for the brush and threaded our way to camp. We waited there until midnight, no fire, no talking.

At last the King said, "Get the mules and the wagon ready. We should be able to make it now." It was two o'clock in the morning.

When we reached the road an hour later, the team set out at a good trot toward Jacksboro in Jack County. We hoped to be well on our way by daybreak. As I have said before about these moral problems, I had learned again to take the easy way out.

I must not forget the evangelical part of this story—it might help you someday. God's in his heaven, it is said.

He may be on the ground, too, if you look long enough. Perhaps that was what the King tried to din into people's minds.

What he had really wanted for weeks was for me and Meander and Chujo to leave the wagon and Effie; now that he knew we would not, he had determined to use us. So for a greater reason we had all done as we had. At least, it was this thought which consoled me.

In Jacksboro, set in its whistling winter winds and among its shaggy hills, the King went to a sawmill and had a coffin made. He also bought a rectangular mirror about two feet in height, a large piece of canvas, and paints in two colors, red and green. By nightfall he was ready for his next chicanery. The canvas had been painted and hung and flapped in the wind before a hastily constructed brush arbor, and already the religious and emotionally starved people were flocking to it. The king stood and admired his canvas.

## DR. ELIAS HOSTETTER

THE RENOWNED INVENTOR OF DR. HOSTETTER'S
STOMACH BITTERS AND SOMETIME EVANGELIST,
WILL PREACH TONIGHT AT EIGHT O'CLOCK.
GOD, WHERE ARE MY SINNERS? IS THERE NOT ONE
AMONG YOU WHO WILL NOT COME TO BE SAVED?
IN THE NAME OF CHRIST, WHO AMONG YOU WILL
NOT COME?

A MODEST CONTRIBUTION FOR THE LORD'S WORK
WILL BE APPRECIATED.

*Elias Hostetter*
*A.B., A.M., Ph.D., D.D.*

Even the King was surprised by the size of his audience. During the day word had gone forth of Dr. Hostetter; the family-laden wagons from the hills and valleys had come to town, and under growing pressure the citizens and bankers and storekeepers had brought bench after bench and chair after chair to set before the arbor for Dr. Hostetter's preachings. Obviously, not all the crowd could be seated within the arbor.

It all looked well enough to those of us who were to take part in the preaching, but we, who were wiser than the congregation and had been taught our parts, waited silently.

The coffin had been placed on sawhorses at the back of the arbor; the King's altar was before it—a barrel covered by one of the Countess's scarves, and then the chairs and benches.

The King had filled the lower end of the coffin with two logs to appear as legs, then a folded blanket for a chest, and he slanted and braced the mirror so one passing the wrapped corpse in respect for the deceased could see his own face. Over all the body but the shoulders and mirror was placed a sheet.

This was Effie's greatest humiliation. She had been equipped with a pair of wings like an angel's, and would stand at the head of the coffin always flapping her wings, made of another sheet the Countess had bought.

I was to be an archangel standing beside the coffin, my willow-wand spear pointed upward, my head half bandaged, the bandage covering only one eye to indicate how blind people were to angels, and perhaps so I could see only half of what went on. Chujo sat beyond the head of the coffin to collect the offering after the deceased had been viewed.

The Countess, who was the Virgin, sat on a ladder to the rear, fluttering and floating while she oversaw the preparation for the massacre. Meander, equipped with a pointed spear and with padded horns and a rope tail which he twitched left and right, was the Devil; he stood at the foot of the coffin.

When the King took his pulpit, he was dressed in black with a high white collar turned backwards; his coat was also turned backwards and buttoned.

By the time the preaching began, people had already fallen to the ground, groaning and shrieking; then with the King's ceremonial appearance, all became bedlam.

But he calmed the congregation with an upright motion of his hand and took his place behind the pulpit. "Ah, my sinners," he cried, "you have all sinned. That is why you are here tonight."

He began a sermon which was understandable to no one save those who writhed on the ground, and at its conclusion he cried, "We have a dear deceased among us. As you pass by the coffin, look deep into that face—it could be yours!"

"Amen! Amen!"

"When you have passed the coffin, leave your contribution at the collection box, please."

Those who were able to get up from their writhing rose and passed by Meander's twitching tail, and by me the archangel, and by Effie who wagged her wings, the Virgin sitting in state high above the ceremonial.

The King's preaching did good for poor humanity, I suppose, for it took strength for people to rise after a hellfire and damnation service, and go up and look into a coffin where each himself might have been, and stare into the mirror at his own agitated face.

Women fainted; men turned green; the Virgin smiled.

When the people passed the head of the coffin and came to Chujo, I never saw money fall from trembling fingers so fast in my life. Chujo's box was full to overflowing.

At midnight we hitched up the mules and started for Tom Green County. If the King's new luck held, he'd be wealthy by the time we reached the Chisos.

There were always small Texas towns or settlements where the old Indian frontier had once been, each ready and waiting to be taken under the guise of the King's religion or some other antic.

But there were also the long days and nights, the biting winds and northers and blizzards as we continued our way between the caprock and the plateau, but these were only name places, since we were too far away to see either of them, one being northwest and the other southeast.

I do not know what to say of Chujo on our long journey, who disillusioned by his people and his father, had followed us into a strange country, and had learned still stranger things from the King.

I do not think that alone he would ever have followed our practices.

# 7

As we made our way deeper into Texas through the old Fort Phantom Hill country of the mirages and Indian battles, the King revealed more of his talent. He would be by turns a seller of windmills, lightning rods, or barbed wire—bob wire, he called it.

He could produce documents to prove his identity, a picture of the installation of a Jarvis Windmill, himself standing before his workers, the picture bearing the printed caption, "Alanzo Jarvis at the installation of a Jarvis Windmill at the home of Caleb Watson, two miles east, three north of Peoria, Illinois."

What made believers in Mr. Jarvis's windmills was the two miles east, three north, talk. This was honest language a farmer could understand; in fact, since he himself lived eight north and four east of some settlement or other, and with distance being fundamental in the new country, a rapport with the King was established immediately.

I always suspected that the King was a laborer on these pictured projects, and had changed to his good clothes before the picture was taken.

After sizing up and coaxing his prospects, the King would remove from his carpetbag a pad of order forms; the farmer would sign for the delivery and installation of a windmill; the King would pocket a substantial down payment, or take a horse in trade. The horse he quickly sold in the next settlement.

With barbed wire it was the same, and with the lightning rods —the King with his on-the-scene pictures, the captions and the order blanks.

We had stopped once at a half-dugout, half-log hut on a barren hillside covered by old thistles. The grizzled farmer was from Iowa, and due to the drought and cow thieves, was abandoning his homestead and returning. "No," he said to the King, "I wouldn't want one of whatever you've got. I'm going back to Ira-way."

"Well," the King said in high good humor, "you go back to Ira-way, and I'll be going my way."

For five miles down the road the Countess chuckled at the King's brilliant retort. Finally the remark became funny to us, and we began to laugh.

How many times the King had worked these schemes in other states we would never know, even though Father Dore in St. Louis had mentioned some of them, but the King was a man of infinite resource. When things went well, he indulged in jocularity or buffoonery, and was equally good at both.

We were getting into the San Angelo and goat country now; not that the cows and cowhands were fewer, but that the goats were increasing. The town had become a center of the mohair industry. It was a busy place, across the Concho from the old fort of the Indian days.

Even miles away, the King had begun to put out his feelers—his inquiries to travelers on the road, cowhands, and goatherds, and to Mexicans who drove their wooden-wheeled *carretas* to market with their wool.

What he learned did not suit him—too many laws and Rangers thronged the country looking for outlaws, fence-cutters and rustlers, and a legendary Fighting Parson, as he was called, a sincere six-gun man with a Bible, preached the word in saloon and prostitute dives, and laid out with his pistol barrel any drunk cowhand who attempted to jeer him down. The parson stood above the inert cowhand and continued his sermon.

"I think," the King told the Countess, "that we must be very careful in San Angelo. I would not like the Fighting Parson to come to our show."

But whatever the King's doubts, we had to stop in San Angelo anyway.

My boots, and those of Meander and Chujo, were frazzled; we had even cut strips from the tarpaulins to keep our bare feet off the ground. The pinto and the mules had to be shod, and we were sorely in need of axle grease; unless some other traveler on the road helped us, the wagon howled like a banshee.

The wagon rolled down the road from an arc of brown hills, the Countess riding the brake handle, and we came to a wide street lined with burros and horses and hitchracks and goats and made our way to a wagon yard.

When the King stopped the wagon in the enclosure next to the livery barn, a long-bearded, tobacco chewing helper in blue denim asked, "Ain't I seen you somewhere before?"

The pompous King acted as if he had been struck. He summoned his courage and said, "Not that I know of, sir, Certainly not that I know of."

Meander whispered, "That helper put the fear of God into the King. But he'd say what he did to any customer—it's just his way of being ingratiating."

The King and Countess climbed from the wagon and stepped aside.

It would take no mental genius to know that the King's dislike of me had increased, and this with Effie's increased independence. Hardly a day passed without her asking me to do this or that for her. Now that we approached the country he knew, the more evident it became that the King wanted to be rid of me, and Meander and Chujo as well. He had even decreed that he, the Countess, and Effie would sleep in the wagon instead of on the ground the way they had done before.

There was one damn mule, a muckledy dun—Old Dun, we called him—and I find that I am speaking more and more like Meander—which sometimes went hee-haw, hee-haw, each morning when he was put in the traces, but tomorrow or tonight he might not even do it. So far, Old Dun had been a good alarm against the King's moving the wagon without our knowledge.

"I don't like it," Meander said, as we padded almost barefoot toward an adobe shop which housed a cobbler. "The King is ready to chuck us, but he might try a get-away first. I'm going back to watch Effie till you two get your boots fixed; then when you come back, I'll go."

Chujo and I were walking back to the wagon yard, our toes feeling leather again instead of picking up gravel, when at a church I saw a fat priest puttering about the wall with a trowel. We went to him.

"Father Dore," I cried, remembering his moon face as he waved farewell to me as I stood on the *Mississippi Queen.* "What are you doing here?"

"Colin, my boy! After all these months, I should ask you that." He embraced me and said, "Now that Los Alamos will be reestablished, I was sent to open a mission there. But a padre here became ill, and I was told to remain until he recovers. As it is, he is almost well, so I can leave with you for Los Alamos within a day or two."

"This is Chujo," I said, and told our story and how we had found him.

"Ah, it will be good to go on together. I have my burro, and will travel fine. But your adventures are unbelievable."

"Do you think the King would have killed Senor Maderas?"

"When I was a priest in San Antonio, and a friend to your grandfather, I heard something of the King's nature. But apart from his minor chicanery, he was very circumspect in what he did, and was the same toward your grandfather in St. Louis."

"But why would he have gone to St. Louis in the first place?"

"Perhaps he was forced to leave Texas, or he may have been sent to watch Don Herrera. After you left St. Louis, I learned that there was once a connection between the King and Don Sostelo, although the King's conduct toward Don Herrera was perfect. I also learned that Don Sostelo has a granddaughter."

"Then Effie could have Sostelo blood?"

"Perhaps," said Father Dore. "Come, I will go to the wagon yard with you and appear to be very casual. In fact, for the sake of both you and the young girl, I will plan to leave the church at a moment's notice. I do not like what I suspect."

"What did you think of the Maderas family?" I asked as we walked.

"They were both good and honest. I believe they were entrapped by Don Sostelo to take Effie to St. Louis where she could influence you in some way, or win you to the Sostelo side so Don Sostelo could gain your property."

I remembered the perfume through the steamboat transom and Senora Maderas's words on the hill above the Canadian, that there was much that she wished she could tell, but could not. And Effie herself had told me almost the same thing when we had galloped away from the wagon that day.

I felt strangely stirred. Whatever Effie had done, it was something she had been forced into, but once in it and when the showdown came, despite her Sostelo blood, she could be nothing but her own dear self.

"Someday," I said, "I will prosecute the King for the murder of Senor Maderas."

"The parchment—is it still safe?"

"Yes," I said. "It is always on one or the other of us."

When we reached the wagon yard, Effie and the King and Countess sat beside a fire they had built in a corner of the boarded fence; from a low window of the livery barn Meander gave the high sign and left to have his own boots repaired.

Father Dore and Effie greeted each other cordially, but this was not so with the King and Countess. Each was surly; while they may have tolerated the little padre in St. Louis, they had no obligation or help to seek from him here. Their eyes were full of hatred.

"Sir," the King said rising, "I had never expected to see you again. I hope your stay with us will not be long."

"Padre, not sir," the little priest corrected gently. "But on the contrary, you will see much of me. I intend to go with the boys to Los Alamos, where I am to establish a mission."

"You have not been invited to accompany us," the Countess said, giving a vicious pull at her whisker.

Before the padre could reply, the King blanched. The high cold wind, as well as the nearness of the fire's heat, had made his jowls more ruddy than usual, but he blanched because three men had ridden into the wagon yard. They dismounted, and walked to the office of the livery barn.

I did not recognize all of them, but one was the man who had come to the hotel in Fort Smith to announce to the clerk that later in the day the King would get his ride on a rail.

But the King had evidently recognized all the men, for he leaped like a bouncing top to the bed of the wagon and hid himself flat between the sideboards. Quickly, the Countess covered him with a tarpaulin. Once more the King faced ruin, all because of a Fighting Parson and three old gambling cronies.

There were the two mules—Old Muley and the dun, cantankerous Old Dun, it was—and it would not have surprised me at all, long before daylight, to hear one of the sideboards crack from Old Dun's hooves, and to hear his raucous hee-haw, hee-haw, as the King tried to put him in the traces.

The padre departed for the church, telling me in a whisper that if the King tried to depart in the night to get word to him, for his possessions would be packed and he would arrange to leave with us.

Now something else happened to complicate things. The three

gamblers came from the livery barn with the wide-hatted owner; it seemed that their mounts were worn from travel, and a horse trade was in progress. But the owner did not easily give in. The gamblers had picked their new horses, but it was a question now of how much boot. At last the gamblers submitted and handed over some money; the trade had taken about two hours and now the men sat in the livery barn office. There had been no chance for the King to do what he had wished to do in town, and the Countess and Effie had sat huddled on the far side of the wagon.

Shortly before dark, the King's head popped from his tarpaulins. He stuffed a few bills into my hand. "Colin, go to town and buy at least three barrels. Buy all the cow or goat bladders you can, and anything else to hold water. Get a full stock of provisions. Have them brought to the wagon after dark. Hurry, now!"

Meander and Chujo, or one of them, started to follow, but the King said, "No, I will need you both here. Get the wagon greased, and get all the tar we can carry. Pay our bill here in full for the mules and include tomorrow's tab."

After I had returned with half a dozen Mexican boys and the barrels and bladders and supplies, I paid them off and they left.

I sat by the fire to have a cup of coffee with Meander and Chujo.

Meander said, "Hell's going to pop tonight. Those gamblers are still gaming in the office—they must be trying to win their money back. I reckon the King will try to skip when the office lights go out. Be ready for anything. The King may have it in his book to leave us."

The King and the Countess would sleep as usual that night, well wrapped in their blankets and covered by a tarpaulin, the King on one side of the wagon bed, the Countess in the middle, and Effie on the far side.

Tonight Meander and Chujo would sleep on the hay of the livery barn, so not to arouse the King's suspicion by all of us being together, and it was my decision to sleep as usual beneath the wagon, trusting Old Dun to awaken me if the King determined to move.

When I woke to the sudden ruckus of the dun and heard the King's plaintive whispers of appeal, I slipped between the back wheels and ran to wake Chujo and Meander in the livery barn. I told Chujo, "Run to the church and tell Father Dore that the King will move to the Desert Road before daylight. He's hitching now."

Meander and I went back to the wagon. Meander spoke to the King, and he jumped a foot. "You'd be better off," Meander said, "if you'd put Muley in the traces first. Muley is gentle, and you'd have something to lead the dun to."

"Do you think I don't know mules?" the King said, jerking at the dun's bit.

Meander said, "You don't know a damn thing about mules, or anything else."

We forded the river and left San Angelo behind in the darkness; a mile out of town we came to a mesa on what was called the Desert Road. A winter sunrise flung its fan-like rays upward. On top of the mesa Father Dore sat his burro, holding an upraised cross.

Chujo stood at his side.

When Father Dore and Chujo came down from the mesa to join us, we drove the wagon into the brush to have breakfast. We had not dared build a new fire or try to eat in the wagon yard.

As far as we could see lay colored soils and desolate growth and barren mesas, golden in the early light, and after eating we were off on the last leg of our journey to Los Alamos, some two hundred miles of it if we could have gone as straight as an arrow. We couldn't, of course, not with the wide swings we must make to places where we knew water could be found. As it was, we would add to that distance, a third or a half. With the long stretch ahead before we even reached Horsehead Crossing on the Pecos, we stopped at the Middle Concho to fill the barrels and bladders with water.

I could not believe, as we wandered onward, that Effie was a Sostelo, and having known of certain things earlier, perhaps it was difficult, too, for her to believe that I was Herrera, or O'Reiley. But neither of us had much time to think of this.

From the Middle Concho, we headed for Horsehead, for there were only a few good crossings farther down the Pecos; once across, we would seek the old Indian trail to Comanche Springs, then continue down the eastern side of the Glass and Santiago Mountains. When we reached Persimmon Gap in the Santiago range we would have our first sight of the Chisos.

But now we had the Pecos to reach; even getting there was a problem, and we never would have made the desert run without the water-filled barrels and bladders. There was Centralia Draw, the Castle Mountains, and Castle Gap, and beyond lay the steep-banked Pecos River.

However much the King might have detested us, his journey would have been impossible had it not been for the hacking of our machetes to clear a way for his wagon. He still feared the gamblers of San Angelo.

"Those gamblers," he would say, "they could be going to New Mexico, to Roswell, maybe. Sure, there's a road of sorts, but we'll play it safe. Unless it's night, we'll stick mainly to the brush."

And that, with the plodding pace of the mules, was all we could do.

In hot unseasonable weather we went on, the bitter alkali filling our mouths and eyes, our stops for water increasing as our supply dwindled; even so, we kept things evened up by always giving the mules and the pinto and burro their scant share from a tin dishpan.

A white salt crust was on our clothes beneath our armpits.

Charles Goodnight in his trail-blazing cattle drive over the same eighty-mile stretch from the Concho to the Pecos had done it in under a four day-and-night running span, but with frantic cows famished for water, not our slow mules which took fourteen days with each deep arroyo to head.

I watched Effie, so much thinner now.

I told her one day as I walked beside the pinto, "I am worried for you."

"Why? You give me half your food and water. You watch me night and day."

I may have jumped the gun, but I said, looking up at her, "I don't care who you are, but I love you."

Surprise showed on her grimy face. Her lips were split and parched and sore, like mine, from howling winds and sand that bit the face.

She said only, "Colin!" and reached down and pressed her hand on my shoulder. I walked on beside the gaunt pinto.

When we came from the mouth of the mile-wide canyon of Castle Gap, we could not believe that only twelve miles separated us from the Pecos. From here, we should have made it to water in a day, but with the exhaustion of man and beast, it was to take two. With the sun on fire, we pitched camp beyond the gap and lay and slept.

But by sundown of the next day we were to have water. Taking their morning drink at the camp, with the first light Meander and Chujo left for the river, laden with our every water bag.

The King had snapped, "Don't take water from the pools you will find. It will be alkaline, and can kill a horse. Bring back water only from the river."

Their boots dragging, Meander and Chujo returned at nightfall, the water bags filled. Now we had another problem—how much should we drink? The water was alkaline, but not as concentrated as that found in the pools. We wouldn't die from drinking it, Meander said, but we could get sick and have cramps. So we went very easy on the water, as Meander and Chujo had done. But that night even the mules and the pinto and the burro drank deeper.

"Was the river high or low?" the King asked, hunkered by the fire.

"Low," said Meander.

"Good. We shouldn't have trouble crossing the wagon."

By mid-afternoon of the next day we camped in the brush within half a mile of the river, but the King had no wish to be seen where traffic might be heavy. As soon as we camped, Chujo and I went for water while Meander stayed with Effie.

On all sides at the steep-banked, sun-struck crossing were the bleached skulls of cattle and horses which had drunk themselves to death after the desert travail.

That night the King made his plans for the crossing carefully. There was a rise some distance to the right; tomorrow, Chujo would climb it, and when the trail back had no horsemen or wagons on it, he would signal the King.

As he talked by the fire, the King grew more excited, as did the Countess. They thought that once across the Pecos, they would find a haven of refuge; they wanted nothing left to chance now.

Even as he talked, the King wiped his cracked and bleeding lips. We were all that way from the long trek; the mules and the pinto and burro maintained their bleary-eyed look.

I have often laughed at the calamity which struck us at the crossing, although at the time it was indeed serious. We had driven the wagon into the water with the barrels empty, planning to refill later, so there would be no additional weight to impede the mules.

We crossed the river, then started up the farther bank, but still in water. Halfway up, with the padre's shoulder at one wheel, and mine and Meander's and Chujo's at the others, Old Dun decided to play the fool.

Having seen and drunk water again, perhaps he thought we were headed for another land where water never grew; he protested with a loud hee-haw and lurched away from Muley.

That was the beginning, or the end, of everything.

In the slippery footing, the lurch had pulled Muley off his feet, and as the wagon tilted he went down, taking Old Dun with him. From the overturned wagon our three barrels tumbled back into the river, and began gently to float away. Supplies were washed away or ruined, and the padre and I barely missed being pinned beneath the wheels we had shoved when Old Dun lurched.

The Countess was sitting in the river.

94

All about was a maze of mules and supplies and wagon wheels; Chujo and Meander swam after the barrels, capturing two of them; then, below the crossing, they found they had caught the barrels but couldn't get them up the steep bank.

I went along the bluff with a rope and hauled them out, and barely in time, for Meander had bogged in quicksand.

Meanwhile, Father Dore and the King had got the mules from their traces and on their feet. We righted the wagon, tied ropes to it from the mules, and with Meander holding the wagon tongue up so it wouldn't be rammed into mud, pulled and shoved the wagon up to high ground, the grunting padre straining with us.

Now we were well into it—one hundred twenty miles to Los Alamos, longer the way we would swing west for the certainty of water at Comanche Springs and Fort Stockton. We were left with no food to speak of, two limping mules, a broken doubletree, and a world as bleak as mesquite in Hades.

Our travels for that day were over; that evening we camped among the bleached horse and cow skulls and stark rib bones; we lifted our two barrels back into the wagon and filled them a skin at a time from the river. There was only one good thing— our axle grease; its cans, stored in large boxes, had been saved. We were all at the breaking point; the padre prayed at the bank of the river.

Just before darkness, the King said sharply, "Effie, go get all the mesquite beans you can find." He kicked the tin pan banging toward her. Frightened, Effie rose, even as Father Dore did. I got to my feet and stepped toward the King; he stepped toward me. Chujo was beside Effie first; she whirled and ran back to his rifle on the sand.

Effie, her tight little mouth stern and uncompromising, cocked the rifle and pointed it toward the King. She said, "If you take one step more toward Colin, I will kill you." She stood very imperious and certain.

The King backed off. Effie had revealed some power she had never exerted before.

95

Chujo took the rifle from Effie; her head high, she picked up the tin pan and walked with Chujo toward the brush.

Meander whispered, "You've got a real girl to side you, but it all proves what I said. The King knows this country, or he wouldn't have known about alkali pools and mesquite beans. You can grind and make a paste out of the beans, and even live on it. That's one thing peons live on. And with this food shortage, he'll have us making food out of old cactus tuna and eating rattlesnakes." Meander laughed. "Still, it's all we'd have anyway."

In the morning, with a patched-up wagon, we hit the brush again, and I want to forget it. For days we obtained our scanty water from depressions in rocks, and battled the desert growth. The western mountains and purple peaks only accented our desolation.

If famished Comanche ponies had died at Horsehead from coming up this trail, what hope did we have, going into it? Comanche Springs at old Fort Stockton would be our greatest hope, if only we reached it.

Late one afternoon, the sky and clouds went crazy. A freak blizzard struck, breaking the heat, and piling two feet of snow on the ground. In the driving wind, with snow as thick as oatmeal, Meander built a lean-to, but it was like no lean-to I had ever read of. I had thought them small cozy places. Instead, Meander first chopped and trimmed persimmon trees from a ghostly grove; then with the help of all of us, placed a long pole across the crotches of two other trees. We slanted more poles against the horizontal one, fastened two tarpaulins in place against the framework, and soon had a fair windbreak with a fire blazing.

I told Meander, "This lean-to looks like one wing of a dead bird stuck in the air."

"This lean-to is an old vaquero custom. It breaks the wind. Like I told you once, I've known cows to freeze to death in twenty-six degrees. It ain't the cold that kills, it's the wind. This way we can stand up and walk around a big fire and all, and don't have to huddle in a hole."

"Ah," said the padre, after we had eaten and had gathered about the fire, "a good game of checkers now?"

The game of checkers was the padre's only vice. He had brought his small folding board from St. Louis; he produced it now from his sack of luggage, along with his red and black men, and in all our worst nights from the Concho to the Pecos, no one had ever beaten him.

"Who will play me?" he asked, rubbing his hands together, his bright face beaming. "You, Colin, will you be first?"

I wanted only to sit and look at frozen Effie, but I said, "Yes, I will play you."

It was the padre's custom to rush his front men forward furiously, meanwhile advancing more slowly from the back line. Just when I thought I had him in a jump, I found myself without three men; one of those idle back men had done the work. I moved again and jumped, then the padre made a double. After that it was slaughter. His first moves had been only decoys.

Effie played next; she lost, then the entire camp lost, although the King had not yet played.

"Will you be next?" the padre asked him.

"Yes," the King said. "And here is where you get it."

Somebody got it, but it wasn't the padre. He won five straight games. He asked the King benignly, "Would you care to try again?"

"No," said the King, bracing himself to go into the snow. "You run a crooked board."

The padre laughed heartily.

It became very cold. The Countess began to weep from despondency, tears rolling down her cheeks, but freezing before they could drop. The King pecked them aside with his fingernail.

When we went to bed, two and a half feet of snow covered the ground. In spite of our discomfort, the snow did mean one good thing—water when it melted, for depressions and rocky basins would be filled from the runoff. Once more we felt safe again.

When we awakened, it was a different story. There was not a

single speck of snow on the ground; there was only the sand. In bewilderment, I asked Meander, "What happened?"

"Sometimes it's like this. A change comes; a dry wind passes and evaporates the snow. It just sucks the moisture up. You won't find water today in any crevice. Now you see what this country can be like."

I began to think the land was haunted. No wonder the conquistadores faltered.

Our travel became slower now, sometimes only a few miles a day. We were lost in great dust storms, the wagon bogging in sand. We would come upon unexpected arroyos, which meant long and tedious detours around their headings, and always there was the search for water. Our pace was as slow as when the King was selling his lightning rods and windmills.

I cannot say too much for Father Dore on our journey. While we made our tortuous way, whether he walked or rode his burro, he always carried his cross before him, and I never knew a man so willing to put his back to a wheel, as he did on the Pecos, or put his hand to an axe or spend his evenings over a cooking fire.

But the padre's joviality only increased the King's and the Countess's antagonism, for many times their wagon would not have gone another foot without his shoving shoulders and those of the rest of us.

And there was always Effie at her menial task of searching for tuna or mesquite beans; she carried an old flour sack, and if the mesquite pods had not burst or fallen from the branches, she gathered them bending from the pinto. Meanwhile, Chujo, Meander, and I helped all we could, filling our pockets with what beans we found in clearing a way for the wagon.

But at times, almost dizzy from lack of food, I felt that the padre was Friar Marcus, leading us to the Seven Cities of Cibola, only in the opposite direction on tags of old cow trails.

Yet the mesquite paste, mixed with our dwindling supply of corn meal and fried in what grease remained from our old bacon rinds, did make the mainstay of our diet, especially when we found no game.

98

It was only that Effie found the beans, mashed them between rocks, and ground them and made the paste, while the Countess rode in state and did nothing.

Except for a snake or rabbit, or some ground bird blown to pieces, the grease was our substitute for meat. The noise of clearing a way for the wagon frightened game away. Fortunately, as we neared Comanche Springs and Fort Stockton, a light rain fell, and we filled our barrels from a rocky creek.

That night Meander suddenly asked the King, "We're not going to Comanche Springs and Fort Stockton, are we?"

Surprised, the King replied, "Why, I don't know."

Only that day we had met some Mexicans who told us the old fort might be closed out soon.

"You know, and I know," Meander said. "This last rain gave us water, and if we went to the springs, we'd end up right back here and still have to go south. We wouldn't gain a drop. But mostly, you don't want to be around that fort, if it's still there, do you? Of course, you would have gone, but you'd rather not."

The King said, discomfited, "Tomorrow, we'll strike for the Glass Mountains."

Meander said, "That's what I thought."

We were well past the purple mass of the mountains when our water ran out, all but one goat bladder and one canteen. That night the King sat before the fire with an empty barrel, reaming small holes in the staves several inches above the bottom. Near him sat the Countess; Effie and Meander and I sat by the wagon, and the padre played checkers with Chujo, who beat him one game.

Meander said, "Do you know what the King's doing? He's been a cowhand, and in dry country. Tomorrow we'll sink that barrel in creek sand where it looks moist, and a few inches of water might seep through those holes. I've seen cows kneel to drink water from creek barrels, and even get their horns stuck and die. I've held back on this trick, just to see if the King would pull it."

Meander swaggered to the King. "If you're reaming out for

99

water, let me help. An old cowhand gets tired drilling by him-self. You can wear a blister that way. Us old cowhands must stick together."

The King could not withhold an expression of surprise. Then he threw his knife into the sand, point down, and stood up. He snarled, "Go to it."

But the retreat he beat to the Countess was almost hasty.

"The fat's in the fire now," I said. "You told him his whole life's history."

"Not all," Meander said. "His life ain't ended yet." His ire was still up at the King's deception about Comanche Springs. "Hey," he yelled to him, "you know more about this country than you let on. Did you ever do any Pecosin?"

The King turned. "I don't know what you mean."

Meander grinned his odd grin. "Then think about it." He turned from the King. "Pecosin," he said to me, "is killing a guy and rolling his body into the river, and I bet the King has rolled plenty."

One morning we awoke in a new world. Overnight the desert had blossomed. The growth we had fought so long had stirred. Yellow and orange and red and white flowers flaunted them-selves on desert and flat-topped mesas alike, and the winter gray of yucca had turned to green.

About us lay a wilderness of beauty and desolation such as I had never dreamed of—the colored earth, the creosote, sotol and cenzio, the all-thorn, guayule and black-brush, and always the yucca and cactus, and the flaming, many-fingered plants. And every cactus bloomed with flowers as delicate as orchids.

We had seen it happening for days in time and slowness—the occasional flower all alone, but now the desert world had burst into color. Moist clouds blew from the south. Spring had come since we left the Arkansas, with its slow cold stars above the *Dewdrop,* and now we moved through starkness and brilliant beauty.

When we reached Persimmon Gap, the pass in the Santiago range, we stopped the wagon on a height. Ahead lay the first sight of the Chisos Mountains, a coffined bulk which reared distantly, mounted by misty white and serrated peaks.

A rainbow hung over the Chisos in all its color, shimmering from red and orange to violet.

Effie drew the pinto nearer.

"But why the rainbow?" I asked. "There has been no rain."

"Don't you know?" she cried, that flop of hair blowing. "It is because of the atmosphere. The old Apaches believed that the Chisos were the place where the rainbows came to wait for the rain. Because of the misty tops, they called them the Ghost Mountains. The old Comanches called them the Echo Mountains."

From the height of the pinto, Effie placed her hand on my shoulder. "Colin, I am so glad to be home. Even older Indians once lived in the mountains—the basket weavers. Perhaps someday we can visit their caves."

We crossed dry Tornillo Creek, and that night bedded down as usual, much nearer the Chisos and Los Alamos.

When we awoke next morning, there was no Effie, no King, no Countess. Only the loose mules and the wagon remained. It was as if a dry wind had passed over the land, taking them all away. Old Dun nibbled at a tuft of grass.

The padre said, "My son, I am sorry."

"But where have they gone?"

"If Effie is indeed the granddaughter of Don Sostelo, perhaps to his hacienda. It is on toward the mountains."

"Well," I said, "I want to see Los Alamos. Let's travel."

We hitched the mules to the wagon and went on, this time riding. A small mesa lay off to the west.

And when I saw Los Alamos, only a mudhole with a few cottonwoods about it, and a dozen lean-flanked cows knee-deep and drinking, I was sickened. In spite of a parchment, I had come so many miles for nothing.

I asked Meander, "Why didn't you tell me Los Alamos was like this?"

"You never asked."

While I stared helplessly about me, the padre said, "My son, it is God's will. Show him the worst," he told Meander.

Meander led us to the ruins of an old hacienda, thence to a stone hut. "This is where you were born, and where your mother was killed."

The padre remained silent, and Meander wandered about the cactus aimlessly. "Here's an old yellow rose bush sticking up," he said.

"Yes, it must be part of a garden where my father first saw my mother. Do you know where she was buried?"

Meander said uneasily, "Over here."

He led me to a small graveyard and to my mother's stone.

He said, "If you will let me have one of those mules, Old Muckledy, maybe, I'll get home by sundown. I've got to skirt the Chisos before I get there. About three days from now, I'll be back with my daddy, and some stock for you. Meanwhile, you and the padre can talk things over."

I watched Meander go with his snaggle-tooth grin, his mouth a little more crooked than usual, and I had never had a better friend in my life.

"Colin," the padre said, "may I place my cross over the stone hut?"

"Yes, padre," I said, and looked at Chujo.

He was studying a small depression which lay between the ruins of the hacienda and a long sand hill several rods beyond.

"It will mean work," Chujo said.

# 8

<<<<<<<<<<<<<<<<<<

It was to be a year and a half before I saw Effie again, but I had
no time to ponder my misfortune. There was much to be done at
Los Alamos, and I had no time for idleness.

On the fourth day after Meander left, Chujo and I saw a
cloud of dust in the south; then we made out Meander and a tall
man who rode beside him. Behind them was a supply wagon
followed by a herd of cattle and another of goats, all watched by
native vaqueros.

But what a change in Meander!

He slid grinning from his horse, a fiery bay, dressed in a flat-
crushed sombrero and cowhand clothes, a pistol tied low on his
leg, looking as much a part of the country as a creosote bush or a
cactus.

"Well, we brung you something. And this is my daddy and your Uncle Michael."

The tall determined looking man climbed off his horse. He was red-headed, with a wide, good-humored mouth, rugged jaws, and slate-blue eyes.

"Welcome, Colin," he said. "But I am afraid you have not come to much, except what we bring you. The cows and goats will get you started. Three vaqueros will stay with you; they once worked for Don Herrera. You will find them loyal, and more of their friends will come, including Miguel, the old majordomo, and Pedro. The pistol, Meander."

Meander took from the wagon seat a Colt .44 and a pistol belt.

"I understand you can shoot," my uncle said. "Wear this gun always, and trust no one not known to you or the vaqueros. When your stock is on the range, you may have Sostelo's men to face."

A toothless old goatherd in blowing tatters crawled his way forward in the sand. Before I knew what happened, he seized my hand and kissed it. "Don Colin Herrera O'Reiley," he cried, "you have returned at last! Now we will again have Los Alamos as it used to be. I served your grandfather. When it is known you are here, many old people and their children will come. We will build jacals and watch the herds, as we used to do."

Don Colin Herrera O'Reiley!

It had a good, if ridiculous sound, but more than that, it showed that I could be of use to the poor peons who had once lived here, and to their families.

"Up, old man," I said. "Do not kneel to me. But those of your people who wish to return will be welcome."

Meander grinned. "Well, Don O'Reiley, will there be room for a country cousin?"

I laughed. "Yes, if he can make adobe bricks, herd cows and goats, and clean up the rubble of the old hacienda."

"Then I'll spend a week every month. I'll start right now."

"You may have noticed that I have ruined Meander's speech," my uncle said. "I turned him loose with cowhands too early. Meander plays the fool, but he is far from being one."

My uncle told me that Don Sostelo did have a granddaughter, Euphemia, and that Euphemia's mother was alive and still lived at Don Sostelo's hacienda. Although he lived far to the southeast, my uncle had inquired closer into the old don's affairs after receiving word of my grandfather's illness, and had obtained what information he could.

He told me that I might expect outright trouble or annoyances from the don's riders, but that if shots were fired at me or my retainers, not to hesitate to fire back. "Get your bluff in," my uncle said. "Let the don know you mean business. Old Carlos there is right. In a week, old families will begin to return. You will have your own men, and in a pinch, I can bring mine. I will take the parchment back with me."

Meander said, while he and Carlos pulled a dozen rifles from the wagon, "Let's get the rest of this vehicle unloaded. You've got grub, ammunition, and all a young don needs to set up in life. The extra vaqueros will go back with the wagon, so you'll have six horses instead of having to ride Muley. If you don't care, I'll keep Old Dun—just a reminder of our trip."

Chujo and Father Dore came and helped unload the wagon; the weapons were placed inside the stone hut, and other supplies piled against the outside.

There was more talk with Uncle Mike—he said call him that, since no one called him Michael—and I agreed to get in touch with him if trouble came with Don Sostelo. Then he mounted and waved good-bye.

I was left with three toothless old vaqueros, a herd of cows, and a flock of goats.

It was as Old Carlos had said that day, the wind flapping his pajama pants, that as soon as the old retainers of Don Herrera heard a young don had taken his place, there would be an influx of people from all the poor and makeshift jacals scattered about the mountains.

I will never forget the day when Miguel and Pedro, the first of Don Herrera's retainers, rode into Los Alamos to give some solace to me and Chujo and Meander on our lonely estate.

They were the long and short of it, with bright serapes over their shoulders; Miguel seven feet tall if an inch, with broad shoulders and fierce upturned mustachios, and there was dumpy little Pedro. He had a narrow forehead, but a full chin and cheeks that bulged downward like a pear. He appeared to be almost stupid, but his sharp black eyes proved he was far from being that.

"Don O'Reiley," Miguel said, "we were here with your grandfather. I was his majordomo. Senor Michael O'Reiley told us you had returned. We have left our goats with relatives, and have come to serve you."

Meander whickered. "Don O'Reiley! I sure like that name!"

"May we stay again at Los Alamos?" Pedro asked.

"You may stay if you wish, only I cannot feed much."

"We will look after the feeding," Miguel said. "Where do we sleep?"

"The ground is free to all."

They left us and walked about the barren stretch and its ruins; to the hacienda, to the depression and the sand hill, and crossed themselves at my mother's grave. Then they walked to a space we had cleared between the ruined hacienda and the church— what we called our plaza.

When they returned, Miguel said, "Don O'Reiley, it is good to be back. Within a month you will have many families here, and they must have water. You will need first a well, for the old one was destroyed. People cannot drink manure water or from the depression where they bathe. It would kill them."

"Yes, I know. But I have hardly thought of a well."

"You plan for the future, don't you?"

"Very much for the future."

"I understand your worry. Let me look after the well. I will go for Astabo tomorrow."

"Who is Astabo?"

"He is the wild man of the Chisos—a water witch. It will take several days to find him. He claims to be sacred, and goes barefoot; the soles of his feet are like leather. He does not use magic wands or sticks to find water, but a cow skull with the long horns still sticking out. But I swear I will bring him."

Father Dore had come up. Pedro asked, "Cannot a man of God find water here?"

"My son, God gives each man a special talent. If Astabo finds water, I will drink it."

It was well that Miguel and Pedro went in search of Astabo; they were gone four days, and when they returned with the water witch five families had returned to the old site to build their hovels near the depression.

But this Astabo—I had never seen anything like him. He was short and bandy-legged, almost a dwarf, with hair which drooped all around to his waist; he wore an animal skin about his middle; his eyes peered, or tried to peer, through the mop which hung over his face, until I doubted that a man was behind this thing at all.

The camp, including the new families and Father Dore, gathered to watch the witch at work. At first Astabo squatted and pronounced a prayer over his cow skull, holding the horns with the long face pointed downward, then he rose and wandered aimlessly as a she-goat, meanwhile giving a series of mutterings, which sometimes Miguel and Pedro were able to translate.

Near the rose garden, Astabo went into contortions, his small body twisting. Miguel said, "He is beginning to feel his vibrations."

To me, so far everything had been reasonable. I had often wondered about the rose garden, why it had been placed there in the first place. If there was some low level of moisture, it explained both the garden and Astabo's vibrations.

Suddenly, Astabo shrieked. In fear, the senoras of the new families fell to their knees and crossed themselves as if against a hairy devil; their children ran screaming and cowered behind the hovels. Astabo, fighting and writhing with the plunging cow horns, which seemed determined to destroy him, continued to shriek.

I glanced at the padre; his round face was impassive.

Astabo was wallowing on the ground, foaming at the mouth, fighting the cow skull, trying to hold it down. But now it flew from his hands to rest lifelessly not ten feet from the padre. The skull could not have fallen in a better place—almost in the center of the plaza. Astabo wiped his frothy mouth.

Slowly, he got to his feet. He picked up the skull. Still muttering, but speaking to no one, he padded back toward the Chisos. Miguel marked the spot where the skull had fallen.

"Is it over?" I said.

"All but our digging." Miguel laughed.

"Don't we owe him something?"

"No, because he is sacred. Money would rob him of his power."

In time we struck water and rocked the well; it was a source of good drink which never failed us.

After the arrival of our first families, others came to Los Alamos, more of the old retainers. They came in rags, most of them gaunt and starved, their rib bones showing, men, women, and children walking, their scant belongings packed upon burros. In the weeks which followed, Father Dore had set out daily to find new parishioners, and his burro carried him to every crevice of the mountains and into the desert draws.

Within six months some thirty families had come to build their miserable jacals or lean-tos about the plaza. I did not see how people could live under these conditions—only a few clay pots or a brazier for their cooking, and a *petate,* or mat, to sleep upon, the women grinding corn and boiling frijoles and making tortillas before those poor quarters. Some shelters were no more than a thatched line of posts set in the ground.

I did not like this poverty, for I had known it, or at least a semblance of it. My poor grandfather had been hard pressed to send me to the best schools; consequently, there had been but little money left for my allowance. I had my meals and room, of course, but among the richer students, I knew the thing of never really having what I wanted to equal their affluence.

I determined to end this poor existence, although the people seemed accustomed to it, and did not complain.

I wanted to learn more of the traditions and customs of the early dons, and the relationship with their people, so one day while Meander and I rode to a goat camp near a bog to the east, I asked him, "What is the real truth about these old dons? I've read about them, but not everything is in books."

"Well," Meander said, "there were two kinds, and each received a grant and authority from a king or queen. One type of grant was the Teopantlalli, which gave some of its earnings to its church and fed its people. Some of the dons on Pillali lands were brigands with court influence, and what you might call armies—proud and cruel men and raising mischief. The Spaniards had built on the old Aztec system."

"Why were dons left in Texas after the War with Mexico?"

"Because there weren't enough up here to matter—mainly old Sostelo and your granddaddy. Sostelo's vaqueros were always up to something, mainly in Mexico, but nothing here was ever proved against him. Your granddad was one who always gave to his church."

"But why did Texans let them stay?"

"Oh, their men were killing each other off, and other outlaws, too. It saved our people having to do it."

"You're pretty tolerant here."

Meander grinned. "Sure, as long as we don't get filled with lead. Besides, we've got our own work to do. We also let rustlers and smugglers kill them. My dad's vaqueros have fought it out with Sostelo's men, even though he never met the don. But he knows all about the old skunk."

As a result of Meander's information and more from the

padre, I called the people to the plaza and issued a proclamation —if it could be called a proclamation—that each family must build an adobe hut of its own, and for those who might come later, they, too must build huts. I would give each family a she-goat and an acre of land for its own use, but there would be a communal acreage where all could work in the cultivation of maize for storage against hard times or winter or drought.

Within days two straight lines were staked out for hut frontages, a street to be between them, and adobe bricks dried in the sun.

With the help of my uncle, I eliminated at least a part of the rags. He established credit for me with merchants at Alpine and Sanderson, on the San Antonio to El Paso railroad. Alpine, to the north, was our county seat; Sanderson lay to the northeast. I took back bolts of cloth for the senoras to make new dresses for themselves and children, and a coarser material for the pajama pants the men wore.

I will say one thing for the new Los Alamos which rose from the old ruins—it was all activity. The street which ran between the adobes was named by the Mexicans the Street of the Dove, although I never knew why. In turn, the occupants of the off-side paths which led to single adobes also named their streets— the Three Flowers, the Path of Pedro, and the Cow and Donkey.

I have perhaps stressed too much the older people who returned to Los Alamos, and have neglected the younger men and women of my age. One nubile girl was dark-haired Teresa, who constantly made eyes at me, and smiled when she bathed in the depression on San Juan's day.

There was much of the old Apache blood among those in the village, and I selected twelve young men of mixed blood—those who demonstrated the greatest ability—and entrusted them with the care and use of rifles. They were quick and intelligent boys, of pride and fierce loyalty.

The mixed breeds, even the oldest men—those like Carlos— had always been poorly armed, but as vaqueros, the ancient trade they knew, the lariat was their greatest weapon. An enemy could be pulled from his horse and killed, or they could lay a frothing bear or deer or javalina in the Chisos.

These expectations lived in boys of five or six, who practiced daily with their lariats, and like their elders could throw a figure eight—the *pial*—catching both hind hooves of a cow or goat separately, even the feet of a human. For this reason, if the youngsters were playing their roping games as I walked about Los Alamos, I wisely kept my sandals low.

My mixed breed young Apaches inherited the tradition of the enslaved, bare-heeled and Spanish-roweled vaqueros of the time of Cortez, whose cattle brand was three Christian crosses, but their fealty to their herds and masters in storm and war, despite their mistreatment and lank lean-tos, could never be equalled.

If another raid came to Los Alamos, its success would not be easily won, not with my young soldados always scattered in the brush as guards, and with the older vaqueros and our herds stationed nearer home. By day or night, at least half my younger men would be on outer patrol; the rest would spend their time watching and living at solitary spots in the desert.

Don Sostelo was not the only reason for these precautions. In fact, I soon bought more rifles at Alpine, and recruited more Apaches for the brush. Los Alamos lay near the cow rustling trail from across the Rio Grande, and if it was not used by Mexican or American thieves at the same time, there were always the smugglers. We lived in constant vigilance.

My Apaches were trained by fiercely mustached Miguel, my majordomo, and Pedro; with Chujo as my steady right hand and Father Dore in his church, we saw progress made. At night there might be the tinkle of mandolins or the strum of guitars from the benches in the plaza.

But the poor padre and his graveyard!

It was not his at all, for in reality it had belonged in part to other friars for centuries. The early missions established for the Apaches had been destroyed by marauding Comanches, and the Apaches had small chance to accept the first friars' faith. Not only the older missions, but also Santa Cruz on the south bank of the San Saba had been lost, so even now the old Apaches still held their ancient Fire Dance in the plaza.

Over the years the small graveyard had received the dead of the padre's faith, those of other faiths, and those of no faith at all. Father Dore was an honest priest, and he was troubled that his own dead did not all rest together, yet there were the Apaches and others to think of.

When a burial became necessary, it was as if the padre played his game of checkers, which was why I thought of the graveyard as a checkerboard. If the dead had been of the padre's faith, he would deploy from a new wall he was building and with a hop, skip, and jump, fly over one alien grave or another to seek the place for a new burial hole, this to be his for this and other dead of his belief. Then with another funeral he would jump the other way.

As time passed, and on sleepless, tossing nights when I left my hut to walk along the Street of the Dove or the Cow and Donkey, worrying for the future and safety of Los Alamos, or went on to the old hacienda or the plaza and on down to the stone church, I often found the padre within his dark walls, standing humped in blackness or moonlight, a stark figure muttering his faith's prayers or his own forgiving words above the other dead.

If this was transgression, or sin, I think in his great humanity he would have been pardoned.

I must not forget the story of how Senora Zelina came to Los Alamos.

Father Dore and Chujo and I had been cleaning the old building blocks of the hacienda, preparing to start rebuilding over the old foundation. The padre could make a single whack of his trowel, and the old mortar broke off like a piece of butter sliced with a knife. My uncle had brought cement from the trading post at Sanderson.

I had raised myself from the stones to ease my back, my pajama pants flapping, and now an old woman emerged from the cactus of the depression, a sack of belongings in her arms. She moved straight toward me.

She was slightly built and bent; her low and ragged dress showed the almost bare ribs of her chest. Her breasts, if she had any, were scrawny. Her long skirt dragged the sand.

When she reached me, she knelt, then fell at my feet even as Old Carlos had done. Her eyes were small and black as raisins, and she looked up pleadingly.

"Don O'Reiley, will you take me back? In New Mexico, I learned you were here, and I would serve you. You are your father all over again."

"Stand on your feet, and who are you?"

"I am Zelina. I served Don Herrera. You would not remember me, for you were only a baby then. But I was your nurse and helped your mother. Before she married, I carried secret notes from her to your father, and from him to her."

"What have you done through the years?"

"I was here when Don Sostelo struck. I helped bury your mother. Later, Don Herrera took you away. Will you let me stay, Don O'Reiley, for what gifts I bring? I have lived long in the Chisos, or with my relatives, but always I have saved something for you."

"What do you bring, Zelina?"

She bent to the ground and opened her bundle, then placed before me a purple cummerbund embossed in gold thread, and a black lace mantilla. "The mantilla was your mother's; the sash belonged to Don Herrera. Both are very old."

"But why do you have them?"

"At the time of the raid, I was washing their clothes—they let no one else wash them. I have saved these for your return."

"Yes, you may stay," I said. "We will build you a hut."

"My son," Father Dore said, putting his trowel down, "may I have the mantilla for the sanctuary? I have already named it the Shrine of Violetta."

"You may keep it, but put it in a place of honor."

Zelina stood again. "I have heard that you have no woman to look after you. I will do your washing, clean your hut, and cook. You already have too much before you, and Zelina can do much to help."

I was touched by this fidelity.

"You may do that, Zelina. Now talk to Carlos there, and he will choose a place for your hut."

The land beneath the Chisos was one of incredible hardship; the women bore their children, made candles of beeswax, wove blankets and clothes and rugs or mats from the hair of the goats, and the hides were made into shoes and waterbags. Men carved cots and furniture, hunted in the mountains, or tended the animals.

We had cleared a large area of brush and cactus; here we planted *milpas* of beans and maize. The families threshed the grain from their own plots on the burnt earth beneath the hooves of plodding burros, then all helped with produce from the greater field.

Zelina, who never washed, made herself the grandmother of the camp; she kept the statuary niches of the huts filled with flowers for La Madonna, or placed prized pieces of lace within, or tended the sick with her priceless herbs and medicinal concoctions. In spite of her age, as she made her rounds of the huts, she was like an affluvial bird hopping from hut to hut.

On the other hand, Old Carlos had proved to be quite worthless. If he were to be told to do a task, he would do it mañana, and mañana would turn into mañana and then into a week.

"*Si,*" he would squat and say, his eyes squinting up from the smoke of his cornshuck cigarette, "I see what you mean, senor. Yes, I will most certainly do that mañana."

"Have you something else to do today?"

"I have given it thought, but have not yet let it master me."

Carlos had given up his life as a vaquero. There were young boys in the camps who needed the training, so he helped train them. One day when I had persuaded him to work with us in cleaning the old stones of the hacienda, and had paused for a rest, I pointed toward one of the peaks away from the Chisos.

"What is the name of that peak?" I asked.

"That is Lost Mine Peak."

"Was gold found there?"

"Some say a few nuggets and fool's gold were found. It was the same in the Chisos. It was a dispute over the mountains which caused the enmity between the Sostelos and the Herreras —that and the waterhole."

"Why has Don Sostelo made no overture against us?"

Carlos smiled his toothless grin. "First, because of our Apaches in the brush. And he wants to know what you plan before he makes up his mind. Perhaps he thought that you and your uncle's friends would make the first move, but you have thrown him off by the work you do. I do not believe he thought so many people would rally to you. Don O'Reiley, we have a little army if we care to use it, and our front line is always out. Don Sostelo knows that."

"I would like," Chujo said, rolling a cigarette, "to know what goes on at Don Sostelo's."

"So would I."

Chujo said, "I would also like to know if a Cherokee could steal through a line of Apaches. Before daybreak tomorrow, I will take food and water and my rifle and go to spy out the Sostelo hacienda. If I am not back in three days, or have been wounded, look for me along Tornillo Creek. I will follow it from Don Sostelo's and I hope through your Apaches again."

"You make our village sound tight."

"It is tight, and we will know how tight when I return—if it is as tight as Don Sostelo's place."

On the first day after Chujo's departure, Meander and my Uncle Mike came in with more barrels of cement. "You've got Old Dun in the traces," I said, and I thought of the days of Effie and the pinto.

Meander grinned. "Old Dun ain't bad, once you get him hitched."

I told my uncle about the risk Chujo had taken. "I don't like it," I said. "I should have done my own spying and not thrown it to Chujo."

"He could get out of a desert scrape better than you," Uncle Mike said. "Not that you couldn't, but he is Indian. You should always be on hand here. You've got to be."

"We've got to tell you," Meander said, "that at Alpine and Sanderson Don Sostelo has been picking up a few real hardcases, rustlers from across the border and outlaws from this side. Chujo will know more when he gets back—if he does get back."

I told my uncle, "I'm selling some cows this fall, and will pay back part of what I owe you."

My uncle laughed. "Save it until next year—I don't need the money. I need it, but not now. As I've told you, the first thing to do is put Los Alamos on its feet. You've done a good job, all but those pajama britches you wear."

"They are cooler, and I've worn out my good trousers."

"The little church," my uncle said, surprised. "You've added two adobe wings."

"Father Dore did that. The senoras decorate the altar with paper flowers."

When my uncle and Meander left, I looked at the barrels of cement. With this second load, work could really begin on the hacienda.

Zelina's bony fingers clutched my shoulder.

"Don O'Reiley, it is three hours before daylight. You wanted to be up early."

"Yes. And fix me a small pack of food, and bring a water hide. I will leave at once."

Chujo should have returned yesterday. But he had not, and I had decided that I and no one else should go after him. I should reach Tornillo Creek in the darkness without being seen, and in a few moments, with Zelina's provisions, I was on my way on foot, as Chujo had gone.

There was the glimmering of a moon as I left Los Alamos; slim shadows of desert growth slanted across the desolate sand, and as I walked it was as if my sandals stepped over the bodies of the ancient dead, the dust of centuries beneath my feet, and that I was some other man who had walked here before beneath unseen mountains, on and on into shadow, wearing a peaked helmet and cuirass, a sword of Toledo steel in my hand.

But I soon put these vagaries aside; I had my own Apaches to fear, yet knowing where each was placed I would be able to avoid them. Having learned of Don Sostelo's increasing numbers from my uncle and Meander, I feared for Chujo's safety.

When daylight came, I followed a bare shelf of talus along a portion of the steep-banked creek, then made my way upward toward a brilliant colored mesa, using the vegetation as a shield.

As I neared the crest, a rifle shot sounded. From the opposite sides of the mesa came answering fire.

"Colin," a voice yelled. "Come on up."

On the summit I found Chujo sitting with his rifle behind a red slab, laughing. Near the slab lay a petrified tree trunk.

"What the devil is this? I thought you were dead and came after your body."

Chujo bent double again with laughter. "Last night I decided to play a game with your Apaches. I've kept them after me for hours. It's good practice for them, and me, too."

"There's movement now from two directions. What will you do before they shoot you?"

"Get off another shot," Chujo said, "and draw two."

At the answering splats of lead, Chujo began to scream. The sound had the quality of pain and fear and agony of a rabbit struck in the throat with a knife. But Chujo did not let the one wail stop him. On and on it went, the eerie agony.

I lay behind a mound of prickly-pear and looked toward the creek. Far apart Miguel and Pedro stood, making distant handsignals to each other. Chujo's sounds were like something they had never heard. Surely a man so badly wounded could not keep up his death cry forever; it was puzzling.

At a gesture from Miguel, he and Pedro came on upward, but one at a time, each covering the other and crawling a few yards behind shelter.

I stood up and shouted, "Miguel, Pedro! It is only a fool you have caught on the mesa, or a screaming rabbit. Rise and come up!"

When we were all together, with Miguel and Pedro seated on the tree trunk, Miguel was disgusted, but Pedro was laughing.

"I will say this," Chujo said to them, "no one would have got through your lines alive last night."

Miguel looked at him curiously. "You are a civilized Indian. Where did you learn to trail?"

"From my grandfather, who was never civilized."

As Chujo and I walked back to Los Alamos, he confirmed what my uncle and Meander had told me. "Yes, Don Sostelo has moved many men to his rancho. They all seem to be idle, but waiting and trying new horses. On the first night I approached very close to the hacienda; it is walled in; there were bushes near a window and I hid there; I saw the old don, and he is cruel. In some argument, he treated Effie harshly. Even her mother protested."

"So you saw Effie!"

"Yes. I knew you would want to know, for I heard your name mentioned. I think she is held a prisoner—perhaps to draw you there to have a showdown on Sostelo soil. In that way you would be guilty of trespass. And I saw the King from a distance—he was with the men."

"Poor Effie."

"Don't worry—she gave the old don as good as he sent. She gave me this note for you."

Chujo handed me a small white paper he took from his shirt pocket, folded once.

"But how did you manage?"

"I think that next morning Effie was still angry from the quarrel; she came early from the hacienda and went to the stables. She made the pinto gallop madly and close to the yucca where I hid. She stopped, and we talked for a moment—only a few moments. I do not think Don Sostelo looked for one from Los Alamos to be so near, and I asked if she had a word for you. She said yes, if she could only send you a note, but she would be watched all day, and it would be impossible to see me.

"I told her to write the note and I would hide in the desert and meet her next morning at the same place. When she reached the yucca, she dropped the note and a packet of food while pretending to look at a rainbow. We had only a few more words together, but that is why I am a day late—having to wait in the desert. Effie told me she would not forget what I had done. Then she rode away."

I tried to read the note as we walked; there was the Sostelo crest at the top of the page, but I bumped into so much cactus and mesquite I soon sat on the ground beside Chujo.

*My Dear Colin,*

*I must tell you why I left as I did so long ago. I was awakened by the King's hand over my mouth and led away into the darkness. The King and Countess disappeared soon after our arrival. I think he is gathering men for my grandfather for something they plan to do. I am never allowed to leave the hacienda; neither is Mother.*

*But Colin, could you do this—in early summer my grandfather will be called to Alpine for a court action your uncle has started with a parchment he has. I will send you a message then, but do not try to get one to me.*

*When you receive my message, on the following day when the first rainbow tops the Chisos, ride to the piñon clump near Paint Gap Hills. I will leave here at the same time, and our distances will be almost equal.*

*I have known Astabo, the water witch, since he took me into the Chisos when I was a child. He says that from now on you must be careful—the King also has men hidden there.*

*I would like to see you again.*

*Your Effie*

My Effie! It was more than anything she had ever said about us in all the time I had known her! I remembered when we had first seen the Chisos and the rainbow together, her hand on my shoulder, and it all seemed centuries away.

"Shall we go?" Chujo asked.

*"Si,* senor," I said, rising. "And *cuanto* manure?"

"Oh." Chujo laughed. "You don't owe me a damn thing. It's been worth it."

"That fits my pocketbook," I said.

But when we came to the mesa which overlooked Los Alamos and gazed down upon the village, seeing the adobe buildings and the short streets, the church and the rising walls of the hacienda, now stoned two tiers above the window levels, I thought that in spite of everything I had done well among the old ruins.

The happy cries which greeted Chujo and me as we walked into the plaza attested this.

# 9

<<<<<<<<<<<<<<<<<<<

After his prank on the Apache scouts and Miguel and Pedro, Chujo had become the pride of the peons. Because of their peculiar sense of humor, it delighted them to see some of their own people fooled by one of a tribe outside their own.

While I had never had a cross word with anyone at Los Alamos, except perhaps Old Carlos, but noticing the increased respect with which the peons held Chujo, and considering that my position as the new don could even make them servile had I wished, I turned the actual management of the huts and *milpas*, or fields, to Chujo. Miguel and Pedro I placed in charge of our field forces.

There was this to consider, too. I did fear an attack from Don

Sostelo, who had been strangely quiet after my arrival, and I wanted each of my chosen overseers to have his own particular job and be expert at it, for in time of battle we could make no sudden or expeditious change.

Los Alamos was fast becoming orderly and regulated by the simple habits of human existence. There could be no sudden change of this in time of emergency; each of us should be assigned his duty now.

There was enough for me in overseeing with the padre the work on the hacienda, and my work with the cows and goats, our only source of income, making the necessary business trips to Alpine and Sanderson, and going on occasional visits to Meander and my uncle.

Chujo could learn from the peons what I could never learn; he could decide a dispute, and the matter would be ended. He knew Cherokee farming and cattle care, and he was an excellent advisor to both me and the peons; he had been educated at mission schools, and no one could have been more devoted to Los Alamos.

And for all his quieter qualities, there could sometimes flash a warning from his snapping black eyes which no one dared ignore.

So while thoughts of Effie dinned my mind, more than thoughts of what legal action my uncle might take at Alpine, or the threatened attack Don Sostelo might try to accomplish, I began daily rides to acquaint myself with the Paint Gap Hills and their great peak.

I found the orange-colored ledges and piñon groves, a small creek flowing, and knew exactly where I would meet Effie. But one day as I sat my horse there, three rainbows hung over the farther mountains; if that should happen on the day I met Effie, by which would she have left the Sostelo hacienda, for as they formed, her first sighting would have been different from mine because of our separate locations, and which would she go by?

Perhaps the dear girl had not even thought of that, but when the day came I would be certain and leave Los Alamos early.

One night I lay on my *petate,* a single candle burning, my eyes straight ahead on the wall. Zelina came into the hut to make her last search for snakes and scorpions. When she finished, she squatted beside me, only the black raisins of her eyes shining in the candlelight.

"Don O'Reiley, you stare so far ahead. What do you see?"

"Only you, the new baby born in the Street of the Dove, worthless Carlos, and all the many, many poor people who have come to make their lives here."

Zelina said, "When you were a baby, you used to stare from your crib, as if reading the whole universe."

"Perhaps I read it badly."

"No. May I roll a cigarette from your shucks? You have read things very well. It is not disloyalty to Don Herrera which makes me say this, but while he was kind and respected, you are loved. No person here but would give his life for you. You have made a new Los Alamos, and given it happiness and spirit."

"Thank you, old woman. Now roll me a cigarette. Tequila and limes and salt are on the chest. Let us have a drink."

"But not me with a don, senor."

"I am no don. And another thing—don't wait until San Juan's Day to take a bath. You smell like a goat."

Bent over the chest, Zelina cackled. "Then I have attracted another—Old Carlos wants to move into my adobe."

"And ever after sit on the cool side of the street, while you do his washing and make his tortillas."

Zelina squatted again, this time with the bottle and the cut lime and salt, her effluvia rising. She said, "You are sad tonight."

"Yes. I wonder if I shall fail these new friends I have."

"Have you ever failed us, Don O'Reiley? Only look about you —see what you have done. No, the peons do not come to you everyday and thank you—they are not made that way. But as I have said, each would die for you, including old Zelina. May I have another cigarette?"

"Old woman, I want a taste of the lime."

"I will give you a taste of that, and something else. I know many strange things that happen in the Chisos. You must take what I tell calmly, for there is no certainty it is true."

"And what is that?"

"I have heard that your father is still alive. Or at least a red-haired man on a big horse has been seen in the mountains."

"Not my Uncle Michael?"

"No, not your uncle, but what I have told you is true, or has been told truthfully. Now I must leave to drag that Carlos out of my hut. When I learn more about your father, I will let you know. Do you want mush for breakfast?"

"No, I want only sleep for tonight."

My father had been dead to me for so long, that he was like the petrified tree on Chujo's mesa. But after Zelina's departure, I wondered if it could be true that he still lived. I put the tale down as something without substance, for a man so devoted to my mother could never have given his son these long years of neglect, leaving a babe for a grandfather to rear.

But even the wayward thought helped give me a restful night, and in the morning as I stood barefoot in my doorway, the mists on the mountains looked clearer. The thought that I still might have a father gave me as much hope as the thought of Effie did.

San Juan's Day was near again, and the women of all the jacals were preparing sweets and foods, for it was the custom for each family to visit its neighbors and share the day with food and drink.

It was also the day when people bathed all over. The men would bathe at the waterhole; the women and girls with their brown flanks and breasts would bathe at the depression between the village and the sand hill beyond. And if I passed the depression as I had done last year, the young women in the pool would only laugh at my presence, meanwhile standing like sleek stone images.

On the day before the celebration, Chujo and I had bought a load of liquor from a cantina on the Alpine road, so I could give one bottle to each family. When we returned, we were tired from fighting a dust storm and ruts and mules, so that night I retired early, telling Zelina not even to make her usual search for scorpions. But my night was not to be restful.

In spite of fatigue, I dreamed of wars and battles, of if my father still lived, or if Effie were standing outside the hut.

In these dreams Don Sostelo's face always appeared. Sometimes the battle might have occurred centuries ago, or else it might have been one from the last war. But always there was the face of the don. I had thought that with the King at Don Sostelo's again, some attack might be made against Los Alamos while my uncle was in court in Alpine, at the time when I would see Effie. I had made provision for this; to have the village on alert that week, and with any sound of prolonged gunfire, to let Miguel choose his plan of defense.

Don Sostelo's face appeared in a swirl of smoke, and I sat bolt upright on my mat. If the don, angered by the reopening of the court proceedings, did plan to attack, what time could be better than tomorrow, San Juan's Day, when the poor would be bathing or going festively from hut to hut, or to the church? To strike on a religious day, a day of feasting and drink? Los Alamos would not be a drunken camp, but with its joviality a tired and unprepared one.

I walked barefoot in my pajama pants to Zelina's hut. I stopped in the doorway. "Zelina, is Carlos inside?"

"He is sleeping against the other wall."

"I dreamed Don Sostelo would attack today. Tell Carlos to get up, to dress and get a horse from the corral and report to me in the plaza. Also, wake the second line of young Apaches under Tomas. Tell them also to get horses, and to come to my hut where I will pass out new rifles. Get Chujo to come pass out ammunition."

In the plaza I told Carlos, "Ride to Miguel and tell him that Don Sostelo could strike today. Tell him I will send the second-line Apaches for support, and for him to go to the old mesa where we met Chujo. Have him come to me at daybreak, when he sees what happens."

Carlos was lost in the night; the new and younger Apaches had been well-trained by Miguel and Pedro; they rode to my half-lighted hut and stopped, receiving their rifles.

Slim and alert, Tomas slid from his horse. "What are our orders, senor?"

"Ride out behind the first line. If there is a raid, retreat when the first line withdraws. All return and hide in the depression at the sand hill."

"*Si*," Tomas said.

For the first time I really took stock of him. He had his lariat coiled over his shoulder, and two knives and a pistol were in his belt. He wore a full bandolier. On his bare heels were spurs with big Spanish rowels. I looked closer at his men; each was as well prepared. A black band was about each forehead, holding the long hair back.

I said, "Tomas, your men are well equipped. If Don Sostelo strikes, you will command both the first and second lines. We may learn something when Miguel comes in, then we can organize. Now ride."

The plaza had filled with men and women and frightened children. "Return to your huts," I said, "but burn no candles. If they plan a raid, and already have men about, we would not want them to know we make preparations. Gather arms and ammunition, but quietly."

"But Don O'Reiley," an old senora said, shivering in her shift, "what came to you in your sleep to make you think there would be a raid?"

"I was restless."

"It was San Juan who warned you. We may be attacked, but Los Alamos will not be taken. The Saint is with us."

Two hours after the first light, Miguel and Pedro galloped in.

Miguel said, pulling his horse up, "They already approach behind Chjuo's mesa, fully seventy-five of them. The don means to end everything today."

Pedro said, "We slipped from the mesa and ran to our horses. The men ride slowly, perhaps fearing our guards, but they come straight for Los Alamos. The man they call the King is with

126

them; I suppose he will lead the raid while Don Sostelo watches. We saw him plainly, because he wears the big batwing chaps."

"You were not seen?"

"No."

Father Dore had hastened up. "Padre," I said, "the bell."

The fat little priest ran to the churchbell he had mounted on scaffolding in the churchyard, and pulled the rope. The clear deep tones would not be heard by the raiders who were still too far away and moving with the wind, but the ringing brought the people from their huts and the nearer vaqueros from the brush.

"Arm yourselves," I told them in the plaza. "It is Don Sostelo. And keep the children in the huts. Senoras, be ready to help the wounded. Take bandages to the church. Word has reached all the scouts?" I asked Miguel.

"*Si,* and I told the outer ring to retreat slowly to the sand hill, as young Tomas said all were to do."

I could not, would not, lose all I had worked for, but my inexperience was great. "Miguel, you will take charge of this battle; Pedro and I will be your lieutenants. Now what am I to do?"

"Watch the sand hill with the boys of Tomas. The hill could be very important. Pedro, take three men and watch the other end of the village."

The hill itself was of no consequence, but it could serve as a point of outer defense while we learned the intention of the raiders. I asked Old Carlos, "Where will the cows and goats be today?"

"At the east bog with their vaqueros."

Our older scouts and young Apaches rode in from the desert. Miguel told them, "As planned, take your positions out of sight behind the sand hill. If Don Sostelo wants only to parley, Don O'Reiley will be on the crest to go talk with him." Miguel looked at our small mesa. "Since the mesa dominates the hill and the camp, they will stop first to spy out the land. If one person rides down alone, I will send someone to meet him before Don O'Reiley goes."

From the crest of the hill, I told Chujo, "If it comes to a

showdown, take four men and defend the hacienda. The rest of us will hold the adobes. Padre," I said to the little priest, who had run up still heaving from his exertions at the bell rope, "You have a spyglass. Will you bring it?"

"Look!" Miguel cried, pointing.

A group of horsemen had begun to gather on the mesa, singly or in pairs. Now more came, until a solid line was arrayed there. A small group in the center waited before the rest.

"Ah," said Miguel, "there is Don Sostelo. I think he is in a cummerbund. He makes his plans with the King now."

I still felt with Miguel that Don Sostelo would want a parley before any attack in force. I saw now that I could make the whole situation ridiculous, as well as giving a threat of our own strength, and turn matters to our own ends.

I called back to Zelina, "Bring me my black sombrero with the gold braid, and the purple cummerbund." I was wearing white, though dirty, pajama pants. I would have told Zelina to bring my threadbare civilized trousers, only they would have ruined my plan. I wanted to appear as absurd as possible.

I put on the gold and purple cummerbund and took the glass from the padre. "Come with me," I told Miguel, and once more we positioned ourselves on the crest.

I raised the glass toward the mesa, and Don Sostelo was drawn toward me.

He was a smaller man under his great sombrero than I had expected him to be; his face was thin, and as best as I could tell at that distance, it was dominated by a prominent and hooked nose.

"What do you think?" I asked Miguel. "Why do they wait?"

"Perhaps to build fear in us. Or perhaps they, too, are uncertain. I would look for a white flag to come soon, since by now they have seen you here."

"Tomas," I called toward the depression, "move your boys close to the first line, but remain hidden. Miguel, I still do not understand why they have not left the mesa."

"Perhaps because of our silence, and they see no one. They

had hoped to battle us in the desert; they do not understand this."

A white flag did come down the mesa. The rider stopped midway between the mesa and sand hill, and waited.

"Here." I took a handkerchief from my pants and gave it to Carlos. "Tie this to a stick and walk to the man. See what he wants."

It was thirty minutes before Carlos returned. Once he had stopped casually on the sand to watch a soaring eagle. I knew his leisurely actions infuriated the don.

"Well," I asked Carlos, "what did the man want?"

"A complete surrender, and you and the people will leave Los Alamos by nightfall."

"What was your reply?"

"I laughed in his face. I told him the man that my master, Don Colin Herrera O'Reiley, who stood on the sand hill in his cummerbund, would accept the surrender of Don Sostelo with the full honors of war, he to keep his firearms, and he could withdraw in honor as if he had been looking for his cows."

"Then what?"

"The man choked with rage. I further told him that if Don Sostelo had matters of importance to discuss, Don O'Reiley would condescend to meet him. The signal for this acceptance will be three rifle shots from the mesa."

"You will roast in hell for your lies."

"Heaven or hell, so long as my feet are warm."

Three rifle shots rang from the mesa, but first there had been a realignment of the don's forces. Perhaps the confident talk of Carlos had made Don Sostelo suspect that he was partially surrounded, especially in the rear; he lost no time in shifting his men, and some swung their horses and disappeared from the crest.

"They go for reinforcements," Miguel said.

At the sound of the shots, I began to walk across the desert; then a single horseman rode down the mesa—Don Sostelo. I thought I knew the way to overpower or even degrade him. It would be done simply by my ridiculous regalia, by my pretense and indifference, and by ignoring his threat of force while mine in his mind was still a question of doubt.

He rode slowly through the brush, disdaining to look either left or right. I stopped my walk this side of the halfway point, letting him ride to me. Don Sostelo halted his horse; his hot eyes glared down.

"Sir, you are Colin O'Reiley?"

"Don Colin Herrera O'Reiley, Don Sostelo."

"Is it your intention to attempt to humiliate me, a man of power, and a don descended from the old realm? I rode down, not because of your threat, but because of your presumption. You possess all the rascalities."

I bowed and said, "By no means, sir. But you might also witness my cummerbund, given by a queen to my ancestors, and equal to yours."

"I order you," he said, glancing at the pajama pants and sandals which I knew irritated him, "to remove yourself and people from Los Alamos."

I watched that beak of a nose, the twitching nostrils. I could understand how, in rage, Don Sostelo could have ordered the earlier raid in which my mother had been killed. He could only be angered at the ragged upstart before him.

"But why should I move my people? I still allow your cows to drink at the waterhole. This is all you want the land for, and you know I have taken no action against your cows or men."

"You have taken no action yet, but I shall take action unless you abandon Los Alamos."

"I will never abandon it. I will fight for it until I and those who fight with me are dead. You have power; can't you be honest?"

"Is it your purpose to insult? What do you mean, sir?"

"The only reason you come to fight is that we have recovered the old parchment, and my uncle has reopened the Los Alamos case in the court in Alpine. Yes, it has been good that your cows could drink at a hole my ancestors deepened and en-

130

larged; I have suspected you would come, but why did you wait so long?"

The hot eyes became shrewd; a sardonic smile showed good teeth.

"Because until now it has amused me to watch you to see what you did here, when I could have crushed you like an ant beneath my boot."

"That would have brought sorrow to one of your family."

"What do you mean?"

"You know what I mean—Euphemia. I intend to marry her. You sent her to St. Louis to ingratiate herself with me and bring me under your control, but she was too honest to do that. She loves me, as I do her. What good did your scheme do? Your daughter, Senora Hernandez, lost faithful servants, Senor and Senora Maderas, and today, if you fight, you will lose all claim to Los Alamos. You will also lose Euphemia, for remember, Los Alamos has eyes and ears at window casements."

The expression on the don's face was incredulous.

I went on, "If you fight me today, my cummerbund is as old as yours, and I would not like to see buzzards in the air at sunset."

"You are a confident tatterdemalion."

"When I came to the Big Bend, I did not know what I was. But now I know. I would rather have the gratitude of one barefooted peon's lips on the back of my hand than all the wealth you could give, or even Euphemia by your intentions. Yes, if you want to fight, we will fight, and to the bitter end."

In his rage, Don Sostelo's face was awesome. "You will never marry Euphemia. At sundown, I hope buzzards do not find you. You have the ears and brains of a jackass, senor."

"And the same stubbornness. But you have made the decision. Los Alamos will await your attack."

"Euphemia . . ." he began, and I knew now I had him. His fierce pride would never let her marry a Herrera. But I was O'Reiley, and O'Reileys had a penchant for marrying into the feminine line of old dons.

131

"Don Sostelo, it is not good for a man to go into battle infuriated; you may need calm judgment. But Euphemia and I do stick in your craw, don't we?"

Without another word, I turned and left him. His anger might be our best ally.

Although Don Sostelo was arrogant and vicious, perhaps I had seen him at his worst. He did have a good horse, however.

# 10

<<<<<<<<<<<<<<<<<<

It began an hour later—the Battle of Los Alamos.

Old Carlos and Miguel and I still stood on the sand hill, the Apaches hidden behind us. When I saw the long line of Don Sostelo's forces ride down the mesa in their great numbers, I said to Carlos, "You are a good rider. Take the fastest horse and ride to my uncle's. Tell him what has happened, and that he is to get all his men and other ranchers here as quickly as possible."

Then I talked with Miguel about the Apaches.

"Hold your ground," Miguel told them. "At the last moment, come up and fire with the older scouts, but not until I signal you. Don O'Reiley, while we wait, bring more men up, and form them behind the others. But if we are overwhelmed, retreat to the adobes. With our loopholes there, we should have things our own way."

I gathered reinforcements from among the vaqueros who had answered the bell summons, then returned to the hill.

Father Dore asked, "My son, is it war?"

"Yes. Don Sostelo is determined upon it."

The padre's church, decorated for San Juan's Day, looked very pathetic.

"But must you fight against Euphemia's family?"

"I do not fight against Euphemia—I fight for Los Alamos."

Don Sostelo's galloping line was closer now, and Miguel raised his hand.

Rifle fire broke from the sand hill; it was not a crackle of fire, but a sudden uproar, accompanied by shouts of derision and triumph. On the desert floor lay dead or dying men and screaming horses. There were men maddened by pain, running on foot across the sand. Perhaps the don's anger had driven his men to this precipitous and thoughtless attack.

Only a few continued to ride into the teeth of the fire, and they were shot down. The remainder fled back into the desert. What surprised me most as I stood on the hill was not the agony in the desert, but the imperturbable posture of the group of men who had remained on the mesa.

I was certain Don Sostelo and the King were among them, for after our first deadly fire, riders had been dispatched over the mesa and down beyond, seeking, I knew, more reinforcements. Even Don Sostelo had admitted our first triumph, but I was still glad that I had sent Carlos to seek help from my uncle. Fully one-fourth of Don Sostelo's effectives had already been killed or wounded, with no loss to us.

The next attack came an hour later, the King leading it. Miguel maintained his position on the sand hill, I with my bloodied Apaches still behind him. The vaqueros I had enlisted were sent to the flanks, and it was as if the King led his men into a pocket of rifle fire. Yet he rode boldly, and although every

134

rifle was leveled at him at one time or another, he seemed to bear a charmed life, and was never hit.

Our flankers swung farther out into the desert. There was danger of the Sostelo forces being surrounded, but the King ordered a retreat toward the mesa. Miguel refused to let our chase continue; he called all men back again.

"What do you think?" I asked, standing beside him on the hill.

Miguel twisted his fierce mustachios. "So far, it goes well. We cannot match their numbers, so it is best we hold here. In the desert, their numbers would count."

The sun was hot and burning.

We barely beat off the third attack, for now we, too, had our dead and wounded. The King had almost flanked our positions; we knew we could not withstand the constant fire which raked us.

Miguel gave his orders. "When they come again, hold the hill and give them a volley. Then retreat to the adobes and the streets. When they charge over the hill, we will give them more fire."

Miguel was right; those of Don Sostelo's men who rode over the abandoned crest were easy targets for the Apaches and other marksmen, especially those who fired from the corners of the huts, or from the loopholes with their pistols.

Some among us might have called this last phase a victory for our side. But Miguel was glum. He had climbed a ladder placed on the inner wall of the hacienda walls; he looked over and beyond the sand hill to the desert. "They come again," he said, "and this time they bring boxes. I think I know what it is— dynamite."

A dog had been wounded in the last attack; it ran yelping from hut to hut until someone shot it. The women, young and old, were in the streets now, bringing chocolate and coffee and tobacco to the men, and leading the wounded to the church.

Miguel shouted from his perch, "Here they come! This time they will take the hill, and throw the dynamite from behind it. Inside the hacienda, senoras and senoritas, inside, all of you."

In the hacienda, Chujo and three more men had mounted ladders; their fire crackled as the first riders appeared on the hill. These fell, but others galloped nearer; the respite for Don Sostelo had been gained.

A stick of dynamite with its spluttering fuse flew from behind the hill; no aim was necessary; it would destroy something wherever it fell. With the explosion, two adobe huts seemed to be lifted from the earth, the debris flying to the very ends of the village. Another, and another; there were the screams of isolated women and children, the noise of falling huts, and the bleating of a goat with one leg blown off.

Pedro said to Miguel, "Let me take men to the desert. We can get behind them. From now on, it will be our only chance."

Miguel knew that, and so did I. So did everyone else, including Tomas and his Apaches, who in the Street of the Cow and Donkey battled hand to hand with knives the first of the King's band to enter the village.

There was a cry from Chujo on his ladder. "Don Sostelo has come. They think the dynamite will end the fight!"

At that moment we had unexpected help from the vaqueros who had ridden in from the east. They galloped, armed with everything from sickles to lariats to knives or old rifles, but any weapon would be good in the brush.

"Pedro," Miguel shouted, "San Juan heard you! Take all these men and go; I will take the opposite flank. Don O'Reiley, you must hold Los Alamos!"

The vaqueros were leaping to the ground, picking up the rifles and ammunition dropped by the fallen. Now they mounted again and flashed down the Street of the Dove and into the brush. Miguel left, and I was left with Los Alamos.

Until we were driven back into our own streets among our own adobes, and I before mine, I had only known a strange detachment about the battle, as if it were something I saw, but had no part in, although I had obeyed each of Miguel's orders.

It was as if I had seen the battle from the letters in a book, its various phases, the movement of men from place to place according to plan. Or that I had seen it all through a series of stereopticon slides, a picture here, another there.

I had fired constantly, but not knowing whether I killed or not. This, too, had been in detachment, almost an unawareness. But as I was drawn by the street fighting to the very door of my hut and had stopped there, reloading my pistol, I saw Teresa, who had smiled at me last San Juan's Day, racing down the Street of the Dove, her arms full of bandages for the church.

At the same time, one of Don Sostelo's Mexicans rode from the Street of the Cow and Donkey, an upraised saber in his hand. He brought it down over Teresa's head, and I fired. I think it was a stomach shot, or near it, for the man sank from his horse with his hands groping his middle, and frighten-eyed Teresa ran on.

I felt only that I had removed an obstruction.

As Don Sostelo's men swept into the streets among the very adobes we had struggled to build, I lost detachment and began to see only the flame of combat. After that, I was no longer the same—it was get or be got, and detachment was lost. I fought for my life.

From somewhere, Tomas screamed, "Senor O'Reiley, behind you!"

I whirled; two of Don Sostelo's riders had cut into the Street of the Dove from Zelina's street, each ready to fire.

Tomas was driving his horse toward the man on the outside. I knew I could not get both before one or the other fired, but judging Tomas's actions, I fired at the inner man. At the same time, Tomas's knife cut the throat of the other.

Two more of our men joined us, and we moved toward the smoking corner of the Cow and Donkey.

The sticks of dynamite continued to fall; a gaping hole showed where the little plaza and well had been. A bench, intact, had been blown to the top of a hut and remained there, as if waiting for someone to sit upon it.

Zelina left her hut, her arms full of waterbags. She was half-way to me when dynamite struck her hut. It was obliterated.

"Don O'Reiley, with the well destroyed, we will soon be out of water."

"Then we must suffer through it."

"No, I will go to the waterhole. The wounded will need water." She left with complete unconcern, walking through rifle fire and the shocks of dynamite.

Now the tide of battle turned again. With the forces of Miguel and Pedro closing upon the rear of the hill, the enemy which had been stationed there with the King and Don Sostelo began a retreat, but an enforced retreat into the village. Hand to hand fighting began again; I did not know how many times I had reloaded my pistol.

It was then, on a corner of the street, that I saw the King. We were not twelve feet apart. We both fired. He missed and I missed. Then he was lost in a swirl of smoke, and someone gave me a cut on the arm.

Now I was in the street with Tomas's Apaches, and it was down this street that the greater portion of the enemy with Don Sostelo moved from the sand hill, although the dynamiters remained on the hill for better height in throwing. In this melee I saw a pistol pointed in my direction. It was held by Don Sostelo. He tried vainly to fire, then he began to reload. I was upon him, my own gun in his ribs, knocking his weapon to the ground.

"Come to the church," I said, "or I will kill you where you stand. I will give you sanctuary." At the church, I left him with our dead and wounded.

When I returned to the battle, Tomas's boys, aided by the marksmen who fired from the ladders of the hacienda, had the situation well in hand. In the close combat, the King's men retreated slowly to the sand hill.

"Colin!" a voice screamed. I recognized Chujo's voice, and looked about.

A stick of dynamite flew in my direction; it was well weighted, for the distance was great, and it seemed to travel in a straight line rather than in an arc. I leaped to catch it, but it was too high. It flew on through an open window of the hacienda, our last resort of safety, and where the women and children were kept.

I stood spellbound, waiting for the explosion. Then Chujo's head disappeared from above the wall. In a moment he leaped through a window, the spluttering stick in his hand. In heavy gunfire, he raced toward the sand hill, or rather toward the street which led to it and which Tomas defended.

It was obvious what he intended to do—destroy the sand hill. This, in turn, brought every rifle against him.

Then Chujo was hit; he stopped running, but still stood in the street, looking down at the spluttering fuse in his hand. He was hit again, then again, and fell on the hard ground. Even as he lay there, his body flinched over and over. With the dynamite still in his hand, he was a prime target for the enemy.

Then, as if some power beyond his own made him rise, he began to push upward with his left hand, his knees wobbling. He stood now, as he had before, looking down studiously at the shortening fuse. At last his right arm moved; with his remaining strength he threw toward the sand hill; a terrific explosion followed. The crest of the hill and the men there vanished; the throw had gone over the crest and into the store of dynamite.

Chujo fell; I picked up the limp body and carried to to Father Dore at the church. Chujo was placed on a cot and immediately stripped; not one inch of his riddled body was free of blood.

"Care for him," I said. "He may have saved Los Alamos."

The casualties on the sand hill were tremendous; the remaining enemy began to retire. Yet even as they did, they faced the increasing fire of the flankers under Miguel and Pedro, and again were forced toward us.

In the village we continued to fight from broken wall to broken wall, the youngsters under Tomas riding their horses to adobes whose roofs remained. They stood in their saddles and clambered upward. Knives in hand, they leaped downward upon the backs of the King's men, stabbing and cutting, or hamstringing horses. Some snaked lariats over unsuspecting riders, pulling them to the ground where fiercer struggles followed.

"Dust, dust!" Zelina screamed, lowering her hot rifle. "It is Senor Michael and his men from the south."

But it was all over now, except for the mopping up.

The Kings men, caught on all sides, once more crawled back to what heights remained on the hill, and only a desultory fire reached the embattled streets.

It was then that my uncle's pack arrived, Meander fully thirty feet in the lead. Somewhere on the mad ride he had lost his hat; he had fastened his lines about the pommel, and he plummeted into the debris, hands free, both pistols firing. Behind him rode my uncle, cowhands and neighboring ranchers.

With the new force, the streets were soon cleared, and the last of Don Sostelo's party retreated to join the King on his hill. Meander led a charge of my uncle's men and other ranchers to dislodge them. The King's only recourse was to retreat into the desert, and he barely eluded the pocket which Miguel and Pedro were closing. He struck hard for the mesa, although some of his men were ridden down by the ranchers and vaqueros.

Meander had returned from the chase and rode to where I learned wearily against a broken wall in the street. Miguel and Pedro had been brought by; Miguel had been wounded in one leg, and Pedro in the chest and forearm.

Meander's grin spread over his snaggletooth. "Well, it looks like you made it."

"Yes," I said, wiping blood from my face and arm, "but barely." I had a bullet-seared neck and a bloody thigh which dripped blood on my sandals.

"These dead," Meander said, "we'd better bury them quick. It gets hot here."

"We'll start soon," I said, looking at the vast sky, and I had never seen one so wide and gracious.

In the morning I went to the church to see Don Sostelo.

"A horse is outside. You are free to depart. But first, look at our graveyard. What value is power to you now?"

Without a word, he departed.

Our graves were many, the flowers few. We continued to place our dead in the graveyard; the others were put in wagons and sent to Don Sostelo.

The hope of peace I held after our victory over Don Sostelo proved to be fruitless, in spite of my having saved his life.

He dared not attack Los Alamos again, but pending the trial in Alpine and while we struggled to rebuild our ruined and broken adobes, he did begin a new type of warfare in the desert. He sent his outlaws to pick off what vaqueros and guards he could, and although we gave him as good as he sent, our new vigilance demanded and took our time from other things.

One was poor Chujo, and we doubted that he would ever recover from all his bullet wounds. While almost all his vital organs and arms and legs had been hit, no single shot had proved fatal.

While my uncle was still at Los Alamos with his men, he was informed by a letter from Alpine that the legal papers he had requested to become my guardian had been approved by the court, and that it was necessary that we come to sign them.

Although the ride would be some seventy miles, nothing could have suited us better, or come at a more opportune time. In Alpine, in view of the upcoming trial, we were told by Judge Howlett, who looked like a red-faced shrimp with rat teeth, and always kept his bottle near, that if I signed certain depositions now, it would not be necessary for me to appear later, since my uncle, who had reopened the case, would be there. This matter was agreed to by Don Sostelo's attorney. It was my uncle's opinion, however, that the attorney did this only to make Don Sostelo appear as a fair and broad-minded man before the court, and that he bore no enmity toward me.

Both Alpine and Sanderson had town doctors, but it was difficut for these overworked men, spending days and nights in the saddle as they did, to make any prolonged stay at Los Alamos to look after Chujo and other seriously wounded.

Yet at a drugstore where we had gone for medicines, we had unexpected fortune. The druggist said, from above his celluloid collar as he wrapped our packages, "Why don't you go look up old Dr. Smedley? He retired from practice in the East a few months ago, and came to live with his daughter. It's the first ranch north of town. I hear retirement doesn't sit well with him; he might be the very man you want. You'd have to ride a few extra miles, but I'd bet he'd go with you."

And Dr. Smedley did go. He was an extremely tall and thin man, with clicking false teeth. He was precise and wore mutton-chop whiskers. At Los Alamos he struck up an immediate friendship with Father Dore, and the two became inseparable over the padre's checkerboard.

But poor Chujo! Never did I know a person who fought so gamely to live.

He had four operations spaced over a period of days, but even then he would carry two bullets to the grave. Dr. Smedley said, his teeth clicking, "One is over the heart, the other near the spine. If you have lived with them this long, why worry? Operations would probably kill you."

Miguel had a leg amputed, Pedro a forearm; now they were indeed a pair. A woodcarver made Miguel a crutch, but Pedro gained nothing.

Chujo tired of his constant seclusion in one of the few un-damaged huts. He begged to be taken into the sun. We cut up a tarpaulin, and the women sewed the outer lengths so poles could be run through the openings. Chujo slept with the stretcher over his mat, but during the days he could be carried outside where the ends of the poles could rest on two piñon logs.

From his new position he could see what went on in our re-building, and watch the mists on the mountains. It is tragic, I thought as I worked in laying out the rectangular adobe brick for baking, that this poor village in the desert, bare and unpretentious, has been destroyed by hate, meaning what it did to so many people and Chujo. The destruction has availed Don Sostelo nothing, but it has cemented the bonds of all of us who remain.

There was a difference in the vaqueros, too, who took more

pride in their work, although at night after drinking too much pulque or tequila or mescal, some might have to be dragged off to their slanting lean-tos or huts, and put to bed in their straw, but even this cemented our bonds.

After two weeks, Dr. Smedley left for Alpine. While not attending the sick and wounded, he had spent much of his time arguing some moot point of medicine or religion with Father Dore. When he left, he surprised me by saying, "I rather like it here. Unless you object, I think I'll come down once a month and stay for a week."

I gave Dr. Smedley our best horse, telling him that he was a friend, and would always be welcome. I lent him six of our best Apaches for the safety of his return, and he rode from Los Alamos clicking his teeth together, as edgy and precise as ever. I will always suspect that Father Dore prevailed upon him to visit us again, for there would always be one illness or another in camp, those too complicated for Zelina to cure.

After the battle, my thoughts had turned more and more to Effie. That she would stand up against Don Sostelo, I knew from what Chujo had told me, but what place would she have for me now in this active warfare against her own kin and the defeat the don had suffered?

Only when we met at our rendezvous would I know.

Perhaps it was the thought of seeing Effie again which made me review my efforts at Los Alamos. For a year and a half I had devoted myself to an almost hopeless task, rebuilding, then seeing all I had created destroyed within a day.

And now the added labor, the lines of baking bricks in the sun, the walls of new adobes rising, clearing our dynamited well, a bandage here, a dose of medicine there, or hearing at night the wailing of some child for a father or mother he would never see again. I had lost weight, and often I walked to the little graveyard where the dead of Los Alamos lay. Or sat at night beside Chujo in his pain, with old Zelina squatting beside me.

I suppose what really saved Chujo—and me—from more despondency in the desolate village, was Meander and Maudine.

One afternoon he and a long-shanked, horse-faced girl galloped into the village, the girl laughing and screaming with big buck teeth showing.

"We got hitched," Meander yelled, then he, too, burst into a peal of laughter.

"Who hit you?" I said, not understanding him in the uproar he and the girl and the snorting horses made.

"Nobody hit us. I said me and Maudine got hitched."

Maudine, fully a foot taller than Meander, jumped off her horse like nothing I had seen before, then Meander followed.

On his stretcher between the piñon logs, Chujo laughed until his sides hurt. It was his first real laughter since the raid.

Meander said, "Maudine, that Injun over there is Chujo."

Maudine whacked me across the back. "Hello, Colin. I've heered so much about you."

"When did you get married?"

"Four days ago," Meander said. "But times have changed. I remember back when my folks had genuine affection for me, but last night Ma and Pa said they couldn't stand any more moon-eyeing about the house, and to go somewhere else till we got it out of our systems. So we come here. You know, I never did like goat meat, but Maudine can make the best frickerseed goat ever. I never et goat till her."

Maudine twisted and giggled. "Now, Meander!"

"You got a place for us to stay?" Meander said.

"The new adobe at the far end of the street," I said. "Unload your packs, then come back and talk."

"We'll be gone a little," Meander said, and they led the horses off.

That night we gave Maudine and Meander a wedding party in the hacienda. It still had not been roofed, and not a stone had been laid since the battle. But the chimney was high enough to draw, and we could borrow tables and furniture from the adobes.

While I sat beside Chujo's stretcher, we discussed the poor banquet we would serve. From the end of the street we could hear Meander's happy cackles and Maudine's shrill hysterical screams.

That night we built a fire in the hacienda, the first since I had come to Los Alamos. We brought small tables inside, and placed them in a line before the fireplace. Meander sat at one end of the big table, Maudine at the other. We placed Chujo on a cot near Meander. Miguel with his crutch and Pedro were there, and Carlos and Zelina and the padre, and we had invited Tomas, who wore his black headband.

It would have been impossible for the villagers to have sat at the table, so we had others placed where the rest of the people could enter, fill their clay bowls and have their drink, then pass outside through the opposite door, although those who wished to dance might remain, yet after the battle few chose to do so.

The fiddlers, the guitar and mandolin and maracas players stood before the fireplace; the native music was excellent.

"Ah," said Zelina, "it is like the old days." She looked up through the roofless hacienda into the stars and moonlight. Then she pointed to the head of the table where Meander sat. "Don Herrera sat there, and after his wife's death, Violetta sat there." Zelina pointed toward Maudine, who was slapping the choking padre on the back. "I was honored," said Zelina, drinking a raw tequila, "to have been allowed to serve in this room."

I said, "Now I remember something. My grandfather told me that a faithful servant recovered the old parchment when it was stolen. It must have been you. How did you do it?"

Zelina said, "The parchment had been stolen long before the raid and the trial. After the raid, some of us were carried away to work for Don Sostelo. In cleaning his hacienda, I learned where the parchment was hidden. I intended to steal it, but first I must have a good story. Give me a shuck, Don O'Reiley. I complained to Don Sostelo that my little money had been stolen, then I stole from others to make it appear that no one could be trusted. When finally I did take the parchment, I stole a horse also and rode to Don Herrera, who was ready to leave with you. I gave him the parchment, then returned to Don Sostelo's. All his servants were under suspicion, so he discharged us and I went to live in the mountains."

"But the mantilla and cummerbund?"

"They were always in my bag, which I had kept hidden and dared not try to reach."

"As a reward, you may always use my cornshucks."

Zelina cackled and reached for a mescal.

Meander had developed a trick of sticking the tip of his tongue at Maudine through the hole in his teeth. He did so now, and Maudine went into shrieks of laughter.

"Colin," a voice said above the music and the chatter of the dancers, "I want a drink."

I turned to where Chujo lay on his stretcher. I looked at his thin face and into his hollow eyes. "Do you think you should have a drink?"

"Yes. I want my stomach to be warm again, although I shall pay for it tomorrow."

I took his drink to him, then pulled my chair away from Zelina and sat beside him.

"It is good to see happy people," Chujo said. He raised his head, and I held the drink to his lips. He settled back satisfied. Later, after another, he said, "I want to walk."

"You have not walked since the day you were shot down."

"You will have to help me," he said, and with effort began to get off his stretcher. I brought him Miguel's crutch.

Chujo and I walked from room to room of the hacienda among the dancers and the clinking of castanets. Some walls were higher than others, although all were intact. Then Chujo walked to the window through which he had leaped with the dynamite. He gazed at the shadow of the mutilated sand hill.

"You know," he said, a strange smile on his lips, "this hacienda must always stand. I have looked for something like it all my life, but have never found it until now."

I recalled the clean-cut Cherokee boy we had first seen at the mouth of the Illinois, his suppleness, his crushed black sombrero

146

and buckskins; now I saw something else, a being who would never be more than a shriveled and shrunken thing, doddering either with a crutch or a cane.

When the wedding party was over, we carried Chujo to his adobe.

From the new hut at the end of the street came peal after peal of Maudine's wild laughter. I looked in on Chujo after midnight; he slept peacefully.

Somehow, he and Meander and I had all grown up since the far off days at the mouth of the Illinois.

Miguel and Pedro took their amputations in good humor. Miguel had his leg tied to a mesquite tree, where soon it was fleshless from the work of carrion birds and ants; Pedro, who had his forearm buried in the churchyard, had it dug up and tied beside Miguel's leg.

When the bones were fleshless, Miguel and Pedro tied them over the doors of their huts.

"If you would do as I," Miguel told Pedro in disgust, "you would get the old Apache flute-maker to drill larger holes into the bone. There is no marrow, and when the wind is up, with tone holes, you would get back a nice whistle, like a flute."

So those who entered the Street of the Whistling Bones, as it became known, paused often to listen to Miguel's flute and Pedro's shriller tones, since he had drilled smaller holes.

Though there were those in Los Alamos who said they heard the sounds regularly, I must in honesty say that I never did.

# 11

A few weeks before I was to meet Effie, fate reared its head again, but this time a pretty head.

It was Teresa, the dark-haired girl who had smiled at me from the pool on San Juan's Day a year ago, and whose saber-wielding assailant I had shot down in the Street of the Dove during the battle.

Unfortunately, she had fallen in love with me, and equally unfortunately, Tomas had fallen in love with her. Before the battle, she and Tomas had sat many evenings in the plaza, and he had bought her dulces and made her silver trinkets.

At last Tomas came to me. "Don O'Reiley, do you love Teresa?"

"Teresa? Not that I have thought of."

148

"It was my hope to marry her, but now she says she is in love with you because you saved her life."

I told Tomas, "You were also on the street then, and you were firing. My pistol snapped; perhaps it was you who killed the Mexican. Tell Teresa that. Her mind has changed only for a little while."

"You tell me the truth, Don O'Reiley?"

"Who knows who kills what in a battle? But tell Teresa you love her. There is something else, Tomas. You neither read nor write, do you?"

"No, senor."

"Then begin to learn from Chujo and the padre. Someday I will need a good man with a good wife to help me here."

"But Don O'Reiley . . ."

"I will give you two she-goats the day you marry. Now go ask Teresa to set the date."

"*Si*, Don O'Reiley."

I was greatly relieved. Teresa could have been disturbing, had I wished her to be. It was hard to look into soft dark eyes that looked into yours, and do no more.

I was standing on the orange ledge in the piñons, dressed in my pajama pants and sandals and rowels, when I saw Effie come on the pinto.

Even at a distance, she was not at all the little ragamuffin I had known on our long trek from the Illinois; a half-child in a gingham dress, who had ridden straddleways with her bare legs hanging down.

She rode in a dignified sidesaddle, wearing an expensive brown riding skirt and a jacket of gold braid; her blouse was green, and her boots were hand-tooled and dainty, although she was bareheaded.

She slid from the pinto and ran toward me, and I still could not believe I saw her again. "Oh, Colin!" she cried, and then with our long and almost frantic kisses we were something which could never have appeared within the chaste pages of *Godey's Ladies Book.*

But it was all as natural as the rainbow on the Chisos, or the cry of a lost bird, the murmur of the piñons, or the gurgling of the stream at our feet.

The surface winds had been hard, with blowing dust and sand. We tasted the bitterness until at last we drew apart.

"Effie, I didn't know it could be like this."

"Neither did I, Colin."

The pinto drooped its head to drink from the stream.

The twist of hair was still over Effie's eye, and she smiled. "There should be something to say besides hello, but it is all I can think of."

"It's enough," I said, "and hello, Effie."

Her voice was just right—not too casual, not too direct, but just right. She said, "I have brought a pack of food. We can have a picnic."

"I brought a pack, too."

"Shall we ride to Lost Mine Peak? I told you of the old basket weavers and their caves. I used to find old relics in the caves."

"Meander and Chujo and I used to ride up to hunt, but not lately."

Effie seemed to flinch. By saying not lately, I had said the wrong thing; I had inadvertently brought the Don Sostelo trouble into the conversation, something I knew we both wished to avoid.

"What did you find in the caves?" I asked.

She said brightly, "Bones, little pieces of silverwork, and arrow-heads. Today, we'll go to my favorite cave."

We mounted and set out on the climb. When we reached the cave near its shelf on the peak and dismounted, I said, "I like your riding outfit, but it doesn't match my pajama pants."

Effie laughed. "Colin, you can afford better."

"No. They are a mark of my trade. I am a carpenter, a stonemason, and a vaquero. Sometimes I am a cobbler, a midwife, or an adobe mixer. And with my lariat, I am also a master of the *mangana de cabre* for four feet and the *pial* for two."

Effie said, "Do you like the smell of piñon burning? I do. We can start a fire with dead wood, then put the green on top."

150

I wanted to seize and kiss her again, but we had forced a distance between us. As we walked about on the shelf, we could see spread below us the blackened ruins of Los Alamos, and Don Sostelo's hacienda and dry Tornillo Creek. What meaning these places had for us, yet how determinedly we avoided their mention!

Effie said suddenly, while she placed a dead stick on the growing fire, "Have you heard of a red-haired man who wanders the Chisos?"

She had become too warm in her jacket; she removed it, and moved about in her green blouse. The outlines of her nipples were as firm as young acorns. I turned my eyes to the broiling steaks again.

At Effie's question, I thought of what Zelina had told me, and laughed. "One of your Apache ghosts? Yes, I have heard of him, but I pay little attention to most of what I hear."

"Remember, Colin, I have told you, and I have heard that someone else is also there, one of importance to you, who remains in hiding."

"Nonsense! Anyone who knows me would come to Los Alamos."

Or would they? Effie spoke from some information other than what I had—I wondered if her informant might have been Astabo. I was convinced that it was he who had talked with Zelina, but now something else had come to light.

Effie's large eyes looked into mine solemnly, but she volunteered no more.

I could have pried into her source of knowledge, but instead, I said, "Meander has married a girl named Maudine."

"Are they at Los Alamos? Why don't you bring them up tomorrow? And Chujo. All of us together again would be like old times."

"Chujo is not well."

A sudden understanding came to her eyes. "Tell Chujo I am so sorry."

Still avoiding everything, we talked only for the pleasure of talking. To make things even more impersonal, I asked the question I had asked Old Carlos. "Was there ever real treasure in the Chisos? More than what peons say?"

"No. But someday there will be a treasure, and it will be far greater than anyone ever imagined."

Effie's eyes were half-veiled, as if she dreamed; she was always enigmatic, and I wondered if anyone could ever interpret her words correctly. I wondered also about her mother, Senora Hernandez, and if she knew Effie was here today.

After eating, we sat on the edge of the ledge together. Effie leaned toward me. "You have not held me since we came here."

"I am afraid to. Suppose we explore the cave."

The wide and circular opening from the shelf gave ample light. As we walked about, we held hands, pretending to be casual. The floor was gray and powdery, as if made from the aged and completely decomposed dust of the basketmakers. In one corner was a small declivity a few feet in width which held a pool of water which trickled from some fissure. It was then drained off by some other fissure or crack, perhaps even ending at the mudhole at Los Alamos, but leaving the pool full.

Effie took great delight in showing me where she had found one oddity or another, even grains of corn centuries old, and once she had found a skull.

"What did you do with it?"

"Ooh! I had Astabo take it out before I came back."

"Someday, I'd like to dig through this dust," I said, letting a double handful sift through my fingers." I saw something white fall, and bent to pick it up. "Look, here is a little pearl. It has been drilled through to make a necklace. You can add it to your collection. We did find treasure, after all."

Effie moved to the mouth of the cave and the stronger light. The luster of the pearl was striking.

"I might look for a year and never find another."

When I left Effie that evening at the edge of the Sostelo land, I asked, "Tomorrow?"

She laughed. "Rainbow time. Colin, before we go, kiss me as you did this morning."

I did, then I said, "You'd better get home now."
My bold, passionate little Effie!

I felt guilty at the thought of leaving Chujo at home tomorrow when we would all go to the peak, so when I reached Los Alamos I rode to the plaza where he lay on his stretcher. "One mescal, senor, then you and I go for a walk."

The hollow eyes looked up from their sockets. "Why?"

"I'll tell you later. What did you eat today?"

Chujo laughed. "That damn frickerseed goat of Maudine's."

While we walked toward the hacienda, Chujo with his crutch and with my arm supporting his waist, he said, "It's good to move about again."

When we entered the hacienda, I said, "As soon as the new huts are finished, we will begin here again." I led him to a corner room at the back. "You have been my right hand, and will continue to be. You will live in the hacienda, and I have picked this room for you. Later, you will have much book work, and the room adjoining will be your office. I tell you now before the roof goes on, so you can have walls or partitions made as you wish."

Chujo turned and hobbled to an open window. "It is good of you, Colin, if I am worth it."

"When we go back to your stretcher, we will seal the bargain with another mescal. And teach Tomas to read and write. He intends to marry Teresa, and it will give you something to do until you can move about."

When Maudine and Meander and I met Effie next day, I was surprised at how well the girls got along. With Maudine's ready exuberance and size, I was afraid she could over-awe Effie. To my wonder, she approached her almost with humbleness.

"Honey," she said, "Meander has told me so many nice things about you, I feel we are sisters." She embraced Effie.

"Then we will be sisters," Effie said, in turn hugging Maudine. "Without Meander our long trip would never have ended."

Meander grinned at Maudine. "See, I said I had friends."

"You wear the little pearl at your throat today," I said to Effie as our horses led the way up the rocky trail to the cave.

"My mother wove the chain from silver thread last night."

"It is a beautiful chain. Could you thank her for me?"

"Of course, if it would please you."

"I worry about your riding alone to meet me."

"My mother has two peons she trusts, Ramon and Gasper. They follow me until they see you, then wait for my return."

"I did not know your mother was . . ." I began, and stopped.

"You did not know what?"

"That your mother was interested or involved in our meetings."

"She knows I love you. Why shouldn't she be? I have a wonderful mother. She loves you, too, Colin. I would tell you more but not now. We have only a few days or a week before the trial is over. Until then, I want these days for only us. There is one thing—when the trial ends, your people and mine will come home. From then on I cannot see you. If you come someday and I am not here, that will be the reason."

I said nothing. I could have railed about the futility of the quarrel between the Herreras and Sostelos, but I did not. And might not some justice, too, be on the side of Effie and her mother? Effie had said there was something else she could have told, but had held it back. I could do no less. While they lasted, we could spend these days in happiness.

"That pearl you found," Meander said when we were in the cave. "I want one for Maudine."

While Meander dug for his pearl, Effie and I explored the mountain. It was all a high wilderness of firs and oaks and piñons. We threw our voices at misty echo places where strange sounds came back. "Hello, Effie." "Hello, Colin." Then there would be the echo of laughter, as if from another world.

Now and then a javalina or antelope ran across colored soil and rock of yellow and red and blue and purple, a flick of life upon fantastic color.

154

A wild peal of laughter broke on the winds. "What is that?" I said.

"It is Astabo. From somewhere he has seen us, or killed an animal. He has a little bow and arrow he hunts with."

"You wrote me that he showed you many hidden places in the mountains."

"Yes, and I love him. We used to spend whole days together."

After the mention of Astabo, Effie became silent. It confirmed my suspicions, but about what I did not know.

Effie pointed to a stand of firs below.

"Look," she cried, "there is a fantail deer!"

I turned to look, but all I saw was the fan disappearing into a draw.

When we returned to the cave, Meander and Maudine sat swinging their bare feet over the ledge. Meander had dug well, like a herd of armadillos coming up in the evening, as the floor of the cave indicated, but had found no pearl. But he had found an old spearhead.

"What will you do with that?" I asked.

"If this durned Maudine don't stop making fun, I'll give her a poke with it." Maudine only laughed harder.

I told Effie as we rode back to the piñons, "You have your two peons. Would your mother let you spend a few nights in the Chisos? We lose so much time riding, we could never stay long if we went by day."

"Colin, of course she would let me stay. What made you doubt it?"

"It would be unusual."

"Were the months we knew of the trial unusual?"

"Then ask your mother tonight, and if she agrees, bring your suggans tomorrow."

We spent our days in the deeper Chisos, among spray and tumbling waterfalls in the peaks, the world far away but at our feet; there was the mystery of green trees and pools. At night, always the twin fires blinking.

Waking from my suggans with daylight.

The quick fire, the morning cup of coffee. "Coffee, senorita?" A slim arm reaching from Effie's own suggans. Putting my jacket about her shoulders as she sat up in the cool air. The bright smile. Sometimes waking after a day of tramping to see the red sun rise, or the early rainbow.

Days of caves and mists and waterfalls.

"Do you know why fish are in the land-locked pools?" Effie asked as we climbed a misty peak one day.

"I never thought about it."

"Astabo says a bird might drop a small fish from the river, or fly in with eggs in moss or slime on its feet. When must we go back, Colin?"

"I think tomorrow, but at least we can still meet in the piñons."

But one morning when I rode as usual to the orange ledge, there came no Effie, no pinto, no silver necklace.

As my horse plodded back to Los Alamos, I thought of St. Louis, the run up the Arkansas and all the rest. It seemed so long ago, but now with Effie and her mother, there was a fissure in the House of Sostelo, regardless of how the trial in Alpine ended.

"Well, here's the account of the trial," my uncle said that night as we sat in the plaza, "and I'll tell you the worst now. The don won a continuance for two years."

"But how?"

"Let me start at the beginning. In the courtroom, I had the parchment present. As you know, the attorneys for Don Sostelo had been lenient in not insisting upon your presence, I think to incur favor with the judge. Don Sostelo claimed that shortly after the old raid, his hacienda had been burglarized, and that a written agreement giving him the rights to the waterhole, and signed by Don Herrera, had been stolen. He swore that he is now at the point of recovering this document, and prayed Judge Howlett for the continuance. It was granted, although disgust and disbelief were on the face of each man in the courtroom."

"Could there have been such a document?"

"It is a complete fabrication. Don Sostelo plays only for time, but for two years your hands will be tied."

"Then nothing has changed."

Uncle Mike cracked his big knuckles. "Do you know what Don Sostelo's story about the last raid is? You were harboring outlaws and he came to clear them out."

"The old coyote!"

"Colin, nothing has changed. You are exactly where you were before, only older and wiser. Hasten your rebuilding, but with the view that anything could happen. The don could stop his desert warfare and strike Los Alamos, or use other means to harrass you. I leave this to your judgment—strike or be struck. Now I must go."

"You will not stay here tonight?"

"No, I overstayed a day in Alpine—the don left yesterday. I wanted to talk with my attorneys about an appeal. Keep Meander with you. Should I ever be needed, I will be here as before."

"Do you believe the talk about my father?"

"Let me say this—I am keeping an open mind."

So it was over, and Effie was gone again.

We continued our rebuilding at Los Alamos, and the intermittent warfare also continued.

We had begun to herd our cows and goats to the eastward on land that even Don Sostelo could not say was disputed, our intentions being to avoid everything but isolated confrontations in the sparse grass among the desert growth. But when these occasions did arise, we were as accurate with our rifle fire as we had been at Los Alamos. The vaqueros lived behind their slanting windbreaks, the kind Meander had built when we came to Texas.

Other things, too, were in my thoughts, and I could not keep from returning to the cave on Lost Mine Peak, hoping against hope that someday I would find Effie again.

I had ridden there, my horse dislodging a few stones from the rocky trail on my way up, and these rattled and bounced their

157

way downward into heaps of boulders or to other ledges. When I reached the cave, the horse's hooves clicking and striking hard on the rock, I dismounted and stood looking down upon the Sostelo lands.

It was then that I heard a moan, or thought I did, and at first it seemed to come from the cave. I paid no attention to the sound, for in the mountains, as Effie and I had learned, weird sounds and echoes from the wind were not uncommon. There could be strange whistlings among the trees and peaks, and any sound, natural or unnatural, would reverberate and echo. Perhaps the closeness of the mists helped hold the sounds inward; near an opening such as a cave's mouth, winds might give an organ tone.

But the persistence of the sound from the cave made me turn, and I walked toward the opening. As I have said earlier, the mouth of the cave was fairly wide, and there was enough half-light to see to the farther rim.

As I stepped inside, the moan became louder. Then I stopped, for the lank shadow of a man lay not three feet from the pool. A pistol rested on the ground near his hand.

I approached; the man's fingers groped for the pistol feebly; when he failed to reach it, the hand lay still again.

He was Mexican, and he whispered, "Senor, who are you?"

"A native of the region," I said, not wishing the Don O' Reiley business. "Why are you here?"

"I am dying, senor. Water, please. My hand cannot reach the pool."

I had one of those little collapsible drinking cups in my hip pocket; I filled it and held it before him.

"I cannot raise my head. Will you help?"

I placed my hand behind his head and raised it; while he drank, or tried to, I saw his face. At first, there were only the haggard eyes; they were haunted and black and deep in their sockets. He had high and wide cheekbones, but a good mouth and chin had there been any flesh on them.

"How long since you have had water?"

"A day, I think."

"Then this is all you get for now," I said, removing the cup. "Later, I will give you more."

"*Gracias,* senor." I laid his head back in the dust.

"When did you eat last?"

"I do not remember."

"If you are sick, where do you hurt?"

"It is not that kind of hurt. It is the wings of vengeance. A thing of the spirit."

"The what?"

"The wings of vengeance. When I can talk more, I will tell you."

There was almost a death rattle in his throat. "You must not talk," I said. "I have food and will bring it in. Later, you may drink again and eat. Now see if you can rest."

The man closed his eyes. I could not leave him here to suffer; when he had recovered to some extent, I could take him to Los Alamos. On the ledge, I built a small fire in the circle of Effie's fire stones, and thought what was best to do. There was a can of tomatoes in my saddlepockets, and a few other foods, including a can of tinned meat, but that would be too highly seasoned for a weak and empty stomach.

I took my rifle and walked up the trail; I saw a partridge in a bush and shot it. Back at the ledge, I heard the moan again.

I went inside the cave. "Are you worse?" I asked the Mexican.

"No, senor. But the shot—what was it?"

"I shot a partridge to make you soup."

"Ah," he said. "May I have one more drink of water?"

I gave him one, then I went outside to the coals of the fire. I dressed the bird, and boiled the breast in my skillet. I entered the cave again, carrying the tomato can and the skillet. I knelt over the man. "Are you awake?"

"*Si.*"

"I will give you a few spoons of tomato juice and partridge

broth. If your stomach holds it, after an hour I will give you more. Tonight you can try solid food."

I stayed with the man all night, burning a large fire at the cave's mouth as protection against some cougar or black bear. With daybreak, the Mexican was better. I was surprised at the richer timbre of his voice, and his enunciation; he was more rational.

"Your pistol," I said, picking it up. "It is a good one."

"Yes, but I curse the day I bought it. Senor, I told you of the wings of vengeance. That pistol is why I am here today."

"How is that?"

"When I was young, I was very foolish. I was good at heart and religious. I shot well, but I allowed myself to be talked into a life of crime. I was vain, and praise pleased me. I must talk, senor, or lose my mind."

"Then talk, amigo."

"I told you of the fiends of retribution. They are so real, senor, that I sometimes see them." He glanced toward the far corner of the cave, as if he expected to see them now. "When I was young, I was to meet a man and kill him. I met him and fired; many people said he died, but I know he did not. I found where he had hidden in a jacal, but he was aided and escaped me and was lost in the desert. Knowing that if he lived he would follow me, I fled to Mexico, for I was no longer proud or vain. I was only ashamed, and fearful. I begged God for forgiveness."

"Amigo, what is your name?"

"Quandaris, senor."

Quandaris! The man who had shot my father!

Now I had found him, and he lay here at my feet, completely at my mercy. He was that other someone reticent Effie had told me of on our first day on Lost Mine Peak.

"Why do you touch your pistol, senor?"

"Habit, I suppose."

Quandaris continued, "Do you know what it is to run, to run always, for years? No, you could never know. When he recovered from his wound, the man I shot learned I had fled to Mexico and followed. Senor, how he did it I do not know, but he found my trail.

"The greatest ill had been done when a hacienda was raided, and a woman killed, but I swear before the Virgin I had no part in it. A powerful don had brought a man from San Antonio to lead the raid, but the man I had shot thought that I, too, had helped.

"For nearly twenty years that ghost has been behind me. I have never had a year, or a month, of peace. Somewhere in Mexico I would find a jacal and be taken in, then there would be word of a red-haired man who came near, and I would flee again. I learned from Astabo, the wild man of the mountains, that I have been trailed even here. This time I am caught. I have fought as long as I can fight, run as long as I can run; I have reached the end. It would have been better had you never found me, and let me die. I had thought that by returning here, where he would least expect me to be, that I could escape him, but no. And I have heard that when he kills me, he will build a band to destroy Don Sostelo."

The words of Zelina and Effie about my father came back to me, then wonderment. Could it be that my father, when he recovered, had heard of my mother's death and thought that I had died also? Now I knew Effie's reluctance to talk when Astabo's name had been mentioned; had she told me part of the story, it would have led to the rest, that my father, himself, would have become an outlaw had he raided the Sostelos, and she had shielded me from this.

"Does the food rest easy on your stomach?" I asked Quandaris.

"I have some pain, but it should soon be over."

"This man from San Antonio—who was he?"

"The King. He was an outlaw and gambler. He knew many outlaws. As I say, he was brought here to lead the raid on the Herrera hacienda."

161

"Where is your horse?"

"Dead, as so many others are. Dead from the constant running and no food."

"Quandaris, I must return to my rancho. Now for you. You have the partridge, and I will leave you a tin of meat."

"Perhaps, with the grace of God, there is still hope, although I always expected to die alone."

"You can't be moved today. At this time tomorrow, I will be here with a horse for you. You will come with me to my rancho."

I packed up and rode down the trail.

Quandaris, the gunman! A beaten wreck!

And a father, I knew now, who still lived.

# 12

<<<<<<<<<<<<<<<<<<<<

That night I talked with Father Dore about Quandaris and what had happened.

"You are more charitable than I thought, Colin."

"I think I could be charitable, if things would let me be. But Los Alamos cannot be brought into another war, even to help my father."

"It is better to be charitable when things will not let you be."

"Do you know what Quandaris must have gone through? Desert sands, no water? I shudder to think of it. Yet I do not blame my father."

"And you will bring Quandaris here?"

"Yes. That will be the best way to find my father. When he

knows where Quandaris is, he, too, will come. I believe what Quandaris says and I will protect him. While we talked, he did not know yet that I was Colin O'Reiley."

"You take a risk."

"Perhaps, but it is all I can do. If my father has followed Quandaris through all these years, someday he will follow him here."

Next day I brought Quandaris down to Los Alamos. When we stopped in the plaza, he gazed wonderingly at the narrow streets and adobes, and at the rising hacienda. His haunted eyes were still deep in their sockets, and he turned toward me.

"Senor, you have never told me your name."

"I am called here Don Colin Herrera O'Reiley, and you are the man who shot my father."

"With your red hair, I should have known. What a fool I was! Have I been brought to execution, after all your attention on the mountain?"

"Had I wanted execution, it could have been done while you were helpless. Come, I will help you from your horse, and we will go to the hacienda."

We found Chujo in his room, the tile roofing completed on this portion of the hacienda and over his office. Chujo looked up from his desk. "This is Quandaris," I said. "He will have his own adobe, and will help you do what you are unable to do outside. Watch his needs, for he is a good man."

Although I had set the inducement for my father's return to Los Alamos, for the next several days nothing happened. Perhaps he was not as close on the trail after all, and must make some other discovery in the mountains before he knew that his son still lived.

Still, there was one almost immediate result from my stay in the cave. A few days later, a fear-stricken Mexican from Don Sostelo's rode into the plaza, amidst the yapping of dogs and the excited cries of those who recognized him. He was accompanied by three of my younger Apaches.

"Don O'Reiley," he said, "my name is Ramon. I was with

Senorita Euphemia in the piñons. I have a note for you, but I almost did not get through your lines to deliver it. You have too many knives ready to strike. Here is the note, senor."

*Dear Colin,*

*Several nights ago I saw a fire on Lost Mine Peak before what could only be our cave. I did not know if it was your fire, or if you wanted me or needed me.*

*If you do, tell Ramon, the bearer of this note, and I will be in the piñons tomorrow with him or Gasper, the two vaqueros we trust, in spite of my grandfather.*

"Tell Effie," I said to Ramon, "that I will see her tomorrow." I told the Apaches, "Let this man through the lines whenever he wishes. Also Gasper."

I wondered if there had been some open break between Effie and the don, that she would meet me so.

When we met in the piñons again, we were off our horses and embracing as before, but now in full view of the vaqueros who had brought her.

We sat on the ledge and I said, "Effie, I have found Quandaris, the gunman who shot my father. I am protecting him at Los Alamos, for my father is still alive."

"I knew that from Astabo, the wild man of the mountains. He came to the hacienda for salt. He detests my grandfather. Colin, I have not wanted to, but now we must talk frankly. After your father kills Quandaris, he will bring a band of men to destroy my grandfather. I must tell what I have never told you, that my own father was killed in the first Los Alamos raid."

I could not believe what I heard. "Your father?"

Effie and her mother had borne their burden patiently, far more than I had borne mine. I had been right in thinking that there might be some justice on their side.

"My grandfather had forced father into the raid, at first to lead it, but he refused, then the King was sent for. You lost your mother at Los Alamos, I my father, and my mother a husband. But these things are gone; they have no right to come between us. I know of the court continuance; it will only prolong our waiting. Nothing now should stop us from what we wish. I no longer intend to put up with my grandfather the way my mother has been forced to do."

"My father must not raid the Sostelo hacienda, especially since you and your mother would be there. I have thought of something, and may have a way to bring peace with the don, and persuade my father that all is settled. Please, could you ride to Los Alamos? You will get through the lines without trouble; I want to show you the hacienda where we will live."

"Yes, I will come as soon as I can."

And the day came when she was there. The villagers smiled, and made love signs to each other.

The tile roof of the hacienda in its regular lines glistened, and the walls sparkled from stones we had quarried and brought down from the mountains.

"It is a Chisos home," I told Effie as we walked through the barren rooms, and I felt once again that the years were rushing.

"Do you remember a little girl who gave me a peck on the cheek on the *Mississippi Queen?*"

"Vaguely."

"You will have dinner in the plaza tonight? *Tamales caliente* and *tamales dulce?* Even frickerseed goat?"

"Of course."

"Then I will send a note to the don, and invite myself to dinner next week."

"Colin, with the talk of your father's raid, I no longer care what happens. If my grandfather tries to stop us from meeting, I will shoot a pistol at his feet." That odd uncompromising expression came to her mouth. "He understands that language. Geneva, my maid, lost her husband last week. He had been sent to steal your cows. This murder must stop. My grandfather is beaten, but he will not give up."

Effie glanced about the large living room. "You have no furniture here a woman would like."

"That one old table—do you call it furniture? If you look carefully, you will see no furniture at all."

166

"Then I beg your pardon."
I returned by Effie a note to Don Sostelo.

*Don Colin Herrera O'Reiley requests the honor of dining
at your hacienda one week from tonight. There are matters of
mutual interest we should discuss.*

In spite of my effrontery, I received an answer.

*The brash and young Don Colin Herrera O'Reiley is in-
vited to dinner at the hacienda of Don Sostelo on Friday next.
The matters he may wish to discuss will certainly be of no interest to the undersigned.*

But the don had at least indulged the invitation, whether it
was his or mine.

While awaiting the night when I was to dine with Don Sostelo, I made a business trip to Sanderson, buying at a general
store a new pair of trousers and what passed in our country as a
dinner jacket.

I had thought first of wearing pajama pants to the dinner, and
so be attired as I was when I met Don Sostelo between our two
armies, but out of consideration for Effie I did not.

At the hardware store I bought an unlimited quantity of
barbed wire, the spools to be delivered to Los Alamos as soon as
possible. The wire had come from San Antonio; since Sanderson was nearer than Alpine, I was able to get a better price due
to the lower freight charges.

The barbed wire, wagons of it, had arrived that Friday afternoon; I had the teamsters drop the spools four at a time in a
long line we marked near the mudhole to extend on each side
through the brush far beyond. The mists were heavy on the
mountains when we finished the unloading, and I went to my
adobe to bathe in a tin washtub.

When I had dressed, wearing the cummerbund, I went outside

to see Miguel and my escort. Strangely, I expected no trickery from Don Sostelo; with his specious sense of honor and formality, he would not let himself enjoy the luxury of deceit in so open a manner; still, I wanted my bodyguard to be in tiptop shape.

I was rather proud of the dozen riders Miguel had chosen; he could ride as well with one leg as he could with two, and he had trained the younger men well.

They sat their saddles erectly, knives in their belts, their black bands on, their rifles in pommel slings, the bandoliers crossed on their chests, their pajama pants clean and white. As befitted the youthfulness of some, they were excited by this armed excursion to Don Sostelo's hacienda, although Miguel had been instructed to tell them that under no circumstance was a shot to be fired, no matter the provocation, unless I fired first.

When we arrived at Don Sostelo's it was almost dark; shadows from ancient trees lay across the low-walled grounds and the long walk which led to the hacienda. The gateway was barred by heavy links of chain which hung from two higher portions of stone. Beyond the wall at the rear were the stables and outbuildings, a well with a spinning windmill, and the huts of Don Sostelo's retainers.

If I had felt proud of the appearance of my bodyguard, Don Sostelo had even more reason to take pride in his. The men were better, almost richly clad, in salmon-colored uniforms, and stood with their rifles erect along either side of the long flower-bordered walk which led to the hacienda, where a few lights had begun to appear.

I was amused by the don's *soldados,* for while the pretense might be to honor me, I knew quite well they were there for another purpose—to awe me—and my own men. If the plan of my visit worked, there would soon be no need for the *soldados* or even the Apaches.

As we stopped at the gate, Miguel hissed to his Apaches, "Until Don O'Reiley leaves us, do not even look at those pretty *soldados.* Keep your eyes straight ahead."

I dismounted with Miguel and walked to the gate. A retainer

with a huge key in his hand inserted it in the locks of the three chains, then drew them aside.

He bowed. "Enter, Don O'Reiley."

As soon as I stood on the walk, the retainer began to replace the chains and lock them.

"Wait!" Miguel said fiercely. He had accompanied me to the gate only as a mark of respect. He asked the retainer, "You are the caporal here?"

"*Sí.*"

"Then you will unlock that chain at once. My don does not visit under such circumstances. You infer that Don O'Reiley is your prisoner."

I had really thought nothing about the chain being locked behind me; in event of trouble with the *soldados,* I could have vaulted the low wall with ease.

"My orders," the caporal said, "I am to lock the chains."

Miguel said, "How sweet you look in your red jacket! I shall look for that jacket in the brush someday. Once more, unlock the gate."

To Miguel, the chains had become a point of honor.

The caporal said, "I am watched from the windows. I am not allowed to unlock the chains."

So this by-play was being witnessed by Don Sostelo, and perhaps by Effie and her mother.

"Don O'Reiley," Miguel said, "it shall be as you said—that if the first sign of treachery appears, we will withdraw." Leaning against the corner block of stone, he pointed his crutch. "Leap the wall, senor, and return to your horse."

I vaulted over the wall and stood beside Miguel. To him, the locked chains were a symbol; he would not ignore them, or what their relocking behind me had meant.

So the dinner battle with Don Sostelo had started even before dinner.

The caporal shook, a miserable man. "Don O'Reiley, if I leave unlocked the top chain, you can step over the other two. That way my lashes will be only one-third as many."

"Craven fool!" Miguel hobbled to the chains and grabbed

the key from the caporal. Leaning on his crutch, he unlocked the chains, tossing their ends aside.

Then, in full view of the windows, he stuck the key into his pocket. He had won the first skirmish with Don Sostelo.

I stepped up the walk between the lines of salmon-colored *soldados*. At the tiled entrance to the hacienda, I saw a bronze knocker on the ornate door. I used it once.

The door opened; an old Mexican maid appeared. She knelt. "Don O'Reiley, welcome to our casa." She, too, appeared to be trembling. What fear the don must inspire in his retainers!

"Rise, senora. Will you show me to Don Sostelo?"

"Come with me, Don O'Reiley. Don Sostelo will be down shortly."

She led me through a dim hall into a brilliantly lighted living room. And I had never seen such a room of gorgeousness, of color, and tapestry. It was quite another world from that of the iron chains across the gateway.

The old servant motioned timidly toward a gold-threaded divan. "Would you sit, Don O'Reiley?"

"May I look about the room? Besides, I see many interesting books on the shelves."

It was to be fifteen minutes before the don appeared; perhaps his delay was due to one of three reasons—or to all three—that he might impress this room upon my poverty, or to recover from his defeat at the gateway, or simply to humiliate me by ignoring me.

The floor of the room was of Moorish tile and thick rugs; paintings of old masters—or by the time of my death they would have become old masters—were carefully placed on the walls, and there were the priceless bookshelves. I was standing beside them, reading a red-bound volume in Castilian, when a dry voice said, "You read Castilian, Don O'Reiley?"

"Yes," I said turning. "I have read this book before, but I have never seen one of the first editions. The binding is beautiful."

The gray eyebrows of a fox raised themselves. "Where did you learn Castilian?"

"I learned at my school."

And I thought, but for a senseless raid, valuables like these might still be preserved in my grandfather's hacienda.

"Will you join me in wine?" the thin lips said.

"With pleasure."

I saw Don Sostelo's eyes rest on my cummerbund, but he said nothing. He pulled a gold cord, and a small gong sounded quietly. A male servant appeared.

"The wine I spoke of, Guillermo."

"*Sí*, Don Sostelo."

While we sipped the amber wine on the golden divan, the don said, his blue eyes sharp in mine, "I have not yet welcomed you to my hacienda. I am pleased by your presence."

"When my hacienda is finished, I shall be equally glad to welcome you. I must assure you, though, I could not out-do your wine cellar."

The don's eyes tightened keenly. "At the risk of appearing to be discourteous, I did not quite expect you to have quite the new manners you show. Have you formerly moved in great society?"

I knew the don talked so only to ignore the more serious business to follow.

I laughed. "No, at my school we were taught all the amenities. It was a boys' school and when we were taught our cotillions, some of us were forced to wear a towel about our waists to appear as girls. If we boys did not present ourselves properly, and bow and scrape to the towel after the dance, we received the administrative coup—a long board across our bottoms. Under such conditions, it was very easy to learn social amenities."

A twist of amusement came to the lips.

"Yes, and the board or lash teaches the same in other fields. What phase of Spanish literature did you like best?"

"Sir, I think the rogue novel. It always intrigued me."

"'A low class thing," the don said.

"Yes, and that is its virtue. It helped bring realism to writing."

"Folly!"

"Let me ask, do you in this great hacienda know how your people live? Do you know what they talk of in their huts at night, how they fear what may become of them, how the peon delivers the child of his wife, how he waits for his thirty lashes? I do not think you see this, sir. You know only the dead side of a person; you do not know that the only life he manages is for you.

"So now the rogue element creeps in, what people must do to keep themselves such, to be themselves, to become secretive or active in their protests, to rob, to connive, to seduce, to be outside a law and live only within the law they build for their own actions, as I am sure you know."

Before answering, Don Sostelo rang for wine again.

What the servant appeared, he asked, "Guillermo, how many lashes have you had this year?"

"Fifty, Don Sostelo."

"Are you a better man for it?"

"*Si,* Don Sostelo. A much better man."

"Then bring us more wine." When the servant left, the don asked, "Now what do you think?"

"That your man is too quiet. Someday, like the rogue, he could stick a knife in your back."

"Rot."

I was becoming impatient with the time-consuming conversation of the don. I knew a decent interval must pass before the ladies—Effie and her mother—joined us, but I had the impression that the don, still smarting from Miguel's victory at the gate, not only wanted to give me a second sizing-up after our meeting in the desert, but also to aggravate or tantalize me by a further delay.

While we continued an utterly specious conversation, I wished only that Don Sostelo would rise and ring some other gong. At last he did, swaying slightly as he walked to a heavier cord and rang a deeper tone.

"Don O'Reiley, we will wait at the foot of the staircase. Soon the ladies will be present."

One, two, three, four, I thought, just as at the school when we walked with our rifles.

Don Sostelo marched me past an unbelievably appointed dining room to a room at the foot of a circular staircase. He said sarcastically, "I will give you the place of honor here, young don," and he marked an imaginary X on the rug with his finely shined boot. "I will stand behind you while you greet Euphemia and her mother."

Yes, I thought, a widowed daughter, and by your own damned folly. I took my place on the X.

"I must tell you," Don Sostelo was saying from behind my shoulder, "that you have surprised me in many ways."

"Before the evening is over, sir, I may surprise you in another."

# 13

‹‹‹‹‹‹‹‹‹‹‹‹‹‹‹‹‹‹

When I heard the light laughter of two women above me, I looked up to the head of the circular stairway, and I stared in disbelief.

I had seen Effie on a steamboat on the Mississippi, dressed no better than some poverty-stricken tramp might have been dressed; I had seen her on the Arkansas, dirty from smoke and coal or wood dust. I had crossed the Territory and Texas with her, she still in her rags and tatters, and we had roamed Lost Mine Peak together, though then she had worn smart riding clothes.

But never before had I seen the vision which descended upon me now.

It was Effie, but how regal an Effie! The eyes that looked down and her hair were the same, but the dress she wore! It was a long interwoven thing of some cross between a light tan and yellow, or whatever name women might in their wisdom apply to such a color. It could not have been less than centuries old; the scent of saffron had already reached me.

Effie's sleeves stopped before the elbows; she wore white gloves, her waist was tight. How the dress blended with the streak of hair over her eye!

Even while Effie smiled down, and while our eyes met and came together with her each descending step, I could not help but be conscious of the beautiful woman who followed her.

She was only slightly taller and golden-haired, but seemed more a sister than a mother to Effie, so well had she cared for herself. Her head was high and proud; she wore a gown of light green. She smiled encouragingly to me as Effie reached the final step.

Don Sostelo moved forward. "My granddaughter, Euphemia, sir. And my daughter, Senora Julia Hernandez." He added with a certain sneer, "Don Colin Herrera O'Reiley."

I bowed to Effie; she extended her hand; I kissed it. Senora Hernandez gave me hers, also.

Don Sostelo said, "Dinner will be a few moments late. Let us sit in the alcove. You," he said to Senora Herandez, "must sit near Euphemia as a duenna, to listen to what she and Don O'Reiley will talk about."

Senora Hernandez smiled. It was a vivid smile. "Of course, I do want to hear what they talk about, but surprisingly, I already know."

"Your pearl," I said to Effie when we were seated, "it is beautiful."

"You gave it to me, and I will always wear it."

Senora Hernandez chided gently, but smiling, "Euphemia, do not reveal your intentions too quickly."

Don Sostelo rang for more wine and said to the ladies, sudden suspicion in his eyes, "You have both deceived me about the pearl."

Effie spoke, and her mouth grew tight. She said to the don,

"From now on, I will make my own future with Colin. I intend to ignore your commands, and see him whenever I wish."

Senora Hernandez said, "Euphemia, do not speak so before dinner."

I was completely at ease now, sensing what was to come. The dinner would be under polite circumstances, perhaps with only a few minor irritations such as earlier had passed between me and the don, but after dinner the fur might fly in more directions than one.

At last we went to the dining table, Don Sostelo at the head and Senora Hernandez opposite him; Effie and I were seated at the sides. The don made his grace at the table, and the servants moved in. The dinner was delicious, but I hardly know what it was, or what I ate.

There was the light gown before me, the openings of the brocade, the frank and amusing eyes that knew they told me more than I was supposed to know.

Don Sostelo, as he ate, drank more heavily. I knew this, because at a new drink the servant had raised his eyebrows slightly. At last the don dismissed us from the dining room—and that was what it was, a dismissal. We sat in the living room, Senora Hernandez taking the traditional place near Effie and me.

This time, Don Sostelo ordered liquor to be set before the golden couch. He sat as if thinking, his head low, then suddenly his fierce eyes peered up.

"Don O'Reiley, what is your purpose in being here tonight?"

Now, I could let him wonder. "I may have several purposes."

"And what would be the first?" the don asked.

"You thought you had killed my father, but do you know he is alive today and has returned to the Chisos?"

Utter disbelief was on the don's face. He placed his glass carefully on the table. "Where do you get this information?"

"From many people, including Quandaris, the gunman you hired to kill him."

"Where is this Quandaris?"

"At Los Alamos, where he will be safe from you."

From their ornate chairs, Senora Hernandez and Effie stared at me and the don intently. I watched Effie's large eyes. By the trend of the conversation, I knew that she had said nothing to the don about my father's reappearance in the mountains. It had come as too great a shock to him.

He was saying, "But what could a gunman like Quandaris do, now that you hold him, even if he had ever worked for me?"

"That is only a part of it. Quandaris and others tell me that as soon as my father finds and kills him, he will lead a band from Mexico to wipe out your hacienda, lock, stock, and barrel. There will not be one stone of this hacienda left standing, no more than was left of the old Los Alamos."

"And your second point?" the don said.

"Euphemia."

"What interest can she be to you?"

"Exactly what you had planned several years ago when you sent her to St. Louis with Senor and Senora Maderas—marriage, but not as you had planned as a means to subject me."

"And what do you mean by that?"

"You sent Euphemia to entrap me, and gain what you hoped would be a permanent hold over Los Alamos. But you did not know your granddaughter—she was too true to herself to have you ruin her."

"And you have sources for this information?"

"I have two sources. The first was Senora Maderas. We were sitting on a ledge above the Canadian, talking, and all she did not tell me I guessed."

"You will never marry Euphemia."

"You sent her to me once; why should you object now?"

Don Sostelo stood angrily. Euphemia also rose, her eyes flashing. "Colin, I will tell you why. He thought you would be easy to control. When he found you would fight to hold Los Alamos, all his plans fell apart. He did not believe you could do what you did, and he hated you for it."

"Who," Don Sostelo asked me in rage, "was your second source of information?"

"I decline to tell you."

"Then you have seen Euphemia more than I thought."

Effie gave a rare tinkling laugh. "Yes, I have seen him often. I told him all of what you had planned."

"Then you will never see him again. Go to your room."

Senora Hernandez said softly, but with flashing eyes, "Euphemia will not go to her room, and I will say what she may do. And I tell you now, she may see Colin whenever she wishes."

"Julia," the don said. "you still live on my charity."

"Yes," Senora Hernandez said, "and that is why I do not intend to see Euphemia live on it. She will have her husband and her home, and never live as I have lived." The senora smiled with irony. "Now, must I go to my room?"

The don sat again, rigidly, and Effie sat again quietly. A strange silence had suddenly filled the room.

The don said, "Then your third reason, Don O'Reiley, since you have saved it for the last, is the real thing you have come to discuss."

"You are correct, although my second point may be more important ultimately. For now, I come to offer peace. I come to give you the mudhole of Los Alamos."

The frosty eyes glinted.

"And why would you do that?"

"Relatives—and I intend to be one—should not war against each other. I have grown weary of the cost of this struggle, both in men and time."

"Your mother," Senora Hernandez said softly, "and my husband—both lost to us. And I have a fatherless daughter."

I did not look at Effie then, but said to Don Sostelo, "When my father and I meet, as I know we shall, I will prevent him from raiding your hacienda. There will be no revenge for twice-ruined Los Alamos."

"And where would your cows drink?"

"We will move them on to the eastward."

"But, suppose," the don said, his eyes flicking like rapiers, "suppose that by some unforeseen chance when the court con-

178

tinuance is settled, the judge would award you the mudhole legally? What would I have besides promises, perhaps empty ones, from you and your father?"

"My father does not enter into this. He and I will have much time to make up together, without seeking useless bloodshed. But I could have papers drawn up, or drop the present case now."

"You have made fine statements, young sir, and many concerning my family. Any other man I would have turned from my home. What present guarantee do you have that I may keep the waterhole?"

"Today I received a wagon train of barbed wire from Sanderson. I intend to run a fence on my side of the hole, and leave the water for you." I heard Effie gasp, and Senora Hernandez clinched her hands tightly. "More wire will be needed, and we must go to the mountains for extra posts for fences. But day after tomorrow we will begin work at the hole and run our fence in two directions from there. Is that guarantee sufficient?"

Don Sostelo rang for a mescal. I could see his mind leap in many directions; should he accept my offer, or wait for what he hoped would be a favorable court decision, thereby gaining most of the other property?

"I think," he said, sipping his drink but offering me none and no wine for the senora and Effie, "I think there is more here than meets the eye."

"Dead men's eyes, senor? Dead men's eyes in the brush? I begin to think you do not care how long the war between us lasts."

The don was in full command of himself now, but a change had come over him. His eyes fell upon Effie's necklace. "I forbade you to wear that pearl. Where did you get the necklace?"

Effie raised her head defiantly. "I will not tell you that."

Senora Hernandez said, "I made the necklace."

The don said sarcastically, "I must commend your craftsmanship. By its excellent quality, I would have thought it made by the silver workers at Taxco."

"No," said Senora Hernandez, her eyes laughing, "it was

made in the House of Sostelo, on a night after Euphemia had been with Colin."

The remark irritated the don. "Julia, you will speak no more in that manner. And be completely quiet. I am thinking."

I rose. "Don Sostelo, perhaps I also disturb your thoughts. I shall go."

His eyes were almost vacant now. He waved an arm almost negligently. "No, pray be seated."

In a low voice, Senora Hernandez asked me, "Will you sit between Euphemia and me?"

"With pleasure, senora."

As I sat, her head was held high, like Effie's, but the beauty of her liquid eyes was haunted.

"Are you well, senora? May I get you wine, or water?"

"Colin O'Reiley, you saw the four walls when you entered the grounds?"

"Of course."

"Since almost the day of your birth, the death of my husband and the birth of Euphemia, I have been a prisoner within those walls."

"What? You mean you have never left this hacienda?"

"My father said I had done enough harm to his name by marrying a coward who would not lead the raid against Los Alamos. But I revere him for his refusal, yet this imprisonment has been my punishment. And when Euphemia was taken from me and sent to St. Louis, I wept for weeks on end. I hope you do not think that I have been forward in helping Euphemia meet you in the mountains. She loves you, and I want her to escape the life I live."

"But you also must escape this place. When you came down the stairway, I might have taken you for Effie's sister. You are still very young."

"But inside I am withered. I want only that you take Euphemia, and let her escape this hacienda."

"That was my purpose tonight, senora, to put an end to these torments, but I have been refused."

On his couch, Don Sostelo had roused himself from his lethargy; he rang for the servant. This time Guillermo brought two glasses on a silver tray; he went first to Don Sostelo, almost with hate in his eyes. The don turned his head to me, almost drunkenly. "Have you met this Ganymede, my cup bearer to the gods?"

"Or to the god? No, I have not had that pleasure."

The servant glanced at me questioningly, and I nodded. He came to me with the tray. As I took the glass, I said in a low voice, "Would you care to work for me?"

"*Sí,* Don O'Reiley."

"When you can, come to Los Alamos. If you are caught in the brush, ask for Miguel or Pedro." There was hardly a flicker in his black eyes.

As I sat with the drink, I said to Effie, "I have never seen so beautiful a gown."

I watched the nobility of the senora's head. She said, "It was my honeymoon dress, and before that, my grandmother's. Someday it will be Euphemia's. It has a going-away cape in black, embroidered with gold threading."

"But why black?"

"In the night, when the honeymooners would leave by horse or carriage, black would not be so easily seen."

"Why did you select the dress for tonight?" I asked Effie.

Effie shook the hair from her eye. "With what mother just said, don't you know?"

"I would ask only a useless question if your mother has already approved."

Senora Hernandez said, "Useless, because I have known my answer for many months."

Effie rose suddenly and kissed her mother. She turned to me, her eyes in mine. "But I want to hear it from you."

I stood beside her. "Effie, will you marry me?"

"Yes, Colin."

I took Effie in my arms; there was one quick pulsating kiss. "But I have no ring," I said, releasing her.

"Here," Senora Hernandez said, slipping the diamond from her finger, "My ring is yours, Colin, until you choose to return it."

Don Sostelo stared drunkenly ahead and from the side of us, oblivious to everything.

So Effie and I became engaged in the House of Sostelo; it had not been among the piñons, or on the ledge before the cave, or high in the misty Chisos, or in the wide openness which had been our home for so long, but it was enough even in the house of my enemy to have been given all a man on earth could desire.

There was a small love seat behind the don's divan; I moved it near the senora, and Effie and I sat before her.

"Listen carefully," I said, "for we may not have long to talk. Effie tells me you have two trusted men, Ramon and Gasper; tomorrow you will have a third, Guillermo, the drink-bearer. Don Sostelo has no intention of meeting any overture I have made. I think I know his mind, but I am not certain. But since Effie and I are now engaged, neither of you can stay longer in this prison. We will set a day through Guillermo when you will ride to Los Alamos. You should gather the personal things you will need, and have them ready. My hacienda will be poor, but there will be a room for each of you, and you will have what you do not have here—freedom. Do not show any enthusiasm before the don; he is like a fox in his instincts, and will suspect you. I must not see either of you again, until I and my men ride to take you away."

"Do you mean a raid?" Effie asked.

"No, not in the usual sense."

Senora Hernandez said, "Colin, you have given me courage. Yes, I will escape with you. But what will your peons do when they learn Sostelos are among them?"

"You will not be Sostelos; you will be O'Reileys."

She rose as I did, and I bowed and kissed her hand.

I moved with Effie to stand before the don. His glazed eyes peered up.

"Goodnight, Don Sostelo. For the courtesy of the evening, I

thank you. May Euphemia and the senora see me to my horse?"

"Of course," he said, his mind awakened and groping. "You say you will begin work on the fencing on the day after tomorrow?"

"Yes, as soon as we get the posts."

The three of us went down the long walk slowly, between the pink-coated *soldados* and their lanterns on the ground.

"Attention!" Miguel shouted, and in a flash the Apaches leaped to their horses.

I asked Effie, "Do you mind if I kiss my new mother goodnight?"

"Not if you kiss me, too."

My new mother said, "Colin, before you entered the hacienda, we saw the battle of the chains." She glanced at the idle coils at her feet. "You have freed me from these. Don Sostelo can no longer be my father."

"I had hoped that reason and my offer tonight might prevail, but it did not."

I left them and mounted my horse beside Miguel. He took the chain key from his pocket and tossed it to the caporal. I heard the chains rattle as they were locked in place again.

As my Apaches rode for Los Alamos, the stars were high and bright. I had done the best I could to bring peace.

# 14

<<<<<<<<<<<<<<<<<<<<

With what happened later, it was not difficult for me to see how Don Sostelo had so often out-smarted my grandfather, whose mind did not run in the don's vein. And within two days from my visit to the Sostelo hacienda, it became obvious that mine did not.

On the second morning, when the oak posts had been brought down to the water hole, and the first were being set for the fence line, Don Sostelo with twenty men and a deputy sheriff from Alpine rode in. It would have taken good riding, I thought, looking at the star on the deputy's cowhide vest, for the don to have sent a messenger to Alpine and have a deputy back with him by now—all in less than a night, a full day, and a full night again—a run of about one hundred fifty miles.

I had known before I left the don's hacienda that night that all his drunkenness had not been stupidity; that he had already formulated some retaliatory plan against what he considered my apparent amnesty. I continued to watch the star and wonder.

I continued to watch the star because I had so rarely seen a deputy, and especially never a sheriff here. Our county—the largest in Texas, almost six thousand square miles of it—had only one town of consequence, and that was Alpine on the San Antonio to El Paso railroad; we were in the loop at the bottom of the county.

Our population was sparse—our few families might ride twenty-five to a hundred miles to visit friends or have a barbecue or a singing or a catfish fry. Between these scattered homes was the merciless desert growth of cactus, and occasional tufts of grass. No wonder we needed our part of these six thousand square miles to graze our few cows and goats.

There were the mountains, dry creek beds, and mesas. If we saw a deputy or a sheriff once a year, he was to be commended in the Big Bend for good riding.

Good riding, if he wasn't trapped or bushwhacked on some outlaw or cow trail, or run into a smuggling gang from across the Rio Grande, men whose knives were as quick as their guns. So if gunfights or vigilante activity took place in our section, they were studiously ignored by most officials; the old families like the Herreras and the Sostelos with their peons were allowed their feuds, the law usually holding hands off for its own survival. As for the other matters, what was one more body found in the desert?

I realized the meeting here at the waterhole was of some importance, or Don Sostelo would not have invested himself with a deputy.

This gentleman eliminated the bulge in his cheek, and rode down to the hole with tobacco-stained mustaches. I could tolerate the stain, but not the brown dribble at the corners of his mouth.

He stopped his horse, gave me a good once-over, pajama pants and all, and said, "You are Colin O'Reiley?"

185

"Yes, I am Colin O'Reiley."

"Here is a summons for you from the court at Alpine." He handed me a large envelope. I opened it, and the summons was from Judge Howlett who had ruled on the continuance of the Los Alamos case.

Having violated the agreement concerning certain properties you claim, and indulging yourself in fencing the disputed waterhole at Los Alamos against the stock of one Don Sostelo, I do declare you in contempt of this court and the agreements upon which the continuance was based. A similar summons is issued against Michael O'Reiley, and you both are ordered to appear within five days before this court to answer the complaint as drawn by Don Sostelo.

I looked up from the summons, knowing what a fool I had been.

There in the don's great living room, even as I talked with Effie and her mother, the drunken mind of the don, even after his defeat at Los Alamos, had continued its devious planning.

After the summons, what trust could any Herrera or any O'Reiley place in the man? I had indebted myself to the store in Sanderson for the now useless spools of barbed wire tossed about us, as well as those placed farther out on the fence lines, and I had done this to bring an end to the deaths in the desert.

Such was my anger at the don's deception that I did not even glance at him. I would not give him that satisfaction.

I said to the deputy, "Get off your horse, please. I want to show you something."

Surprised, he did so, standing bowlegged and uncertain.

"What is your name?" I asked.

"Haymaker." He had pale blue eyes.

"That's what we are going to make while you are here—hay. I want you to watch carefully what I show you, because you will be subpoenaed to testify before the judge as to what you found here."

Haymaker said, "But I ain't got authority."

"No, but you'll make a damn good witness, or every family in this end of the county will see that you are impeached for failing in your investigatory duties. Those duties are part of the law, aren't they?"

"I reckon."

"Now walk around this mudhole with me."

I showed Haymaker the line of posts which were beginning to run outward on either side of the hole. "Now look at this," I said, and led him around the hole away from the Sostelo side. "Do you see the holes on my side already dug for the posts? Do you see my workers with their posthole diggers making others? Do you see the first poles already being tamped in and beginning to close my cows and goats from my own water?"

"Hmm!" Haymaker said, biting a chew from his plug.

"If I violated any terms of the continuance, I hurt only myself, not Don Sostelo. I was at his hacienda two nights ago and told him I would fence the hole, giving it to him, to stop this warfare. I know now what a conniver I dealt with. He has twisted the whole matter in order to influence the court."

Haymaker's pale eyes looked straight into mine. "Yeah, I see them stringing bob wire now. You've got a few points. That wasn't meant to be funny," he added hurriedly.

"When you are subpoenaed, I hope you tell the truth. These peons and my Apaches have heard us talk; in the desert there are many quick knives."

When Don Sostelo and his party left, and Haymaker rode on down to my uncle's, I told Miguel and Old Carlos, "Take down every line of wire you have stretched. Take up every post. We can use the material elsewhere. Miguel, from now on, I want double the number of men in the brush. This time it is not the Herreras at war; it is the O'Reileys."

I still wondered about my father; if he knew he had a son at Los Alamos.

I wondered and worried for several reasons. If he still searched for Quandaris in the Chisos, he possibly could have seen no one who had told him of me, or where Quandaris remained. And if he did know, could he change his plans and destroy first the hacienda of Don Sostelo, then turn his attention to Quandaris?

I had kept in constant touch with Guillermo, the don's cup-bearer, through Miguel and Pedro, leaving them to decide the time and the meeting places. I sent messages and notes to both Effie and her mother, and in return received messages from them.

Another incident had cracked the walls of the Sostelo hacienda. I learned that Senora Hernandez no longer came down to dine at the great table; she took her meals only in her rooms. I suppose Effie might have done this also, but by dining with the don it afforded her a better contact with Guillermo.

But my father—what would he be like? What terrible vengeance must he have borne, a thing which had driven him almost all the days of my life from one endless Mexican desert or mountain to another, to one lost wilderness jacal and then to the next, and small towns and villages and watering places? And places where no water existed, save the few drops obtained by cutting the head of cactus in some sandy waste?

I had seen the wreckage of Quandaris; would my father, too, have been wrecked, but for another reason?

Would he be a man of hatred, one whose old self had become lost in a new and alien one, a man who had relentlessly driven himself for that single moment when he would face Quandaris again?

Or would he have qualities like Uncle Mike, who rode with me to answer the summons of Judge Howlett's court at Alpine?

Uncle Mike had stopped at Los Alamos with about thirty of his own men and neighbors. "If it suits you, Colin," he said, "take an equal number of your men. If you can't spare them, get other peons from the brush. This is a game of bluff as well as law; we do not intend to be bluffed. Arm each man well. With elections near, we'll let Judge Howlett know we mean business."

To our surprise, we were to find that many people in Alpine meant business, too. The town was on the railroad, which gave it certain advantages; it was more or less cultural, and seemed to have hatched from an egg in the sand, and the courthouse, while small, was adequate.

Under honest law enforcement, Alpine was reasonably peaceful, but now that Judge Howlett's clique was in power, a certain tenseness always prevailed.

Another thing—the people of Alpine and those of the distant ranches had begun to tire of the violence in the Big Bend; there was talk in Alpine about Don Sostelo and a certain Colin O'Reiley, and there had grown a resentment about the outlaws the King had held in the town.

We learned, too, that upon our arrival a number of armed citizens and cowhands would be on the street corners to see somp'n happen, in case the forces of Sostelo and O'Reiley shot it out without benefit of court sanction.

From Los Alamos, we made a leisurely two day trip to Alpine, camping out one night, and discussed our plans along the way. The moment we struck town, we began to move like clockwork.

Tomas and twelve of his Apaches boldly took over the hitch-rack in the street before the courthouse, and already Judge Howlett's pink face looked down through a window of his chambers.

The Apaches bore their usual equipment—the lariats, knives, and rifles, the black bands about their foreheads. They dismounted and squatted at their horses' forefeet. They were known, of course, as Mexicans, but their fame preceded them.

The walks of Alpine were rapidly becoming crowded; Uncle Mike and I and three of our leading ranchers dropped our reins before the courthouse steps, and stepped upward. The rest of our army continued at a slow pace around the square, speaking, as we had decided earlier, to no one.

As our rowels jingled up the steps, the sheriff and two deputies came down and mounted their horses.

"After reinforcements?" I asked Uncle Mike.

"Hell, no." Uncle Mike laughed. "Just out to save tail. They'll light for the Davis Mountains, about five thousand feet up."

Within the courthouse, the halls and doorways were jammed

with men of good cow and goat smell; the courtroom overflowed. As we entered, still wearing our pistols, Don Sostelo turned from a window where he had watched the streets.

We marched in a body to our pine table and sat with our attorney.

Judge Howlett entered from his chambers; everyone stood up, then he sat at his rostrum in his robe, banging his gavel.

"This honorable court is now in session," the bailiff, a political-bellied bald man called. "The people from Los Alamos will remove their concealed weapons."

An uproar of laughter came from the spectators.

"Correction!" Waving his arms, A. B. Champion, our attorney, leaped to his feet. "Is there a man in this room who sees a concealed weapon upon my clients?"

A lank cowhand stood up. "Most open weapons I ever saw, lawyer, 'cept this one," he said, lifting his own and putting a bullet through the ceiling.

"Arrest that man," Judge Howlett shouted to the bailiff.

"What man?"

"The one who fired his pistol."

"Judge, I don't know which man to arrest. I can't find a single man in this courtroom with a concealed weapon."

Don Sostelo sat at his table, pulling his long nose reflectively. I knew one thing—after the falsity of this summons, I would never speak to him again on any subject whatever.

The bailiff had returned from a window, after watching our parade of horses about the square. "With that many animals, somebody's going to have a time cleaning those streets tomorrow."

"Them Apaches still out there?" Judge Howlett asked, licking his rat teeth.

"Still there," said the bailiff, "under their horses sharpening their knives."

Then Uncle Mike snapped his big knuckles; it sounded like a six-shooter going off, and Judge Howlett jumped a foot. "All participants in this case will retire to my chambers," he said.

After the judge lowered his head for a few brandies, he asked my uncle, "Why is it that you have fully a hundred mounted and armed men surrounding this hall of justice and patrolling the streets?"

Uncle Mike said blandly, "We are squirrel hunting."

"I never knew it took that many men to catch a squirrel."

"A squirrel or a skunk, it wouldn't matter," Uncle Mike said. "Judge, when I'm in a game of poker, I like to play honest. But if things don't work that way, I believe in having that ace up my sleeve. Like playing with old Judge Roy Bean one time on the porch of his Jersey Lily down the railroad at Langtry. Roy was a great one for poker, and due to his judgeship, always the banker. He didn't have poker chips, so he substituted shelled corn instead. The old conniver always kept a good hand in his lap or pocket to use when he needed it, and I decided to match his own game. I brought along a good supply of corn in my pocket and joined in. After some tolerable luck and a high-priced bottle of the judge's cold beer, I cashed in with my own corn before the game ended. The judge paid off in money, as he always did.

"When the game was over, there wasn't enough money in the bank to cash the other corn. Everybody in the game believed they were up against another of Roy's shenanigans, but they couldn't prove it. Nobody ever out-talked Roy Bean. Now here's the situation—I'm involved in a court case, a contempt case. If I can play it fair, I will. If I can't, those men in the streets are my ace, just like my corn. No Sostelo is going to dominate this court. If force is needed, we've got it, also the power of impeachment if there's anybody left to impeach."

The spectators who crowded at the door laughed and guffawed; some moved forward and clapped Uncle Mike on the back.

Don Sostelo was furious. I formed a new opinion of Uncle Mike; he had helped bring me up and get me started here; he was always so unassuming that I had thought little of what he could be. Now a man spoke who was as hard as nails.

The judge rose and stared into the street. Then he sat and

asked about the fence. I explained to him its original purpose, but that I had now removed it, thereby whipping the don's chicanery back to him. No word had yet passed between us.

Deputy Haymaker, summoned by the subpoena, rose to testify. He looked vainly for a cuspidor; he left the room and returned almost immediately. In addition to testifying under oath, I think Haymaker had some other calculation in mind.

Judge Howlett asked, "Did you see the fence being built?"

"Yes, I seen the fence. It was going up, but on the O'Reiley side of the waterhole."

Uncle Mike said to Haymaker, "Maybe that honest testimony will get you a few votes from the Big Bend when you run for sheriff."

"I would sure appreciate that," said Haymaker, as if the idea had just occurred to him.

"Silence in the court," said the judge, searching vainly for a cigar in his vest pocket, but settling for a bite from Haymaker's plug. As soon as it was partially digested the judge said, "It is the opinion of this court that the conditions of the continuance of the previous case have not been violated. Case dismissed, and retrograded to the previous decision."

Retrograded was right. I stood up.

"Not quite, judge. Until now, I have tried to live in peace with Don Sostelo, and by building the fence to bring a measure of good will. But your officers are so few in our country that we must take our own measures. I declare that from this moment on, in defense of my property, I shall make my own war against Don Sostelo."

I looked at the don, and his pale lips twisted.

"Now, now," said Judge Howlett, who owed the don a few political favors, "No threats, young man."

"It is not a threat, judge, it is a fact."

My grinning uncle left the room with me and we went down the stairs to gather our riders.

My every thought from now on, considering what action my father might take against Don Sostelo, and the increased warfare which might erupt as a result of my statement before the judge—a statement I intended to abide with—was to secure the removal of Effie and her mother from Don Sostelo's hacienda.

It was not that I thought my father had become so brutalized that he would raid a hacienda and take vengeance on all he met, including women and children, but there was no way of knowing what any outlaw band would do in the excitement of attack.

I could not know what might happen; Effie and her mother could both be killed, or even worse.

When we returned from Alpine, my uncle, who never seemed to have an aching bone in his body, rode on in a night ride to his rancho, and I immediately called a council of war in the hacienda. The tables were brought in and placed end to end before the fireplace. The food was prepared outside; even before the meal began tired Miguel sank with his crutch in a chair. *"Dios, but I am weary!"*

"We are all tired, old friend. But if what I hope comes to pass, before too long we all may rest."

Our council consisted of Pedro and Meander, Chujo, Old Carlos and the padre, Zelina and Dr. Smedley, who was here on one of his periodic visits to the village.

I set the best wines we had on the table, the mescal and pulque and tequila. When the food was brought in, I, like Miguel, was too tired to eat. I sat and simply stared.

Dr. Smedley clicked his teeth. "How was the contempt trial?"

"Status quo, except that in the presence of the Judge I declared my war on Don Sostelo. My statement is a matter of record—his clerk took it down."

"You have reached the end of your patience."

"I know, and I don't like doublecrosses."

The padre said, "My son, you have called us here. What is your plan?"

"Within a week, I plan to raid Don Sostelo's hacienda."

Miguel sat bolt upright. "To raid the don?"

"I am engaged to Euphemia Hernandez, and I admire her mother. The hacienda might be raided by others, and the women harmed; I intend to strike first and bring the women here."

"Impossible," said Pedro. "Don O'Reiley, you are out of your mind."

"Am I? Who has fought for peace here, and who has lost it? I have lost, Pedro, but that time is over. Don Sostelo has ridden the top horse; now he will know the burro."

Father Dore said, "Think of the loss among your peons."

"Not my peons. Each is his own master. But those who help, I will reward. If all goes as I plan, few will die, if any."

"The thing is," Meander said, "we'd better stop gabbing and get down to business. If you want those women, I'll help get them. I know what Maudine means to me."

"Miguel," a voice from the outside called.

Miguel said, raising his pulque pot, "Pedro, see what he wants."

"I will go," I said.

It was Guillermo who waited. "Don Sostelo has returned. He is in a fury, and swears he will wipe out Los Alamos within a week."

"Then at daybreak, day after tomorrow, have Euphemia and her mother ready to leave. Have your horses hidden and ready. We will raid at sunup." I returned and told the council what Guillermo had said.

"Colin," the padre spoke quickly, "what is your plan?"

"Zelina," I said, "go to Chujo's room, and bring pencils and paper."

When Zelina returned, I drew a rough map, showing the location of Don Sostelo's hacienda, of Tornillo Creek, and Los Alamos. There was a long ridge to the west of Don Sostelo's hacienda, and a smaller one lay to the north. I sketched in the two ridges.

"These are our points of attack," I said.

Miguel had risen and stood over me. "But that far from the hacienda?"

"The point is, there will be no attack. It is simply a ruse."

"But how?" asked Meander.

"If Don Sostelo plans to attack within a week, we must strike first. Miguel, how many new men from the brush could you

194

have here by tomorrow night? Each man who goes will get a she-goat."

"I could gather perhaps seventy-five. We will scour all the brush, and those who have been with us at Alpine will not have gone home yet."

"Good," I said.

"But the plan?" Miguel said, looking with Pedro at the map.

"We will leave after nightfall tomorrow. We will go in three groups—you and I will lead one, Pedro one, and Meander one. We will be in position before daybreak. I would like two-thirds of our men here with Pedro," I said, pointing to the longer ridge, "and the rest here on the shorter ridge with Meander. Miguel, you and I will ride directly for the hacienda with the Apaches."

Miguel's dark eyes glinted. "Now," he said, "for the strategy."

"As I said, we will leave after dark. Tornillo Creek will be our guide line. We will move up in small bodies, six or ten men, and if apprehended we will say we are going to visit a sick relative or a dying one. Make a wide circle of the Sostelo land, and Pedro and Meander, be in your places behind the ridges before daylight. Wait for shots from the Apaches before firing.

"But when they do fire, I want all hell to break from the ridges, so Don Sostelo will think it is the Apocalypse. Every man will fire repeatedly, but after ten minutes, break away from behind the ridges and cut back in a wide arc for Los Alamos."

"But with them gone," Miguel said, "what about us and our Apaches?"

"That is the point—Don Sostelo will rush every man except his household guard toward the ridges. He may not even have extra men, since he would not expect me to attack so quickly, or he might think my father attacks. At any rate, he will find the ridges empty. That is when we move in with the Apaches to take the women. Don Sostelo's main force will be too far away to stop us."

"Colin," a quiet voice said, "may I ride with your Apaches?" It was Chujo, his eyes darkly circled.

"You?" said Dr. Smedley.

"I can sit a horse."

I looked at the doctor, and he nodded.

"Then you will ride between me and Miguel," I told Chujo.

At midnight, I left my adobe and looked at the half-moon. Tomorrow night there would be just enough light. I walked down to the church, and Father Dore was there, digging a grave in the hard earth.

"Why do you work so late, padre? You are like a spider making a web."

The little man sighed wearily, sitting and dangling his feet in the grave. "I work to bury our dead tomorrow. Dr. Smedley says he will ride with you."

"No, Dr. Smedley must be here in case we bring wounded in. He could do nothing with pursuit on the desert. I will caution all wounded to ride straight for Los Alamos. But I think there will be no graves; it will be a clean, swift job."

"Colin, you have iron blood in your veins."

"No, it has changed, but it is not iron."

"Don Ruiz Herrera," the padre said. "He was a great man."

196

# 15

<<<<<<<<<<<<<<<<<<

The night was still as the horses clumped their way on stone, or lost their sound in sand. The half-moon was high, ideal for the light we needed. The night before, Miguel had sent Ramon and Gasper back with a dozen bottles of mescal to be given to the nearer of the Sostelo guards; as Chujo and I and Miguel led the Apaches onward, we hoped these guards would be half-drunken or asleep.

We reached our position behind a dune to the side of the hacienda wall and waited. Daybreak came, and rainbows flickered over the Chisos.

Miguel whispered, "Is it time for our shots, Don O'Reiley?"

"No, they would still be asleep at Don Sostelo's now, all but the cooking women. Let the men all get awake to know what the other shots mean when they come from the ridges. How tired are you?" I asked Chujo, who sat his horse beside me.

"I am all right."

"Good. It should soon be over, and we will be back at Los Alamos."

"Colin, I will never get there."

"But why?"

"Something I feel. But do not worry. This is something I want."

When our first volley burst from the dune, such an answering roar followed from the distant ridges that it could have waked the dead. Men rushed from the hacienda and from the jacals toward the stables and the corral, the don at the lead. There was hasty saddling, then the pell-mell rush toward the longer ridge. It was then that Meander's men fired again, shot after shot; it was almost a miracle that it was so sustained.

There was a shift in the don's forces now; believing the main attack would come from the longer ridge, and ignoring my first fire completely, perhaps thinking his house guards would take care of us, most of his riders had plunged with him in that direction; but now uncertainty pulled them up sharply. The don made his first error, dividing his forces to send fully half his men toward Meander's ridge, although in view of our plan of retirement, this would not have mattered anyway.

No sooner had this body departed, than an even greater blast came from Pedro's ridge. Don Sostelo's men were falling, and the greater body withdrew in confusion. At last the don succeeded in rallying his men, and pressed on toward Pedro's ridge.

"Now," I cried to Miguel and the Apaches, "Ride for hell and okra!"

There is something I will never forget about the Apaches, the galloping hooves, their thunder, the wild shouts. There were cries of alarm from within the walls of the hacienda; I could see Guillermo and Ramon firing at the pink-shirted guards from an upstairs window, and as we pulled up at the wall we saw the other guardsmen fighting among themselves.

"Enough," cried Guillermo to them. "Don't you wish to be free of Don Sostelo? Look behind you—Don O'Reiley and his Apaches are at the wall. If you fire again, you will lose everything."

Ramon had disappeared from the window; now I saw him with Gasper and two other servants race across the yard toward a single jacal not far away. Then from its narrow doorway two saddled horses were led. At the same instant, as if the appearance of the horses was a signal, Effie and her mother ran from the rear of the hacienda. Two pack horses were led from the jacal.

Effie and Senora Hernandez had mounted now, and with the other horses following, rode around the corner of the wall to come in our direction.

"No!" I shouted, for we had come under heavy fire from a die-hard portion of the hacienda guard. "Start for Los Alamos. We will follow you."

Other guardsmen ran toward the corral, where Ramon and the two other servants had mounted, and were breaking corrals and driving the Sostelo stock to freedom. These guardsmen also caught horses, and galloped with Ramon and Guillermo to follow Effie and her mother. We had things under control now—Effie and her mother free, and ourselves well-protected by the wall from the remaining guardsmen.

Our difficulty now lay in making our own retreat. The wall had given us protection; not one man or horse had even been wounded, but in withdrawing from the wall we would be thrown into the open. Another servant appeared in a window and fired into the guard; an answering shot made him stand rigidly for a moment, then he bent like a string of rope and tumbled to the ground. He bounced once, and lay still.

Then, with the last shot from within the walls, Chujo sighed, for the remaining guardsmen had thrown away their weapons

199

and stood with upraised hands. I said Chujo sighed—it wasn't a sigh, it was a noise in his throat. He had been struck with the last shot, and the front of his shirt was bloody. I tore it open, and could see the blue hole and stream of blood.

"Hold your pommel," I said. "We're going now, before Don Sostelo's men learn of our trap. Old Doc Smedley will fix you up."

Chujo nodded, and deliberately placed both hands to hold the saddle horn.

Guillermo rode back from Effie's guard. "It is all over here, Don O'Reiley."

When we rode up to the women, Effie paled at the sight of Chujo. "We'll have to hurry," I said, "before the don's men return. We must get Chujo to Dr. Smedley."

As we galloped, Chujo's head bent to his chest, as if he slept. The firing from the ridges ceased; I knew that Pedro and Meander were leaving their positions and beginning to lose themselves in the desert, starting their long arc to avoid what men Don Sostelo might start in pursuit, if, indeed, he knew which direction to take. Our two groups would be gone before Don Sostelo's men gained the ridges to spy them out.

Senora Hernandez galloped her horse back from the front.

"Senora," I said, "you are not sorry to leave?"

"No. For the first time in years I feel free. But at such a cost—poor Chujo!"

"You must go back to the front. It is not safe here."

As we galloped onward at breakneck speed, I lagged behind to steady Chujo. He raised his head now and then, but by now a red froth had come to his lips. There was no lack of courage in his eyes; in spite of pain, he smiled wanly.

Once he said, "Colin, it was a good raid, a clean one. I am glad I came."

"Do not talk," I said.

Effie dropped back and rode on Chujo's other side; the senora rode onward with Miguel, surrounded by the Apaches.

Chujo spoke again. "Euphemia, it was wonderful on our long trip, wasn't it."

"Chujo, I shall never forget it."

Chujo swayed left and right.

The poor boy was like a sack of grain Effie and I shoved back and forth between us to keep him seated; we were both smeared with blood, but we could not stop, no matter how much we wished; the chances were too great that a wait would allow us to be overtaken. That could have meant death for all of us, Chujo included. This way he had a chance.

A single shot was fired from the brush; I felt my horse lose rhythm. He seemed to stagger, then pulled on again. He had been shot from before, perhaps by a Sostelo guard; already I could see blood dripping on his withers.

Chujo tried to hold a handkerchief under his shirt, and I was never so sick in my life of listening to driving hoofbeats.

At last we passed the mudhole of Los Alamos and pulled up in the plaza where anxious people waited.

Maudine ran to my horse, looking up to me and screaming, "Meander, my Meander! Is he hurt?"

The other women of the camp, and those whose husbands had served only for the night, also ran forward. "My husband, is he all right?"

"Quiet," I shouted. "The others will not be here for an hour, at best. They have a longer way to travel. Now fix your men something to eat, or when they come in they will beat you."

Effie had leaped from her pinto; she had her hands up to help Chujo, and now Maudine, suddenly calm, raced to his other side. I was out of my saddle, also, and held Chujo around the waist. By then Dr. Smedley and the padre were there.

We carried Chujo to one of the adobe wings of the church, and placed him on a cot. Dr. Smedley already had his instruments out; they had been placed on a white cloth on a table. A pot of water boiled over a brazier.

The doctor approached Chujo, who made a feeble motion to

wave him aside. "No," he whispered. "I have something to say."

"Man, what is more important than your life?" Dr. Smedley said.

"Give me something to stop the pain. That is all I want."

Senora Hernandez stood silently, her face stricken at the thought of the death of one who had given himself for her freedom.

Chujo was muttering, "Colin, has Meander come in? I can barely see."

"No, but some of Pedro's men have come. Meander should be here soon."

"Is Euphemia here?"

"She is beside me."

We heard horses plunge into the plaza, and shouts of triumph. Meander, dirty and smoke-grimed, rushed into the room. Maudine was in his arms; he shoved her aside. "Chujo, is he bad? They told me he was hurt."

"Meander," Chujo's whisper said, "you made it?"

"Sure," said Meander, bending over the cot, "and we'll get you out of this, old man."

Rousing himself, Chujo muttered, "Colin, I am glad to have been a part of Los Alamos." He looked deliberately at each of us. "I thank all of you for letting me be your friend. Colin, I want to be buried tonight."

Then the Cherokee composed himself and died.

It seemed that some invisible hand shoved Effie and Meander and me from the room, and we stood outside, oblivious to everything. People stared, but made no effort to approach.

There was so much behind us at that moment. It was the days of hardship over long miles, miles of blizzards and northers, desert heat, and what might have been our own battle for survival against the King and Countess, each of the four of us branded by a bond which could never be broken.

This was understood by the villagers, who had known of our trial.

Meander said, "Damn it, it would have to be Chujo. I guess

about the happiest days in my life—except with Maudine—were being on the rivers and meeting him. Do you remember the night the wind changed, and there wasn't snow?"

Senora Hernandez and Maudine and Zelina stood apart, watching us.

I said, "Chujo told me that if anything ever happened to him, Meander and I were to share his rifle. Effie, you were to have the little turquoise talisman in his desk drawer."

"Oh, no," she cried. "He loved it so."

Meander said, "Didn't Cherokees paint the faces of their dead with red? Some Indians did."

"I don't know," I said dully. "We'll get the Apaches to seal his eyes with clay—some tribes did it. Maybe Cherokees did."

Meander said, "We'll give him a light-colored paint. That ought to even it up. Anyway, I know they faced east."

Dr. Smedley came up and said, "He has been bathed and is in his best clothes. He is in the coffin now. You may see him whenever you wish."

It was Senora Hernandez who smoothed the red powder on Chujo's cheeks and forehead. The Apaches sealed his eyes.

That night we buried Chujo, who always described himself as a back-sliding Methodist because of the mission schools he had attended, but this posed no problem in Father Dore's church-yard. Standing over the grave he had dug two nights ago, in the flickering light of many piñon knots held by the Apache honor guard, the black-robed padre said, "This was a good man. He had his old gods; perhaps that is why he never accepted others. Yet without him, there would be no Los Alamos tonight, and we would all be dead. To his ancient gods, I commend his spirit."

Meander and I with the Apaches shoveled the dirt upon the coffin.

Dr. Smedley was unable to save my wounded horse. For my next mount, I chose a reddish sorrel of Meander's string, and I named him Chujo. It was hard at first to call him that, but as the months passed on my desert rounds from cow camp to goat camp, it was to become easier, until I could say it lightly, and call Chujo as if someone, a good and close friend, rode laughing across the desert with me.

What Father Dore said was true—without Chujo there would have been no Los Alamos.

For several days after Chujo's burial I was quite lost in our village.

There were two adjoining rooms in the hacienda, a wide doorway between them, and these I gave to Senora Hernandez and Effie. Effie and I wandered the small streets of Los Alamos, visited the adobes or walked to the mudhole, or sometimes stopped at the churchyard. It was as if we walked as ghosts among our people, and they, understanding, avoided us.

Sometimes we walked to Meander's adobe, and sat with him and Maudine. But always the past came back; perhaps I, and even Effie, had known too much hardship in the past and had been kept apart too much here beneath the Chisos; we were in a state of lethargy, content only to be with each other.

Yet in spite of this feeling, I could not help but wonder why there had been no retaliation from Don Sostelo. It was because of this threat that I had doubled the outpost guards beyond the waterhole, and lest Don Sostelo might take some idea from what I had done in the raid against him, I had placed guards all about the camp.

I had enough men now to supply an army, had I wanted one. Word had reached outlying districts that a crazy Colin O'Reiley at Los Alamos always paid a peon two goats for a day's—or a night's—work, and we were deluged by applicants, many of whom had suffered under Don Sostelo. These people I could not keep, of course, yet they remained.

Dr. Smedley had insisted that for reasons of sanitation these penniless must stay beyond the camp; they were fed and given a few clothes to cover the nakedness of the wives and children. But the impression had grown that Colin O'Reiley had a thousand men ready to fight at the drop of his sombrero.

But why had the don not struck?

Was it because he had been so completely duped by the raid, and had lost confidence as well as a good portion of his men as they approached the ridges, or was it because he had lost both his daughter and granddaughter, and had not yet determined a way to get them from Los Alamos safely?

"Senora Hernandez," I said one night, watching her sparkling eyes as we sat with Effie at our poor dinner table, "are you happy at Los Alamos?"

"Colin, why should you ask that? I go among the people every day, and you do not know what that means to me. I find sick children, and Dr. Smedley has given me and Zelina medicines to care for the croup and colics of the poor camp. For the first time in my life, I am free and of use to people."

"I hope you can endure the poor furnishings here."

"Poor? To see Euphemia happy makes each bare wall rich. I have hesitated to mention this, but if there is a question of money to complete your furnishings, I have more than enough for all of us. We can have furniture sent from San Antonio, or Mexico City, or Vera Cruz."

I laughed. "No, I find I can live better on my good credit than I can on cash. And if Effie is to become the mistress of Los Alamos, she will find that the way will be hard, and there is no better way for her to learn than now."

"Colin," Effie said, "you have eaten my burnt bacon for hundreds of miles. Why do you appear so virtuous now?"

"So fifty years from now I can look back and say I told you so."

"You will be as poor then from grandchildren as you are now with cows and goats."

"I'll shut up then."

Senora Hernandez asked, "What will you do with the barbed wire?"

"I think I will fence some space for better cattle, or I may give it to Meander. He has some idea about the old bog to the east. It's beginning to hold water, but our well here is failing. I've got to get a windmill. Meander thinks the dynamiting opened a new, fissure to change the water flow. I never did understand that bog."

Since her arrival at Los Alamos, a great change had come over Senora Hernandez. She had always looked young, but now younger than ever. Perhaps it was the free life she led which made her so. There was a deep bond between her and Zelina which, although I may have suspected it, I did not know its true nature.

I glanced across the table at Effie, and there sat a creature as beautiful as her mother, only in her there was the first fair flush of womanhood. "Then you will agree," I said to her, "that you will walk barefoot among the rattlesnakes and scorpions, hoe the frijoles, gather the maize, tend the sick goats, and look after your husband."

"I had never thought," Effie said, fingering the pearl at her throat, "that it would be necessary for me to answer such a question. And mother, you have insulted Colin. He would not take money from anyone."

Senora Hernandez's eyes sparkled. "Then I beg your pardon, Don O'Reiley."

"It is Don O'Reiley one moment, and Colin the next. Let us have a drink of good wine and forget it."

The happiness I knew in those few short days I would always remember.

They were times when Effie and I rode or walked together, sometimes her mother with us; the sites of the goat and cattle camps we visited, the *milpas* hoed by peons for the grain for tortillas. Rainbows subdued the Chisos, and sometimes we visited the old caves, or found new ones.

Sometimes I talked with fearful Quandaris and thought of my father. When I found him, or he me, my life would be complete. Yet winds, as I had learned to know in the Chisos, were often deceitful, as were its rainbows.

One day Miguel with his Apaches rode into the plaza, with ten drag-tail followers of Don Sostelo under a white flag.

"What is this, Miguel?"

"I must apologize for this delegation from Don Sostelo, but upon his return from the ridges, he had his remaining house guards executed. But the matter of importance is this—when he found how complete the raid had been, and when he learned that his daughter and granddaughter had been stolen, he fell in a stroke. He has been kept in his great bed, completely paralyzed on his right side, and can hardly speak. His servants have deserted him; he babbles constantly of you and Senora Hernandez and Euphemia; he wants them to return to care for him until his death."

"Another of his schemes."

"No, it is true. I have heard it before, but you have been happy and I did not wish to disturb you. The don sends these last of his men as a token."

"What shall I do, Miguel? Befriend my greatest enemy—a man who has declined every overture I have made to him?"

"Don O'Reiley, I tell no man what to do. That is within his own conscience."

"You make it hard," I said.

"Perhaps I do."

"A good friend is buried in the churchyard. Am I to forget him, too?"

"Once more I say that I do not intrude upon a man's conscience."

I walked to the hacienda and found Effie and Senor Hernandez seated in the living room. Effie said, "Colin, you are late. We were to have coffee."

"Something has happened," I said, looking directly at Senora Hernandez. "You must prepare yourself for it. After the raid, when he found you and Effie gone, Don Sostelo suffered a stroke. He is confined to bed, paralyzed and barely able to speak. He has been completely deserted. His last men are here to see if you and

Effie will wait upon him. I will send the answer back immediately."

Senor Hernandez rose, her eyes flashing. "Colin, is this another of his tricks?"

"No, Miguel says it is true. Let me say first that I will understand and not blame either of you for the decision you make."

"And you?"

"I cannot go. Something inside will not let me."

Effie took my hand. "Colin, we have been so close here."

"Perhaps I was not meant to marry into the gentry of the Chisos. I have been forced to do many things I have not wished to do, but until Don Sostelo asks for me, I cannot go; it goes too far back, the wounds are too deep."

I dared not look at Effie.

Senora Hernandez said, "I have never been so stricken in my life. I do not know what to do."

"You are Sostelos, and you must go to him. When you pack your belongings, your horses will be ready. I will be back in thirty minutes to lead an escort for you."

I led the silent escort and it was as if I tore my heart out. At the Sostelo hacienda, I left Effie and her mother at the gate of the unguarded wall.

# 16

<<<<<<<<<<<<<<<<<<<

A small village had grown up near my Uncle Michael's ranch.

They called it Pack and Tote, for a log supply house had arisen there. Although prices were high, they were still within reason, for Karl Steuben, the fat beer-swilling beard-to-the-waist German owner, had his supplies shipped on the railroad to Sanderson, then brought them down by wagon himself, avoiding the longer rail route to Alpine and saving the additional freight.

And Pack and Tote certainly beat the long miles we stretched out to reach Sanderson and Alpine with our small wagons and wooden-wheeled *carretas*.

With the supply house and the influx of new families, we now had a voting population of at least twenty in our section. Then two cantinas sprang up, one run by a bulky Mexican named Luis Peinados, the other by an ex-outlaw, Deb Kessinger, and these were followed by a barber shop run by a straw-haired old woman, Minnie Barr, three hundred and thirty pounds avoirdupois, then a grocery store and a dulce shop opened their doors.

In time a down-at-heel cowhand put in a cobbler's stall, perhaps for his own convenience, but for other cowhands, also.

Minnie Barr had also put in a line of patent medicines and grain alcohol. She is worth a paragraph to herself, and wore a wide dress of print sacking. Due to her weight and varicose veins, she couldn't stand on her feet to do her barbering, so she sat on a stool three feet high, with a smaller one on the floor between her sandals.

On this stool sat the cowhands for their clippings and ablutions, a sheet wrapped about their necks. When a cowhand came in for a shave under Minnie's razor, it was said that he rode for a toot, the belief having grown that he could get as drunk on the alcohol Minnie rubbed on his slashings as well as he could by having a beer at Luis Peinados's or at the Outlaw Saloon.

I have said that Minnie deserved a paragraph to herself—perhaps she deserves more. On a visit to Alpine she had stopped at a general store; here she found a set of four vari-colored bowls of different sizes, bowls for flowers to be kept in, and she had bought the batch.

She now had a bowl size for each cowhand's head; the bowls were red and blue and green and yellow, and sooner or later she found the perfect fit. The cowhand sat and was helmeted, and with her hand-clippers or scissors Minnie cut the hair to the rim to the bowl; she then removed the ornament, and whacked a few hairs with her scissors to even things up. That is why I had let my hair grow long, Apache style, to avoid Minnie's infernal machines.

And if, during his hacking, a cowhand squirmed on the lower stool, Minnie pressed her big thighs against his neck like a vise, holding him as helpless as a maverick being branded, until the last hair was mutilated. She didn't have a styptic pencil to stop the bleeding from shaving—that's why she used grain alcohol.

Pack and Tote was quite respectable now, and the two cantinas served their purpose. Pack and Tote—you packed, then toted—was near the old rustler and smuggling trail from across the Rio Grande, and after driving a herd of wetbacks to some point to the north or east, the gentlemen of these trades made the cantinas their stopover to wet their whistles, as did the various runners of contraband liquor and narcotics. For the mangy crew they were, they spent lavishly, and the village began to prosper.

Some twenty adobes were built and two hitchracks stood in the street, as well as watering troughs.

At Los Alamos we could say, almost with honesty, that we now had a road to Pack and Tote. It was on the old trail to my uncle's ranch, but within sight of it branched off to the new village. We hacked off mesquite branches which overhung the trail, and dug up cactus and other desert growth. Not all at once, understand, but simply when convenient or when we were snagged. Our Mexicans often used the road and they, too, helped widen it when they took the trinkets or carvings they had made to Pack and Tote to barter for pulque, or the women taking the mats and clothing they had woven from mohair, someone always slashing away with a machete as he walked or rode.

There is something else to mention about Pack and Tote. It also became known as Shootout Town, for reasons which were obvious. Even I had winged an outlaw—one who had wounded one of my Mexicans.

One day I asked Quandaris, "Why don't you go down to Pack and Tote with me? I want to see Karl Steuben about a windmill."

Quandaris had been brooding in the graveyard too long, pondering his own fate, or staying close to his hut. His answer was direct and simple. "I am afraid to leave Los Alamos, senor." His fine features were still harrassed with worry. His only recreation had been an occasional game of checkers with the padre.

"My friend, you cannot hide forever. I have told you that you are safe with me. A tequila in Luis Peinados's cantina will do you good; you must learn to talk with people again. Now go to the corral for a horse."

On our way to Pack and Tote, the wind suddenly came right, and we heard the bawling of many cattle. Then we came to signs where a herd had crossed the road.

A yellow mesa reared its height off to the right. I said to Quandaris, "Let's ride up the mesa and see what this is about."

From the summit we looked across the road and on beyond at a moving cloud of dust, the small and half lost figures of cows and cowhands in the distance.

"Rustlers," I said, "and at least a thousand wetbacks. It is a good haul."

What I could not understand was the direction of the drive; it was on a line away from my uncle's ranch, and pointed northeast, a direction which would take the cows to the vicinity of Sanderson, if the drive were a long one.

Something else, too. Wetbacks were generally scattered quickly or sold shortly after crossing the Rio Grande, and were certainly not driven as an entire herd into a populated area.

Quandaris said somberly, "They will be stolen again and back in Mexico within a week. I would not care to be a cow, especially near the Rio Grande. I would become too tired."

"I disagree that this herd will be stolen again. There is too much method, and too much control over it; that means good organization. They know exactly where they go."

While the horses clambered down the mesa, I noticed for the first time that Quandaris wore no pistol. "Where is your gun?" I asked.

"Never again, senor, will I wear a pistol. Since coming to Los Alamos, I have had much time to think, as well as to fear. I remember a vain and foolish youth, and what a single shot did to his life."

"I know what you did at one time, but I know you would not do it again. A gun may be necessary to save your own life. Had we met the rustlers we have just seen, what would your life, and mine, have been worth?"

"Nevertheless, I will never carry a gun."

"Have you discussed this with Father Dore?"

A faint smile came to Quandaris's lips. "Yes, and for a padre, he is a practical man. He says that a man who has come to salvation should not needlessly risk his life, when by living he might impart salvation to others. While I am afraid even to be here with you, I am glad I came. It is not the same as when a man is followed forever. I think, senor, that someday I shall belong to the priesthood."

We reached the road again, and Quandaris's eyes were fixed straight ahead.

I said, "I should hate to see a good man die for want of means to defend himself."

"Would not death be my final atonement? You ride with me as a friend, but have you thought what I have done to your life, and your father's?"

"You may have made my life."

When we reached Pack and Tote, we were thirsty from the long ride. We left our horses at a hitchrack and crossed the dusty street to Luis Peinados's cantina. Luis had a long plank bar, a few tables and chairs, and the usual open urinal trough on one side. As we entered the bead-strung doorway, we walked straight to the bar, hardly noticing the other occupants.

Luis swung his bar rag at a hornet. "Well," he said, "how is my niece, Teresa, who married that worthless Apache?"

"Tomas is far from being worthless, and Teresa is expecting. Give us two beers."

Luis beamed expansively. "With the news you bring, the drinks are on the house."

"I thought my credit was still good."

"It should be; I have enough of it."

As I raised the glass of beer to my lips, a quiet voice said, "Colin O'Reiley, you still owe me for a horse."

I turned in surprise, and at a table Captain Vale of the old

*Dewdrop* of the Arkansas and Illinois sat smiling, his captain's cap askew on his head, its bill shoved back. Vale laughed at my astonishment. "Bring your friend and come over."

"Yes," I said, moving forward with Quandaris, "I owe you for a horse, but you still haven't sent me a statement."

Vale said, "Yes, that was our agreement."

I grinned. "Anyway, I still couldn't pay you. In fact, I'm in the village to buy a windmill on credit." I introduced Quandaris and we sat with the captain. "In a pinch, I could pay you," I said. "Why don't you ride up to Los Alamos? I'll pay you or give you another horse. I've still got your wagon and one mule—Meander has the other. But why are you here?"

"Do you remember a little fat man called the King?"

"How could I not remember him?"

"He robbed me of my liquor at the grog shop on the Canadian. He stole my wagon and mules. I won't make bones, Colin; I am here to get him."

I recalled something Captain Ferguson of the *Mississippi Queen* had told me—that Captain Vale was an easy man to get along with, but he would follow a man who had cheated him to the ends of the earth. And that, I thought, watching Vale steadily, is just about where you've come.

Luis Peinados brought another round, and put a plate of red sausages before us. "Who is this Don Sostelo?"

"You remember Effie, of course. He is her grandfather, with a great hacienda."

"But what does he do? Where does he make his money?"

"First, tell me how you found out about what the King did, and how we left the Canadian."

"It wasn't difficult. McAuliffe and his men arrived after the flood struck. When the waters went down, they talked with a few people. It wasn't hard to figure—some said they had seen the whole bunch of you set out with the wagon. Since I knew where you were headed, I didn't waste time on a desert chase. I knew there were river captains on the Rio Grande, and decided to become one, too. You know of Captain King of King's Ranch—he had a steamboat before he fell in love with cows. I don't care for cows that much. I'm after a king, but another King. Now tell me about this Don Sostelo."

Captain Vale, the whimsical lines at the corners of his mouth creasing, ordered a bottle of tequila, a basket of limes, and a shaker of salt. Somehow, although I knew what he was, it was good to have an old friend near me again.

After we had a round of tequila, I began the long story of the Herreras and the Sostelos. How the don had sent the King and Countess to St. Louis to watch my grandfather, how he had sent Senor and Senora Maderas with Effie for her to intrigue me so he could take the Los Alamos property, how he had again raided Los Alamos with the King. And of my own raid against his hacienda, and the taking of Effie and her mother and their loss again.

"Let's have another tequila," I said.

Vale placed his cap on the table. Two more than tipsy Mexicans got up and swayed to the urinal. Luis flapped his dirty apron and tried to drive a herd of flies through the doorway.

"Colin," Vale said, "mentally, you are no match for anyone. Your mind does not run in a certain groove, but mine does. I can learn more in one day than you can in a year, because by nature you are not suspicious. I am always suspicious. Do you know why Don Sostelo was rich, while you and your grandfather had nothing? I will tell you why; it is because the don for all his life has managed the border rustling, but keeping clear of any activity himself, and selling to ranches between El Paso and San Antonio. Meanwhile, your pious grandfather starved, and if the don recovers, so will you. I understand he will steal you blind."

"How do you know this?"

"Maybe I know the right boys."

"But if you saw Los Alamos, you would say it has all been worth it."

"For your information, the wetbacks are taken toward a small hacienda near Sanderson, where the King stays."

"Sanderson!" I said, and Quandaris was looking at me significantly and nodding. "What happens next?" I asked Captain Vale.

"The herds are sold before they reach the hacienda; meanwhile, the King and the Countess spend their spare time riding the railroad between San Antonio and El Paso, working their shill and con games."

"That is why he is never around the don's hacienda."

Captain Vale was saying, "You have a good phlegmatic mind, Colin. You know what you want, but you are too patient in getting it. You plan each step too deliberately. Your mind is not geared to suspicion. By chance, did you see a herd of cattle as you rode down today?"

"Yes, Quandaris and I watched from a mesa."

"It goes to the King. Well, how do you like my haircut? I got it next door at Minnie Barr's."

"It looks like hell. Which bowl did she use on you?"

"The red one. What's this about her cutting a man's ear off when she shaved him?"

"She didn't. It was a prank of my uncle's cowhands. They were tired of being bloodied, so they made an ear out of colored wax and took a bottle of catsup along. Someone shot a pistol outside and claimed Minnie's attention, and the catsup was smeared on the cowhand's head, then he yelled that Minnie had cut his ear off. When Minnie saw the bloody wax on the sheet, she fainted. She was so heavy, it took twelve men to get her on her feet."

Vale laughed. "An odd sense of humor you people have."

"How did you get the *Dewdrop* up this far?"

"When we reached the Gulf of Mexico, we stuck to the coast. That way, if a storm came up, we had inlets and rivers to help us. And we ran between the coast and spits of land like Matagorda Island, and they broke the big water. Once we reached the mouth of the Rio, there was no trouble, except waiting for a rise up-river."

216

"Senor," Quandaris spoke slowly, "why should you pursue a man like the King so?"

Vale said surprised, "Since you are with Colin, I thought you would know that."

"Being with Colin is exactly why I do not know."

"You will return to Los Alamos with us?" I asked Vale.

Vale nodded. "I have a horse."

"Exactly what is your profession here?"

Vale laughed. "Mine? A smuggler, diamonds, liquor. Anything I get my hands on but narcotics."

"But why?"

Vale clapped me on the back as we rose. "As I told you long ago, for excitement."

I think Captain Vale was rather sobered, and in a new way, when he saw Los Alamos.

"That hacienda," he said. "How did you build it?"

"From stone quarried in the mountains, and the timbers of oak and piñon brought down. We are working now on a patio to run across the back. It will have high walls for defense, if we need them."

Vale walked among the adobes. "You said it was all leveled to the ground when you came here?"

"As flat as a pancake."

We went inside and sat in Chujo's office.

"I want to see the rest of the kids again."

"They are no longer kids. Chujo sleeps in the churchyard, Meander has married and has a child, and Effie is with her sick grandfather. She has changed, too. She is older and different."

"And you did all this building with your phlegmatic mind?"

"Yes, looking at nothing."

"By God, I wish I could be like you. What you need is a woman for this hacienda. A quick raid could do it, Colin."

"No, I returned the women voluntarily. There will be no more raids."

"But how long will you continue to wait?"

"Until Don Sostelo sends for me. When he does, it will be the true sign that the warfare of centuries for a mudhole and fool's gold is ended, and I will be there to see him die, as I did my own grandfather at St. Louis."

We went outside into the night; the moon and stars were high and glittering, the Chisos were a black bulk, and dogs sniffed our legs. Some peed against the huts. Captain Vale said, "Where do I stay tonight?"

"In Chujo's old room. I will go back to my hut."

I had not seen Effie since the night we had parted before the gate of the Sostelo hacienda. Then after months I received a note from her—only the question, could I meet her in the piñons tomorrow?

She did not mention the time, and I supposed we would leave the two haciendas at the sign of the first rainbow. She had been offended, I know, by the manner in which I had almost insisted upon her departure from my hacienda, not even asking her if she would prefer to remain there. But no longer would I go to Don Sostelo's under the slightest guise of a suppliant. I had made my gestures of peace too often. Not staying with Effie and her mother was something I regretted, but could not help, although I had sent Dr. Smedley to visit the don.

I did not worry too much about Effie's coming to the piñons. The range had been quiet since Don Sostelo had sent his last men to seek Senora Hernandez and Effie.

I was in the green trees first, and saw her come in her old cowgirl clothes, with only a ribbon tied about her hair. When I stepped toward her to help her from her horse, she was as quiet and composed as ever, but slightly austere. But even this did not keep her from smiling. "Hello, Don O'Reiley." She still wore her diamond.

I helped her down; if she thought this pretense of formality would ease what might be a tenseness between us, I, too would play the game. *"Buenas dias, Senorita Hernandez."*

218

We sat on the orange rocks, and she asked directly, "Why haven't you visited me and Mother?"

"I told you why I could not go. It is still Don Sostelo's hacienda."

"You could not call it that now. When my mother first saw my grandfather the night you took us there, she exacted harsh terms if we were to stay to nurse him. He was never again to make one move against Los Alamos, and we were both to have complete freedom. You would hardly know him now, so shrunken and still he rests."

"I am sorry for him, and for all of you. Dr. Smedley says another seizure will mean his death."

"Do you mean you will return to the hacienda with me?"

"Effie, I have set foot in the don's house for the last time, or until he himself asks me to come. His last deceit was too much."

"Have you noticed that there has been no firing on the range for months, that Sostelo cows no longer go to your waterhole?"

"I had wondered about the lack of firing, but I saw Sostelo cows at the waterhole yesterday."

"Then they were some which escaped our vaqueros. As terms for remaining to stay to care for Don Sostelo, my mother insisted that the brush fighting cease. Anyway, we have only four vaqueros now, parentless little boys, only children. They cannot watch things as men do; they cannot even throw the *pial*. Some can hardly ride, but we have done our best."

"You know I cannot look at a famished cow. Why did your mother have the watering stopped?"

"Oh, you silly goose. Because of you, of course."

"I would never ask that your cows die of thirst. Please, beg your mother for me. She is welcome to use the waterhole."

"Then why won't you ride back with me?"

"When Don Sostelo asks me to, I will come. Effie, what do you really know of your grandfather? How has he made his money?"

"Why do you ask that?"

"Captain Vale of the old *Dewdrop* has brought his sternwheeler up the river; he searches for the King, and he told me that the King is the link between the rustlers and Don Sostelo, who has controlled them for years. Did you know this?"

"Colin, I never knew, and I doubt if my mother did, since she had been allowed outside so little. What will Captain Vale do if he finds the King?"

"He already knows where he and the Countess live—it's a small hacienda near Sanderson. There the stolen herds are broken up and sold. One day Quandaris and I saw wetbacks driven in that direction. Knowing the King as I do, I think that with Don Sostelo stricken, he will turn the opportunity to his own gain."

"It is odd to hear Captain Vale's name again."

"He never forgives an enemy. He plans to capture the King, and let the law punish him for at least some of his crimes. Your mother should be very careful. The King could turn even against your ranch, for no one would know as much about it as he."

"But if that happened, what would Mother do? She has no men left, and not a servant within the house."

"But she knows Colin O'Reiley and the people of Los Alamos."

"Do you mean you would help us?"

"You and your mother, yes."

"You sound so desperately serious."

"I am serious, because I know the King."

"Could I ask you—would you meet my mother here at this time tomorrow?"

"Yes, I will be here, and will also bring a good force of men. I will bring Miguel to be your majordomo, and you may have Carlos and Zelina for the house."

"My same sweet Colin," Effie said.

I made no effort to kiss her good-bye, for there had always been one thing in all our miserable lives together—no intrusion upon the will of the other.

Next day when Senora Hernandez rode into the pinons, I was already standing before Miguel and his Apaches, and helped her dismount. She wore a pert riding hat instead of a flat-

220

brimmed sombrero with silver bells she sometimes wore, and she had a neat pistol at her waist.

"Good morning, Senora Hernandez."

"You will not kiss me, Colin?"

I took her hand and bent over it.

"Not that," she said, "and especially among relatives. We still are, aren't we? My cheek, please."

After I kissed her, she sighed. "Colin, I am trying hard to make a new start in the world, but I need someone to help me. Euphemia said you would. Is it true?"

"You see Miguel and half my Apaches behind me, and Carlos and Zelina and four house servants. From now on they are yours."

"You are such a combination of softness and hardness."

"Did you let your boy-vaqueros drive your cattle towards the cottonwoods today?"

"Yes."

"Then we will sit and talk." I led her to a spot where Effie and I had often sat.

"How can I face things, Colin?"

"I talked everything over last night with Captain Vale and our council of war. There will be constant contact between Los Alamos and your hacienda. To the east, we will send our men out beyond our line of cattle and goats; some will work closely with Captain Vale, who is moving a few of his trusted men toward the King's hacienda. We will make no move against the King until he commits some overt act. Captain Vale wants to take him alive, to be tried for the murder of a Negro boy on the *Mississippi Queen* and for the murder of Senor Maderas and the raid on Los Alamos."

"But if the King attacks us, as you did?"

"We will have warning; our other men under Pedro will be in a position to defend Los Alamos, or to help Miguel if your hacienda is attacked first. I am worried about one thing—unless Don Sostelo recovers, there could be an outbreak of lawlessness when he dies. While he has kept this section of the county in some order by force, someone must rise to take his place. There can be no feuding between Mexicans and whites, or incursions across the border. You must begin to think of such a man, one the people will accept."

The senora rose and her laugh was like a tinkling bell.

"Don't you know, Colin? You are that man. You have been the master of the Chisos for years, the one who has broken my father. I only hope you will continue to love my daughter."

# 17

<<<<<<<<<<<<<<<<<<

It was remarkable how the King blossomed forth during the illness of Don Sostelo. I had known little of him since our arrival at Los Alamos, whether he stayed at the Sostelo hacienda or at some distant place. I had been in contact with him only once, and that when he led his second raid against Los Alamos, and I had known that he had been recalled from his other activities for that purpose only.

But now Captain Vale had filled in the picture.

The King, Vale said, was cocky and confident, certain that he would take Don Sostelo's place in the county when the old man died. He had been seen more and more in public places, in Alpine and Sanderson and even in Pack and Tote, for he was placing himself before the people like Deputy Haymaker, who wanted our twenty-or-so votes—twenty-six now—in the upcoming election for sheriff.

The King strove for one thing, Haymaker another.

The deputy dropped by to see me one morning, the same star on the same cowhide vest, the same tobacco-stained mustaches, the same pistols, the same unwashed pants and dirty boots.

"Light and rest," I said in the plaza, and he climbed from his saddle.

"Well," he extended his hand, grinning like a cat eating bootblack, "I reckon you know why I've come."

"I reckon. Sit on that bench and I'll get you a drink."

Haymaker waved his hand deprecatingly. "No, Don O'Reiley, not on the job. I like my drinks, but not while working. In that respect, I am opposed to the present sheriff."

"Do you think you will win the election?"

"Well, I don't know," Haymaker said, releasing his wad at a galloping goose, "but it will be a hard fight. I don't want to spread rumor, you understand—that's not my purpose in coming here—but word has done reached me that the present sheriff has been on Don Sostelo's payroll. Now, I wouldn't believe that statement for a minute, for I've worked with the present sheriff diligently, and I never saw a payoff in any way, or in any direction. You can believe that, can't you?"

"I can certainly believe you never saw it."

"Which brings me to the point," Haymaker said, crossing his legs on the bench. "Now, if you could have a sheriff, one as honest as the present one, but one who would look after the interests of all the pee-pul better, and especially in your section, who would you vote for?"

Before I could answer, Haymaker raised his hand to admonish me. "Friend, let me remind you of something. You remember when that old don squawked because you fenced off your own waterhole, a deed against yourself? Now who was the man who testified for you before the judge, without thought of gain for himself? Do you remember that man?"

"His name was Haymaker," I said, but didn't add that he had been brought in under subpoena.

"What I'm trying to convey,"—Haymaker bit off a chew—"is that my heart is in my work. When I see the lowly down-trodden, my heart bleeds for them; that's why I want your vote and influence in the upcoming election."

Haymaker knew as well as I that with the illness of Don Sostelo, the political winds were shifting. But had Haymaker actually been held down in the performance of his duties, was he trying to escape from something as I was, as Quandaris was, as we all were?

"I'll take a chance," I said, "on one condition. If I ever send for you, be here with enough sworn-in deputies to handle the situation. Yes," I said, extending my hand, "you can count on my vote and influence."

Haymaker shook hands and said, "I want to give you the evidence; I ain't afraid of man nor beast except that goose out there—I got picked bare-bottom by one of them things once—but here's my evidence as a law man."

Haymaker pulled his britches legs out of his boots; he extended the right leg. "See in the calf here? That's where I got one bullet. See this other kneecap? That's why I walk kinda stiff-legged. I'd show you on up, but I can't remove my pants publically." He opened his shirt and pulled his tails out. "You see this belly scar? See this one over the heart, this one in my side?" Haymaker rolled up his sleeves. "Look at this wrist." He lowered his shirt. "Look at these wounds in my upper arms."

"Get dressed," I said. "I've got to ride to Pack and Tote with some of my boys. I'll give you a good campaign spiel."

"I just want this job for my wife and children," Haymaker said, pulling his shirt on. "It will bring me fifteen a month extra."

My windmill had come in at Karl Steuben's, and since it would be loaded and carried back in sections in our wagons, I picked our best men for the task—Meander, Pedro and Quandaris, and Captain Vale also wanted to go. We had sent the wagons down yesterday, but I wanted experienced men to load the equipment.

Now that the bog was filling, Meander and I had made a deal. I would deed him sufficient range and living space; in return for a thousand cows he would throw in, we would become partners on the eastern land. Nothing could have suited either of us better.

"Cousin," Meander said, "from now on with that water, we've got it made."

We set a good gait from Los Alamos, and by noon the wagons were on their way back to Los Alamos. We left Karl Steuben's and walked past Minnie Barr's and to Luis Peinados's cantina.

The street was dusty, or clay-baked, depending upon how much sand had blown in, and where. Our horses still stood at Luis's hitchrack, watered and rested. Mexicans, men and women, held a few goats in the street waiting for buyers, or sat on the plank walks before the cantina and store fronts, waiting for some interest to be shown in their hand-carved furniture and woven mats. Hogs rooted around for dropped corn kernels, and a long-horn steer wandered down the street.

As we reached Luis Peinados's door and dusty windows, some instinct made Captain Vale turn suddenly. "Look," he said, "since we left Steuben's place a dozen horses have been tied in front of Kessinger's cantina. What does that mean?"

"Some outlaw bunch," I said casually.

"Hell, no," said Vale. "Somebody means business. Who knew you were coming here?"

"I suppose everyone in Los Alamos. I haven't added any new people, and I trust all the old ones." I took my own dig. "You're too mercurial."

Vale laughed. "That's a good one. Perhaps it explains my character."

Haymaker said, "Gentlemen, don't worry about it. You are protected by the law."

We took two tables in the cantina, meanwhile talking and laughing with Luis. A few Mexicans were standing at the bar, and two others had taken a table of their own.

226

Vale, who was always generous on these occasions, ordered the usual bottle of tequila, the basket of limes, and the salt. Suddenly, almost with my first drink, I began to worry about the horses at Kessinger's cantina.

"What's the matter with you?" Vale said.

I stood up and stepped to the door. The horses were still in front of Kessinger's; nothing moved in the street except the old longhorn which was wandering back from its previous direction. But something had happened—the street was deserted of people.

"Colin," Captain Vale called, "sit down and take another drink. What is the matter with you?" he said as I sat.

"I don't know. It's too quiet outside. Even the Mexicans are off the street. I've got a feeling a dozen things could happen."

The old longhorn wandered back the other way now.

"Have another drink," Vale insisted.

"I don't want another."

"This is tommyrot," Captain Vale, "you are too excitable."

"With my phlegmatic mind? Before we step out of this place, get your pistol ready."

A man carrying a pack of supplies came from the grocery store across the street. Sensing something unusual, he mounted a horse and galloped from town. It was impossible to see well through the cantina window, flyspecked and dusty as it was, so again I rose and stuck my head out the beaded doorway.

Since we had entered Luis Peinados's cantina, another group of horses had been tied to the hitchrack before Kessinger's cantina. From the shouts and laughter which came from the end of the street, it seemed a drunken brawl was in progress.

I returned to Vale. "At least two gangs are in Kessinger's now."

Two Mexicans hurried in from the back door. They whispered to Luis behind the bar. He nodded, and they went directly to the other Mexicans. Luis reached beneath the bar for a shotgun and two rifles; he placed half a dozen pistols beside them on the bar, and ammunition. Quandaris rose. "I will go to the dulce shop next to the grocery store. I promised to send Zelina some sweets."

"'Watch your step," I said, since he was going into the street unarmed.

Luis had heard me, but his heavy face was inscrutable.

Quandaris slanted across the street and entered the dulce shop. I went to the window. There may have been sweets inside the other shop, but all I could see through Luis's dirty windows and the equally dirty ones across the street were fancy flowers made of colored paper and strings of long red peppers which drooped down in semicircles.

At last Quandaris left the sweet shop. He stood on the plank walk, a paper bag in his left hand, gazing toward the other cantina, as if puzzled by the uproar there. Then, as if his curiosity had been satisfied, or that he knew it could not be, he turned and started back across the street to the cantina.

My attention was attracted by another horseman.

A stranger in a dusty hat rode down the road from the mountains. Two empty supply sacks drooped from his pommel. Through the dirty window, the man appeared to be almost ghostlike, or like a Chisos mist. I stepped to the doorway to see him better.

He wore grimy and thorn-torn chaps, a blue shirt open two buttons down the throat, and a slouched bandanna. Another outlaw, I guessed.

The horse pulled up, and for an endless moment the rider stared toward Quandaris, who still walked with the candy in his hand.

"Quandaris!" he cried in ringing tones.

Quandaris, who had not noticed the rider, stopped and stood motionless.

I stepped farther out on the walk.

Quandaris gazed intently at the rider, whose voice cried, "You know why I will kill you!"

Recognition flashed on Quandaris's face, but he waited without a flicker of fear.

Then he shrugged and made a slight deprecatory gesture with his right hand, as if in resignation, as if he could do nothing about a fate which had overtaken him.

228

Now I noticed more about the man on the chestnut. He was strangely like my Uncle Mike, his features were rugged, and yes, beneath the low hat were long bristling red sideburns.

Suddenly I knew him.

That man was Coley O'Reiley. That man was my father, and to save Quandaris, I must shoot or kill him before he drew, for he must not take vengeance on an innocent man.

I do not believe my father would ever have drawn a pistol against an unarmed man who did not intend to draw against him, but the little gesture of resignation from Quandaris's hand had made my father believe that Quandaris reached for a pistol.

His eyes had been so intent upon the face of Quandaris that I doubt if he had even noticed the bag of candy he carried, and only movement caught his eye.

It was when my father's pistol began to clear leather, that I was drawing mine.

"Father!" I called. "Don't shoot! Don't kill that man!"

I doubt if Coley O'Reiley even heard me; I only hoped I could hit where I aimed.

There was swiftness in his draw, and even with my own gun out, I barely beat him to the shot. My bullet struck his right shoulder; his body seemed to be jolted by an electric shock; his pistol fell into the street, and he fell after it.

I ran and looked down at his red head in the dust, hatless now.

"Father," I said, as I bent to hold his head on my knee, "I am Colin, your son. I know you think Quandaris killed my mother, but he did not. He was not even on the raid. God forgive me for shooting you, but it was the only way."

The blue eyes which looked up were glazed. "You are my son, and positive of Quandaris?"

"Yes, I know everything."

Quandaris had knelt beside my father, also. "What Colin says is true, Senor O'Reiley. I did not kill your wife, Violetta. And for my folly in shooting you, I have paid for it in a thousand ways, as you well know."

"Yes," my father said, regaining some strength and looking up into the dark face, "and I have known the dry hell of other

229

things. Colin, let my shirt go; stand up, so I can look at you. We can take the bullet out later. Yes, you look like a good man. God, I am glad to see you."

"It was the only way, Father. I had to stop you."

"I had thought you dead, but in the mountains I learned you were alive, and at Los Alamos. I had planned to see you after I found Quandaris. Well, get me to your cantina, and we will get the bullet out. And I might like a good drink to go with it."

It was then, as Quandaris and I set Coley O'Reiley on his feet, that a pistol shot rang from the farther end of the street. At the sound of my shot, fully a dozen men had raced from Deb Kessinger's; they stood watching us, a short fat man in sombrero and batwing chaps before them—the King!

This was how the battle began which put Pack and Tote on the map, and almost obliterated it. Perhaps the King had recognized my father at that distance; he certainly knew me and Quandaris. Haymaker rushed from Peinados's place.

We made it safely to the door of Luis Peinados's cantina, moving through a hail of rifle and pistol fire. Pedro and Captain Vale and Meander met us at the door, and began to fire down the street.

"Luis Peinados," I called. "I have shot my father. Take the bullet from his shoulder."

We placed two tables together, then stripped Coley O'Reiley of his shirt. Luis Peinados was an expert at this operation; he had forceps and cutting tools and probes, mescal, and tequila, and fortunately the bullet had not gone too deep. Luis also had a bit of chloroform. Luis swabbed the wound with a charge of Minnie Barr's grain alcohol; old bar rags and a clean towel were the bandages, and then a sling; Luis stood back and laughed.

He laughed, that is, until a fusillade from a building across the street cut his windows to pieces, and the doorway beads, whose strings had been shot away, rattled about the floor.

Meander and Pedro and Captain Vale tumbled back inside. Haymaker fired another round, then he, too, came in.

230

Vale said, "The King sent some of his men around the far corner and down the rear of the opposite buildings. I imagine they'll soon have some at the back of this one."

Deputy Haymaker took a drink of tequila. He had been completely casual, almost indifferent, throughout the preliminary gunfire, even to the shooting of my father. Now Haymaker said, checking his pistols carefully, "As it must to all deputies, I've got to earn my job."

Luis Peinados had taken a crowbar and axe and was splintering the wall between the cantina and Minnie Barr's barber shop. He worked like a brown Hercules, slapping boards left and right. "If all the gunfire comes from that one building, we can't all stay here. With some of us in Minnie's place, we can throw a little flanking fire."

Tangle-haired old Minnie was already at a window, firing some antique blunderbuss of the time of Columbus at regular intervals. Then that damn longhorn walked down the street again.

"Colin," my father called weakly from his two tables, "what is back of all of this?"

"I'm not sure I know." I told him everything which had happened since he left the country. "With Don Sostelo dying, the King might be ready to move against Senora Hernandez, or even Los Alamos, and was collecting some of his men at the other cantina. When they heard my shot, it put the fat in the fire."

The firing had become desultory, and Captain Vale came back for a drink. "I didn't tell you, but I have called upon Senora Hernandez. She is a beautiful woman. I intend to mend my ways and marry her." The old whimsical grin came back. "Provided I'm not killed in this ruckus," he added.

Coley O'Reiley said, "Get me to my feet, son."

"You can't fight, the way you are."

My father grinned. "I'm a fair left-hander. Put me in a chair in the corner by the broken windows. I'll wing a few before it's over." He was put in a chair; Luis brought him a pistol.

"Witness," called Captain Vale, laughing and holding a mescal glass high, "if I don't make it, my sternwheeler, the *Dewdrop*, is hereby bequeathed to Colin O'Reiley, Meander O'Reiley, and Euphemia Hernandez. Have I been heard?"

A bullet spanged into the mescal glass, shattering it. Vale looked up into the air where the glass had been, surprised.

"You done been heard," said Meander, "but if that damn boat will float on sand, I'd rather have it here now than when you're dead."

"Gentlemen," Captain Vale said, "the doors across the street have been opened. It means a charge."

The longhorn walked down the street. "Damn," said Meander, "I sure wish I was a cow."

Half a dozen Mexicans, all armed, beat on Luis Peinados's back windows. Pedro opened the back door, and our numbers were almost doubled. Vale, by whose authority no one knew, seemed to have placed himself in charge of our defense. He sent three Mexicans to guard the rear; we feared not only a frontal attack, but a surprise from the back if others moved down from the rear of Kessinger's. Vale sent two other Mexicans into Minnie Barr's through the opening Luis had made.

"Gentlemen," Haymaker said, "let's meet the charge. They'll come in a bunch and be pickings."

"Agreed," Vale said, "but once we're through the door we'll spread out on the walk." He peered through one of the dirty windows which was still unbroken. "They are crowding the doors." He called to the Mexicans at the back. "Two of you come up here. The others call if you need us." He told those who came up to spread behind the windows and fire to our sides on the walk—"not straight ahead," he said, "or you'll kill us."

Quandaris had buckled on two guns; his long fingers smoothed their crossed belts over his belly.

When the King's men burst from their doors, led by the little man in batwings, hoping by mass superiority to subdue us, Quandaris and Deputy Haymaker were first outside. Already I heard my father firing from his corner.

One thing was wrong with the battle—the King had thrown all his men into a single attack, as he had at Los Alamos. He

232

held none in reserve, or for using as cover from the other buildings. As the mob rushed toward us, Deputy Haymaker took his stance on the plank walk. And what a stance!

He was tall and impressive, the brown juice dribbling from the corners of his mouth; he held two pistols, and began to spread his legs apart. I had seen supposed fighting stances before, but none like this, Haymaker's boots three feet apart, now almost four, as if with his many wounds he hoped for all the flying lead to go between his legs.

We were there spread out on the walk beside him—Quandaris, Luis Peinados, Meander, Captain Vale and Pedro, facing the brunt of those who raced nearer. Even as I fired, I could not help but notice, or feel, the methodical and calm firing of Haymaker. I could almost sense the man he aimed at.

One-armed Pedro had decided his method of firing; he couldn't reload easily, so now and again he backed to the open window, thrusting his empty guns inside and receiving in return two more fully loaded. Pedro held one in one hand; the other, he stuck in his belt.

A cloud of smoke engulfed us. Someone who had remained behind at Kessinger's had fired two plank buildings on our side of the street; Karl Steuben's log store burned, and those who fought were almost hidden by swirling smoke.

Now the direction of the attack changed. Under our heavy fire, a segment of the King's force under Deb Kessinger broke and ran toward old Minnie Barr's door. Minnie saw the movement through the broken windows. Her blunderbuss empty, she seized her big barber stool and stepped behind the half-opened door, out of sight.

With some Mexicans, I ran back into the cantina to reach the opening Luis had made in the wall; we burst into Minnie's shop just as Deb Kessinger entered from the front, his pistols out.

Deb took one step beyond the edge of the door, but that was one too many. Minnie's stool came down and splintered over his head, and now she became the heroine of the fight.

Kessinger fell flat on the floor, his head and lank face bloody, then at last managed to get to his hands and knees. I doubt if Minnie had ever heard of a mare other than the farm or ranch variety, and certainly not a flying mare, a little trick of wrestling.

But she used it now; as Kessinger stood half erect, she seized his hand and in the scuffle, her ponderous body twisting, jerked him over her back. As Kessinger struck the floor and struggled to rise again, she flung herself, big belly and all, on top of him. His breath came out with a whoosh! which escaped through every crack and opening in the building.

We were firing over Minnie at Kessinger's men jammed in the doorway; they had enough and left, and meanwhile, as Kessinger struggled to force himself upward, Minnie accommodated him by raising her own avoirdupois by a good foot. But this was no generosity on Minnie's part; she raised herself only for the pleasure of dropping her blubber again on Kessinger's body, wrestling his tossing hands, and bringing from him a greater whoosh! than ever. Her big thighs straddled his legs, keeping them still. Again and again, that monstrous weight bounced down upon Kessinger.

Haymaker had come through the hole in the wall. His boot kicked Kessinger on the chin, then he dragged the limp body to handcuff it to the bar rail in the cantina.

Minnie stood heaving and panting, running a hand through her tangled hair. Sweating, she went back to reload her blunderbuss, and Kessinger came to nursing a fractured jaw and four cracked ribs.

Then Pedro shrieked; he had been hit, and half-lost in the heavy smoke, he spun like a top, then tumbled off the walk into the dusty street. In the middle of the street the other dead and wounded lay. And there was Quandaris—I don't know whether he would have made a good padre, but he was one hell of a torch with his six-shooters.

Perhaps the smoke of the burning buildings had made us more difficult targets after all, and when the King led his retreat to the opposite doorways, we retreated also. We had all thought Pedro dead, but now from inside the cantina we could see movement and hear Pedro's moans from the dust.

"I'll bring him in," Vale said.

His pistol holstered, he walked into the street and bent over Pedro, placing his hands under and around Pedro's back. He began the slow drag to the walk.

The King appeared in a doorway briefly, his pistol firing. He emptied it at Pedro's limp figure and at Captain Vale. Vale suddenly loosened his hold; he had been hit. Pedro bounced and lay still.

The captain rose and stared back to us in the cantina, almost amazed that such a thing could happen to him, an expression of ludicrous disbelief on his face. Then he tumbled into the dust, his officer's cap bouncing three feet away.

"Well," said Meander, "I hate to get a steamboat that way."

I saw my father sitting stiffly in his chair, watching for a shot at the King. "How are you?" I said.

"All right. I've seen worse."

From behind the buildings held by the King, a veritable fusillade rent the air. A larger group of Mexicans from the brush had ridden to our defense, and the King's men burst from the store fronts. Then we had our turn in that hard and brutal land, and the King's men dropped as they ran down the street to their horses. The other side of Pack and Tote burned now, all but the adobes.

We were loading the bodies of Pedro and Captain Vale into a wagon borrowed from Karl Steuben, ready to leave for Los Alamos, when Uncle Mike galloped into the ruins with his cowhands. He said, "We heard the firing. We didn't know the reason, but we thought it best to ride in." He gazed at the smoldering buildings. "My God, what a wreck!"

A deep voice said, "Hello, Mike. Thanks for what you've done for Colin."

Uncle Mike turned and climbed off his horse. My father extended his left hand. Uncle Mike said, looking everywhere but at my father, "Coley, it's good to see you again."

I do not think that the King, when he brought his own force in to meet the outlaws already gathered at Kessinger's, had the slightest idea that we of Los Alamos were also in Pack and Tote.

The events were purely circumstantial, but when my shot to save Quandaris was heard, it precipitated our battle, and the meeting was as great a surprise to one side as to the other. Later, I was to learn the falsity of my reasoning.

The sudden appearance of so many Mexicans fully armed and ready to do battle had caused the King's retirement, and also aided his escape, for we who remained had our wounded, all hurt in one way or another, and we had the bodies of Pedro and Captain Vale to look after.

It was my opinion that the Mexicans who had entered Luis Peinados's cantina before the battle and talked with him at the bar had some knowledge of the King's approach; this was why Luis had placed his firearms on the bar in readiness.

It would not have served any purpose to ask Luis this: he was not secretive, but in affairs concerning others he preferred to keep his mouth shut.

And I wished I could forget the memory of that longhorn walking the dusty street.


So we took the bodies of Pedro and Captain Vale to Los Alamos, but Uncle Mike insisted that my father remain at his ranch for a few days, when he would bring him up on a mattress in a spring-bed wagon. But my father wanted Los Alamos. Next morning Pedro and Vale were buried in the churchyard.

Two days later, I found my father seated with Quandaris on a settle beside the grave of my mother.

"You know," I said, "the peons call this the Shrine of Violetta. It is a nice name, don't you think?"

"Yes, I have always liked old names," my father said.

Quandaris rose and left, and my father said, "I understand you know Euphemia Hernandez."

"Yes, very well."

"Do you like her?"

236

"I love her. I intend to marry her."

"A Sostelo?"

"I loved Effie before I knew she was a Sostelo."

"I knew her father. He was a good man. But the don has ruined many good men. Nothing would change you from your decision?"

"Nothing could change it."

"I have no right," my father said, "to question anything you do." He glanced about the village, the orange rose garden the padre had started from cuttings from the old rose bush, and then toward the hacienda. "How have you done all this?"

"When I returned, I suppose I felt an obligation. There was nothing here, but the people began to come back, and in some way they needed me. We have only all worked together on things."

"I understand your cows and goats are in good condition."

"We have good vaqueros."

"I have never met Euphemia's mother. You are not afraid of what consequences might follow your marriage?"

"Senora Hernandez is too wonderful a person. No, I am not at all afraid. When Effie and I are married, this long quarrel will be ended. I am riding to meet Senora Hernandez near the Sostelo hacienda tomorrow. Would you like to go?"

"I would like it very much, and to pay my respects to Euphemia, if she is there."

"Why do you say Euphemia, and not Effie?"

He turned his eyes toward the distance. "As I told you, perhaps I like old names."

# 18

<<<<<<<<<<<<<<<<

Next day as we rode across the desert, my father said, "When I began my chase for Quandaris, I did not think I could ever cross this land. Some peon found me, and when I was healthy again I began my long trail, one of desolation and bitterness. I will say this for Quandaris—he fought for his new way of life as hard as I fought for my old one. But not everything was wasted. I learned very early that Quandaris had fled to Morelos, deep in Mexico, and I stayed with a family in a jacal in the mountains.

"Have you heard of the Ajusco Range, north of Morelos? Beneath it I found a village surrounded by a ring of mountains, very high, and from the heights it looked like a pinhead in the

238

bottom of a tea cup. I stayed with this family often, and one day I was fortunate enough to find a silver vein."

"You have a silver mine?"

"A small one, but good ore. I shared it with those who had taken me in. It was through them that I knew when Quandaris had come again to Morelos—to Cuernavaca and Tepoztlan or Tlaltenango—for he seemed always to return there. They had various friends in the cantinas, and means of learning things from others who lived in the mountains. So I would get word again, and the chase would end in Oaxaca or Mexico City or Guadalajara, with always the terrible land and blistering rock to cross. Yet Quandaris always escaped me. Perhaps time had developed his sixth sense, and he always knew when I was near."

"But in all the years, you never saw him?"

"No, although I later learned that one night in Vera Cruz, each unknown to the other, we had stayed in the same rooming house. Yet out of everything came friendship with others, jewelers and buyers of silver from Mexico City and elsewhere, so I cannot say all was lost. Using the mine as a headquarters, I enlarged it, meanwhile continuing my hideous search." Then under his craggy brows, Coley O'Reiley's eyes twinkled. "I will return to Mexico for a few months, sell my mine, and come back to Los Alamos, if you will have me."

"Los Alamos is always yours."

"No, you have the Herrera blood, not I."

When we reached the piñons the senora's horse was there, but she was not in sight. "Let us go to the ledge," I told my father.

Senora Hernandez was there as I had supposed she would be, seated on the same orange ledge. She wore the same small hat and pistol.

"Colin," she cried, rising and rushing toward me, "I have so much to tell you. So much has happened, or almost happened." She laughed. "Or at least, Euphemia and I thought it would happen."

"First, Senora Hernandez, my father, Coley O'Reiley."

The senora extended her slender hand. "I am happy to greet you. We heard rumors that Colin had found you, and that you had been shot."

My father extended his left hand, his right arm still in its sling. "Yes, I have been shot, and would you believe it, senora, by my son—this Colin O'Reiley you admire so much."

"But how?"

"To keep me from a greater wrong—killing an innocent man."

"Quandaris?"

"Yes."

We moved down and sat together on the ledge, the stream at our feet.

"I have said that Colin could be hard, but also soft. Remember that, Senor O'Reiley."

The mists gathered on the mountains, and I said, "What troubled you and Effie, senora?"

"One morning a group of riders appeared on the northern mesa. Even Miguel did not know them. We feared a raid and took precautions, but nothing happened. By late afternoon a rider galloped toward them, and they all fled from their positions. Why?"

"The King was defeated at Pack and Tote; that is why he did not send more men for the raid on your hacienda. The village is burned, but we will rebuild it. I was wrong in thinking there would not be a raid here that late in the day."

Coley O'Reiley said, "So we did serve a purpose at Pack and Tote."

The senora asked, "But should we still take precautions?"

I said, "As much as ever. Had you heard that Captain Vale and Pedro were killed?"

"No."

"I think the captain could have been a good man."

"He was a good man. I felt it when he called upon Euphemia and me."

"If the King strikes again, it will be at Los Alamos, since now

240

what force he has left will be stationed to the east. In that way, and in addition to Miguel, we will be able to protect you."

The senora rose, and we helped her on her horse. "Thank you, Colin. I will try not to trouble you again."

Coley O'Reiley said, "Senora, perhaps within a few days I could help you."

"Your son will not visit us until Don Sostelo asks for him. I am afraid your visit would not be approved by your son."

"Oh," said Coley O'Reiley, and I would swear I saw something pass in their eyes. "So that is it. But after all, I am O'Reiley; he is half Herrera."

Senora Hernandez said, "Senor O'Reiley, perhaps I will see you here again with Colin. *Adios, senores.*"

I do not think I was gulled by Deputy Haymaker's statement that he wanted me to take the campaign route with him in the Big Bend. I thought his motive was deeper—that what we really looked for was some trace of the King, who had not been seen since the Battle of Pack and Tote. It was possible that he might have some hideout nearer than that at Sanderson.

But both of us, although I was not the same Colin O'Reiley who had come down from St. Louis so long ago, endured the pretext of campaigning, although we were in reality manhunters, and it was Haymaker's greatest disappointment that he had not been wounded at Pack and Tote, so he could have another wound to show.

His usual method of presenting his qualifications was first to clear his wad, then address his audience of two or three whites and a dozen indifferent Mexicans. He would praise first the qualifications of the present sheriff and all the deputies, himself included.

"But there is one thing different," he would wind up, "have you ever known one—yes, a single one of my opponents—to be shot down and wounded in the line of duty?"

Always some cynical bystander would say, "Maybe your hoss couldn't run."

"Run?" Haymaker snorted. "He can run better than any hoss in the county. And it's always frontwards; it ain't backing off from a fight. You brought up the point, now let me show you something."

If no women were present, Haymaker would pull off his vest and shirt and show his battle-scarred torso. "Now this wound,"—he would point to it—"this was from that Albuquerque outlaw, Calendar Ace, they called him. It was a close one, but he's toes-up now. This scar is from Memo Jacks; now he's sprouting cactus. This here one is from that Mex rustler, Juan Peña. I don't know where he is, for he fell in the river."

Haymaker would drop his pants and go over his entire body. He did look like a sieve, only the holes had healed. However, and for modesty's sake if women were present, he would pull his britches only from his boottops and show the scars up to his knees.

Then he would finish his speech. "Now, I am an honest campaigner. Some folks say that the present sheriff gets a pay-off from Don Sostelo, but have you heard me say it? No! Still other folks say that my fellow deputies get pay-offs from outlaws, rustlers, and smugglers. But, fellow citizens, have you heard me say it? No! Whatever happens, remember I have run a clean campaign."

Having raised his doubt as to the character of his opponents, Haymaker would step from his stump or desert boulder to a yawn of applause.

But privately, Haymaker worried. His pale eyes would look at me honestly over his tobacco-stained mustaches. "If that damned Sostelo would die, that would help me win—he's been running things too long. As I see it, me and the other candidates are about neck and neck; I'll have to do one big thing to get the vote out."

"Your part at Pack and Tote was pretty good."

"Yes, and hanging on to your coattails is good, too. And that's what I'm doing, only I'm honest enough to tell you so. When Sostelo dies, you're the coming man in this county, and I'm going to be there with you."

"At least we know where we stand."

"Right now, we both want the damn King. You're looking for him as hard as I am. If I get him alive, he'll be convicted sure for killing Captain Vale in cold blood. This drowning of Senor Maderas on the Canadian, we've got a chance there, too, and maybe with this Negro boy on the *Mississippi Queen*. But the other things would go pretty far back. If Sostelo lives, his lawyers could turn the other cases upside down. But I'm giving a personal reward to any man—white or Mex—who turns the King in. He's got to hide somewhere, and these peons like money."

"As long as things are quiet at Los Alamos and at Don Sostelo's, I'll keep riding with you. You're right—we want the same thing—the King."

Although I continued to make a determined search for the King and his men, I was often disturbed by some rumor which reached me—that he had been seen by some isolated peon or other, or by a jacal of frightened children, all very near Los Alamos. Once an old senora who had ridden in on a burro told me that she had seen the King and Countess walking together across the desert.

If these rumors were true, what did they mean?

Did the King's losses at Pack and Tote indicate that his force was so depleted that action against Los Alamos or the Sostelo hacienda would have been useless? Was the King resigned to his fate? After the battle of Pack and Tote, he had even sent the rider Senora Hernandez had told me of to withdraw his men from the ridge.

Did his walking the desert with the Countess mean that he had lost his horse from our last fierce fusillade, and that he was confined to his boots for traction?

Yet I had known his resourcefulness for too long; he was most dangerous when counted out, and for that reason I did not trust the rumors. There was the possibility of truth, yes, but nothing was certain. I had even sent a younger group of Apaches with Captain Vale's last men on a reconnaissance of the hacienda near Sanderson. They reported that there was no activity near the place but that of the servants, that no herds of cattle were near.

So I was left with one thought—that the King still wandered near Los Alamos. I would return to my hut after nights and weeks spent in the brush, tired and hungry and stinking from old clothes and sweat, caked with the filth of riding, exhausted with hardship, the night shadows, the blaring days of sand and cactus.

There was one place the King and Countess might be, and I went to the hut of Tomas and Teresa. Teresa was sewing a dress for her expected baby. "Tomas, you and Teresa have never been on a train, have you?"

The dark eyes showed surprise. "No, senor."

"Get your best clothes together, and I will give you more money for clothes in Alpine. You will board the train and go to El Paso, then get tickets back to San Antonio. Do this for two weeks, back and forth. I want to know if the King and Countess are working their gambling games on the train, if that is the reason we have not seen him again."

All went well on the train, except that Teresa had her baby in the ladies' room a month early, perhaps due to the unaccustomed vibrations. She named him Taza, after an old Apache chief, and they came back three instead of two. But the King had not been seen on the train.

So it was all closer home now, very close. The King was still near, but with or without his men?

In spite of my constant riding, there was still time for long talks with my father in the plaza. One day while we sat on a bench with our chicos beside us, he said, "You have sent Zelina and Old Carlos to help Senora Hernandez and Euphemia with the don."

"Yes."

"Yet you will not call upon them yourself."

"They both understand why."

"It is odd, Colin, that a man will send his best fighters under Miguel, and his best house servants, to help people he will not call upon."

244

"I have said that both Effie and Senora Hernandez understand why I do not call. I will not go until I am called by Don Sostelo."

"Have you thought that perhaps you wrong others?"

"Father, I did not make this feud. It lived when first you met my mother. I was born into it, and I saw my grandfather die in a miserable shack where he had lived for my sake; when I came here, I made every possible overture to make peace with Don Sostelo, even offering him the waterhole. At every turn he has rebuffed me; he has raided this camp and caused the deaths of my friends; he has deceived me; in his pride he will never make peace, but he wishes me to humble myself again by going to him. For what? To beg? To beg for what? I have all I want."

"If you wished to see a man die today, who would it be?"

"The King."

"And next?"

"That hopeless man, Don Sostelo."

"And you say you have all you want?"

"Yes."

"You are not honest with me. More than anything in the world, you want Euphemia."

Coley O'Reiley rose and paced before the bench. "Do you think I do not know your provocation? I let vengeance rule me for almost the whole of your life. I know what I became inside, and what Quandaris, an innocent man, endured. I do not want you to become what I became. Senora Hernandez would give that entire ranch to see you set foot in her hacienda."

"Then you have been seeing her."

"Every day, Colin."

"Are you in love with her?"

"I would not say that, but I am attracted to her."

"So," I said.

"She loves you as a son. After having her and Euphemia stay at your hacienda and arousing their expectations, now you mistreat them terribly. I know you look after the material things, but not really what matters."

"A bundle of sticks," I said.

"What?"

"Nothing. Only something I remembered."

"I, too, Colin, want to see the King out of the way, but legally. I cannot see you become the manhunter I became; your treasure here is far greater."

Father Dore was herding a flock of geese into a pen.

"There is a loyal friend," I said. "It was he who buried Don Herrera. Let me ask you a question—Don Herrera did not like you, or did he?"

"He may have respected me."

"Effie is to me what my mother was to you. Before you married Mother—when you eloped—what would you have done had Don Herrera come upon you with his pistols?"

"To have defended myself and Violetta, I would have shot him."

"And you can understand my feelings toward the King?"

"I can understand them, yes. But if vengeance and hurt must be your guide, you will find many jacals where you will sit alone; your belly will cry from hunger, you will know the fear of famishing from thirst. When you are stretched face down in the sand, each wind and mirage will bring only dust. Your legs will be torn by thorn, one horse after another will die. All for one thing—vengeance. Ask yourself if it is worth it, with all the goodness that is here for the keeping. I see back down the path of years; your road is still ahead. Never take mine, Colin, I beg you."

Deputy Haymaker rode into the plaza; he dismounted, and led his horse to the watering trough.

Rising from the bench to stand beside my father, I said, "I must go with Deputy Haymaker now. Father, I will think of what you have said."

My father turned. "Thank you, Colin."

In spite of my determination to find the King, day by day the words of my father loomed larger and larger. The time came when words put themselves together as thoughts, and thoughts threw me into meditation. Combing some lonely stretch, with or without Haymaker, I would think suddenly of Los Alamos as I had first come upon it.

I remembered more and more Chujo, Meander, and Effie as we were then. I remembered the desolation of the waterhole as I first saw it, my mother's grave, the sand dune and the single rose bush. And Uncle Mike the day he had come with Old Carlos and my first herds of cows and goats.

Without knowing quite that I did so, when I was in camp for any duration, I found myself wandering the crazy quilt pattern of streets, looking in at this hut or another, remembering when this was built or that, or viewing the calm of the padre's church and graveyard.

I might pat a stump-tailed dog on the head in the Street of the Whistling Bones, and turn and look back at the splendor of the risen hacienda. I knew every part of the new Los Alamos very well, for no part of it had been built without my own sweat and grime, and sometimes blood of battle, for the blood and sweat of all of us had renewed it. And every day I became more conscious of what I owed those who lived there and who trusted me.

I would not yet admit it to myself, yet somewhere in my mind my father's words still lingered—must I give up all of this for vengeance and the King? My life was in every adobe brick of every hut, in every stone of the hacienda.

I was in this state of mind one day when I received a message from Senora Hernandez, who would meet me in the piñons tomorrow. But my choice had not yet been made.


Senora Hernandez sat on the orange ledge as usual; the vivacity and gaiety were gone from her eyes, and only a great seriousness remained.

"You have beaten me here again," I said.

"I had to come early—it is so important."

"The King?"

"No. You and Euphemia."

"What about us? Nothing has changed."

"Since you intend to search down the King, Euphemia weeps day and night, but still wears your ring. Colin, she says your marriage would end all the old wrongs, that something new would begin, but you must never become a man such as your father was with Quandaris."

"I have known the King too long; even before I knew him, he had formed my life. I intend to find him, just as Captain Vale did."

Tears in her eyes, the senora shook her head. "Colin, my love for you is the same I hold for Euphemia. Please think of her; I beg this for your happiness. You must not become a searcher, a killer, for revenge alone. Can you throw away all you have won so lightly, and hurt those who depend upon you? That is what you would do, Colin, should you persist."

Those had been my father's arguments; now they were the senora's, and I wondered if they were not almost mine, too.

But I said, "The King must be punished. Think of the ruins of Pack and Tote."

"And you would destroy yourself and Euphemia."

"I would come back to Effie."

"Would you? As what? Would she even want you then? Would you want her, after both your lives were wrecked? Some deaths I can understand, but not this from you. Believe me, I know, Colin. I have been hurt, too."

"I don't know all the answers, but only what I feel now that I must do. I suppose my father will see you tonight?"

"Then you indeed know more than I do."

Senora Hernandez rose. I helped her to her saddle; she turned her horse and left me in the piñons.

It was perhaps well that Haymaker and I rode out on our usual quest next day, our horses packed to the limit for a week's stay in the desert, for within a few hours the matter of the King was settled.

It had all begun when Haymaker said, "The way I've got it figured, about every candidate has the same number of votes. But

248

I was at Pack and Tote, and I've been campaigning in the Big Bend where the other candidates haven't come. Now as I see it, this district holds the balance of power." He cleared his throat and went on. "If I could do just that one big thing, I'd win the election."

"For your information, in the registration drive, we have a total of thirty-two who can vote. Women can't vote, of course, but they boss the men."

"That was why I was modest in showing my wounds," Haymaker said.

We heard a crackle in the mesquite, and through it ran Father Dore without his cassock, clad only in his underpants; he was so intent upon reaching some unknown destination he did not notice us.

"Padre," I called, "what is the matter? Why are you running?"

He stopped, his fat belly quivering, and approached panting. "The King," he said breathlessly. "The King caught me."

"The King?"

"Yes. He and the Countess. They were running through the brush when they saw me. I was on my burro on the Lord's rounds to the vaquero camps, and the King at the point of a pistol took my cassock and burro. Then he put on my cassock and mounted. He fired two shots at my heels, and here I am."

"You don't know why they were running?"

"No, unless they were discovered by the vaqueros. Far behind them, I could see horses starting in pursuit from a lean-to."

"Now," said Haymaker, stroking his chin, "which direction would you say the King rode on your burro now?"

The padre continued to pant. "I would say toward Sanderson."

"Here is my jacket," I said. "It will help cover you. Tell them at Los Alamos what has happened, and that we have gone on."

At a good clip we started our horses toward the King's hacienda. Here it was, the long awaited moment—the showdown.

Yet we had not gone more than a few miles, when stopping in the brush to listen better for some distant or revealing sound, we heard great shouts and laughter.

"Look at that *carreta*," Haymaker said suddenly, drawing his pistol.

The *carreta* and its oxen stood near a heavy stand of cactus. I gazed and drew also, and I knew it was the end of my search. The wooden-wheeled *carreta* had been completely poled in, sides and top, front and back, the poles tied together with rawhide. Within that cage a violent, red-faced man in a cassock shouted obscenities and danced about, stopping now and then to shake the poles.

That man was my quarry, the King.

Haymaker and I galloped in, our pistols pointed, and we pulled up in a crowd of mounted vaqueros and standing women and children, all in high merriment. The women all held pointed goads. A tall, thin woman, the Countess, sat in their midst straddleways on the padre's burro.

Now and then the King was goaded by a woman who had lost a husband or relative at Los Alamos; he squealed in despair and jumped about or held frantically to the poles with his fat hands.

"Colin," the Countess cried, "this treatment is inhuman. Stop it! It would be more merciful to shoot him." Tears streamed down her cheeks. I remembered other tears, icy tears which in the old blizzards were picked off her cheeks by the King. I saw laughing Padillo, my caporal, and asked, "What has happened?"

With much pride, Padillo twisted his mustache and said, "We found them in a senora's jacal where they had hidden since the fight at Pack and Tote. My senora had gone there to borrow a few frijoles, and found them armed and in Mexican dress. She did not betray herself, and said nothing until she came to me. It is good, is it not, Don O'Reiley?"

"In whose jacal were they found?"

Senora Sanchez stepped forward. "In mine, but the King always kept a pistol on me or my husband." Big-toothed, she laughed pleasantly and goaded the King again.

"Padillo, how did you capture them?"

"When they heard our vaqueros coming, they ran from the

jacal into the desert. Then we caught them, the King on the burro in the priest's cassock, and the Countess walking beside him. We built our cage on a *carreta* at another jacal, and are taking them to Alpine."

"Now, now," said Haymaker, biting into his plug and tapping the star on his vest, "I am the deputy here, and I am with Don O'Reiley. We also were searching for the King. He is in our custody now, so your responsibility is relieved."

"But, Don O'Reiley," Padillo said, "we wanted to take them ourselves."

"All who wish, may go, but the deputy is in command."

Haymaker said to the panic-stricken King, "In the name of the State of Texas, and Brewster County, I arrest you for the raiding of Pack and Tote and for the murder of one Captain Vale and of one Senor Maderas, also for malicious arson. There are other crimes I will bring against you. Now who will lead this *carreta?*"

"I, senor," said Padillo.

"Colin," the King cried, "they can't do this!"

"Someone give the woman a poncho or blanket for her shoulders," I told Senora Sanchez. "It will be cold on the desert tonight."

"Colin," the Countess said, "think of the many times we have been together."

"I am sorry, senora, but I have no say in the matter."

The King, goaded and hopping about in his cage, screamed to the Countess, "My dear, my dear, what have I done to deserve this? What can they prove against me? The first man to fire a shot in Pack and Tote was Colin O'Reiley, not I. Who even knows the exact spot where Senor Maderas went down? How could I be extradited? Who could prove anything?"

The Countess said gently, "Do not worry, Mr. Jarvis. All will come right."

Haymaker edged his horse toward me. He said in a low voice, "You've been too quiet about this. I think I know why. When these women tire of their sport and go back, I can slip some thongs and let the King out of his cage. He'll run, and you can plug him."

"A shot in the back."

Haymaker said, "It's customary—the flight of the fugitive, you know."

"No." I holstered my gun. "I have come to my senses. I wouldn't shoot that miserable man if he ran toward me."

Haymaker extended his horny palm. "I'm right glad to hear you say that. I never made that offer to anyone in my life."

And looking into his dog-like eyes, I believed him.

"Ready to go?" Haymaker asked the caporal.

"*Si*," Padillo said.

The deputy turned to me. "Your vote, Don O'Reiley?"

"Yes, and maybe thirty-one others. But on that old condition —when I send for you or a deputy, I want a man here pronto. This useless trouble must end."

Haymaker squirted his wad. "It won't be a deputy to come—it will be me."

The *carreta* pulled out, the blanketed Countess riding the burro beside it, the King jumping up and down in his cage like a monkey.

I continued to sit in the late evening among the shadows of cactus and mesquite and yucca. I could hear the screams of the goaded King, but the women would soon tire of their sport and return to their children in the jacals.

". . . can't prove a thing, can't prove a thing!" I heard the squeal from the distance.

Sunset came, and still I sat as one drugged.

A laden moon swung up in the east; stars breaking through a glimmer of white clouds were like lanterns, and the long shadow fingers of the tall ocatillo lay on the sand like writhing snakes.

And there were other sands—sands where I might have lain stretched flat in exhaustion among other ocatillo, my hands, my own fingers, groping endlessly for water.

And Effie, and Senora Hernandez . . .

A hell of a manhunter I turned out to be!

252

When I reached Los Alamos late in the night, I stopped my horse at my father's adobe. I dismounted and stood in the doorway.

"Awake inside?"

"Yes, Colin. I have stayed awake until you returned. Come in."

There was the flare of a match, then my father lighted a beeswax candle. I saw him sitting on the mohair mat and squatted beside him. "Any liquor here?"

"Tequila and salt and limes."

I could see something in his eyes as the light flickered on his craggy face, something he hoped for. After we drank, I said, "I am glad you and Senora Hernandez talked with me."

"Why?"

"I see what you meant. I think I did before, but I didn't know. I had my chance at the King today."

"When the padre came in, he said you would find him. Did you kill him?"

"I let him go. Haymaker has him."

Coley O'Reileys big hand grasped my shoulder. "What is really on your mind, Colin?"

"Tomorrow, I will send a message to Senora Hernandez, and ask if I may have dinner with her and Effie."

"I will go there in the morning. Could I take your message?"

"If you would. Will you go to dinner with me?"

"No. That will be your occasion. Will you see Don Sostelo?"

"Yes," I said.

# 19

When the ladies came down the circular stairway, as had happened so long ago, they were more beautiful than ever.

Effie came first; I awaited her at the foot of the stairs as before, but without Don Sostelo behind me. She was dressed in a shimmering gown of another cut, tight-waisted and long-skirted and her mother wore a similar gown.

Effie's head was high, as was her mother's; the thought crossed my mind again that they could easily pass for sisters.

I had left my cummerbund, coming simply as Colin O'Reiley, and not as an off-breed don of the Herreras. At the foot of the stairs, Effie extended her hand; I bent to kiss it; her mother's ring was still on the other hand.

"We are still engaged?"

"If you have time for such things." But Effie's smile was a happy one.

I kissed Senora Hernandez's hand in the honor due her. Our greetings over, we drew apart. I noticed the strain on their faces from the fatigue of constantly waiting upon the stricken don.

The senora asked, "Shall we go to the great room, or to the alcove?"

"If it pleases, to the alcove."

A flash of understanding showed in her eyes; she knew I did not wish to be reminded of the unpleasantness with the don in the living room on my earlier visit.

We seated ourselves in the alcove; Effie placed her hand on mine. "Colin, you look tired, and older."

"You can never know what the senora and my father saved me from."

Senora Hernandez said, "Your father told of the King's capture when he was here today."

"I wonder what I would have made of my life. What I would have given up—you, Effie, Los Alamos, to go through what my father did when he pursued Quandaris."

The impending death of Don Sostelo hung in the hacienda like a mist; our conversation was limited. The excellent wine brought by Carlos did not help.

A gong sounded on the floor above, and Senora Hernandez rose to go upstairs.

I asked Effie, who watched me curiously, "You told your mother the rumor that Don Sostelo headed the rustlers here? That the King was only his understudy?"

"I told Mother, and she asked Don Sostelo. He was stricken that she knew." Effie tossed her head impatiently. "You do intend to see him?"

"Yes."

"Did you know it is the only thing that will let him die in peace?"

"I did not know."

"He wishes greatly to see you, but do not be shocked when you see him."

"But why?"

"There is no flesh on his bones; he cannot talk. Only a few syllables come from his lips, but Mother and I have learned to make some small sense from them. Why have you waited so long to come? The real reason, Colin."

"You saw my grandfather buried. His death is why. Perhaps I am not big in heart at all. I don't know."

"We each lost a parent in the first Los Alamos raid, but we put that behind us. We must do so with this, then there will be only ourselves as we used to be."

"Shall we go up to the don now?"

"No. He is in a seizure, or Zelina would not have rung for mother. When mother comes down, we will have dinner, and by then he should have recovered enough to see you."

It was an excellent dinner with catfish brought from the Rio Grande, but none of us did more than nibble or occasionally raise a wine glass.

The beautiful senora glanced toward me suddenly. "How strange it is here now, as if I am no longer in my own house, as if none of it is Sostelo anymore. Herrera vaqueros tend our cows, the guards are yours, and the servants are yours. Your father gives advice and counsel. It is the ruin of an old world, Colin."

I said abruptly, "Shall we go upstairs?"

"If you wish."

I held the senora's chair, then Effie's. Together we moved up the wide red rug of the spiral stairway.

When I saw the canopied bed of Don Sostelo in a room of gilt and gold, with Zelina sitting close, I could not believe that the human wreck before me was the Don Sostelo I had known.

A coverlet was pulled to his chest, and over it his arms extended downward. But what a face, and what bone! It was only

256

a shrunken skeleton which lay in the splendor of the room, almost featureless except for the cruel beak of a nose.

As we stood in the doorway waiting for a sign from Zelina, Senora Hernandez whispered, "Colin, if you can, be kind."

Yet all I thought of was a bare shanty in St. Louis, and another aged man who waited for his last moment on earth.

Zelina motioned, and we moved forward quietly. I told the senora, "When you tell him I am here, do not use the words don or Herrera. Simply say Colin O'Reiley is here."

"There was a reason, Colin, for your not wearing the cummerbund?"

"Yes."

A weird sound came from the canopies. "Ah, ah?"

"What is he saying?" I asked.

"He knows someone is here. He is saying, 'What, what?' We have learned to understand some of what he says. Euphemia is better than I. Father," the senora said at the luxury of the bedside, "you have a friend to visit you tonight, Colin O'Reiley."

"Ah, ah?"

Zelina rose and placed her hands behind Don Sostelo's head, turning it toward us.

"Ah?"

"Your friend, Colin O'Reiley, has come to pay his respects."

"Oie Oilie?"

"Yes, father. He wishes you may soon recover."

With what happened next, I thought I was in a house of dementia. A gush of tears flowed from the old man's eyes. One would have thought, as they continued to flow endlessly, that he would have made some effort to wipe them away, but then I remembered that he had been paralyzed on one side, and that the paralysis might have spread to the other. He was incapable of movement.

He called my name, "Oie Oilie."

I took my handkerchief and wiped his tears. The fleshless mouth and throat struggled, but only gibberish came from his lips.

"He says he is dying," Effie said.

More gibberish.

"He says to you, God forgive him for what he has done."

I bent over the bed. "Don Sostelo, I bear you no ill will."

"Ah-me, ta-cah-o-Eumia-an-er-moer."

"What?" I said.

"Promise him that you will take care of me and Mother," Effie said.

Still bending, I said, "I will always take care of them. Do not worry, Don Sostelo. I love them both."

Gibberish again, ending with Ietta, Ietta.

Effie said, "There is no church here. He wishes to be buried at the Shrine of Violetta."

I could not help but glance at Julia Hernandez, who stood close to the canopies, her face drawn and hopeless. It seemed my very soul was torn from me, but I saw Effie's tense face and turned to the bed.

"Yes, Don Sostelo, you may be buried at the Shrine of Violetta. But I should go now before I tire you."

"Is-ing-or-gines."

Effie said, "Kiss my ring for forgiveness."

I took the wrinkled hand, and the fingers were like another bundle of old sticks I had held once, and I kissed the Sostelo crest, not in submission, but in pity. I dropped the hand back to the coverlet.

"Go with God," I said, and turned to the doorway.

Senora Hernandez and Effie followed. The senora said, "Colin, your face is as white as a sheet. What this must have cost you!"

I smiled, or hoped I smiled, for I was thinking of Don Herrera and my mother. "I will leave now, so not to keep you from Don Sostelo. I will be back tomorrow."

I had no sooner stopped my horse in the plaza when Miguel galloped in from the Sostelo hacienda.

258

"Don O'Reiley, Don Sostelo died soon after you left. They need you at the hacienda. Could you return?"

"Yes. Go to the stables and have two horses saddled. I will rest this one."

I walked to my father's hut. "Awake inside?"

"*Sí*, Colin."

"Don Sostelo has died. Dress, we must go back together. I must tell you, I promised he could be buried at the Shrine of Violetta. Do you object?"

"No, son."

That day we brought the body of Don Sostelo to the empty hacienda of Los Alamos. The body lay in state, cummerbund and all, but few came to view it.

Next morning, the don joined the dead in our graveyard.

Other things had happened in our county. When the election returns came in, Deputy Haymaker swept to a landslide victory in our section of the Big Bend, getting twenty-eight of our thirty-two votes. But even this small number, after the returns from other districts were counted and recounted, put Haymaker in the sheriff's office by exactly that. He was jibingly referred to in the sister towns of Alpine and Sanderson as the sheriff of Pack and Tote, although Sanderson was in Terrell County.

A week after the election, Haymaker stopped his horse in the plaza.

"Light and rest," I called from a gabfest with the padre and Meander and my father. Meander had been talking about a small hacienda he and Maudine planned to build on a rock ledge over-looking the rapidly filling bog.

Haymaker cleared his wad at one of Father Dore's geese; he climbed.off his horse and walked toward us. "Well," he said, hunkering in the general pileup, "you boys put me over and got Judge Howlett out, too." He stood up as if suddenly embarrassed. "I just wanted to tell you, Don O'Reiley, that I made you a campaign promise, and I rode down from Alpine just to reiterate

259

it. If you need me, send for me. A man can't speak more honest than that, can he?"

"I guess not, old friend."

Haymaker, under the weight of his new responsibilities, seemed to stagger back to his horse. Once mounted, he waved back. "Adios, gents."

Meander said, "There goes the most honest bowlegged man I ever saw."

Effie and I were courting again, and I said to Julia Hernandez at her hacienda, "I'm trying to establish credit in San Antonio. When I get it, I will have several sets of rings sent to Sanderson for Effie to look at."

"I don't need my ring, Colin."

"I don't think you do either," I said, and she flushed.

One day while Effie and I sat in the Chisos, she said, "Colin, why don't you write a book about us?"

"Us? Why us?"

"It wouldn't be just us—it would bring in all sorts of people."

"Not this vaquero."

"Don't you love me?"

"That has nothing to do with it. And don't try to work that woman stuff."

Effie became serious. "What I really mean is this. When I become an old woman, or while I sit waiting to bear Augustina and while you paddle Coley and Euphemia and the twins, I would like to pick up a book, and in all the happiness of our hacienda, whether we are young or old, be able to remember how frightened I was when I first kissed you on the *Mississippi Queen*, to know the sting of freezing snow and sleet in my face at Fort Smith; the morning the desert bloomed, and after our long trip, the arc of our first rainbow together. Then, after reading, I would look across the fireplace to the man I had loved so long."

I grinned. "You have a point. What is your title?"

"The Treasure of the Chisos."

"Why?"

"Like Lost Mine Peak, there was always treasure here, even if no one found it. But it is more than that, and someday you will know. You have always known, but the thoughts have not come. But you did find a pearl on the peak, and here is your dear little Effie beside you."

"Yes, if you would get that hank of hair out of your eye. You make me want to kiss it away."

"That's why I always leave it."

"Oh, God. I'll write your book, Little Treasure."

She put her arms about me and I forgot all about the book.


My father had said to me, "Colin, here is a little package I received from Mexico City. I hope you and Euphemia will like it."

I opened the small velvet-bound box and saw a beautifully matched pair of rings, a diamond in one which glittered and almost knocked my eyes out, and there was the simple elegance of a wedding band.

"But why?" I said. "I would have bought the rings."

"I have an old silver craftsman at my mine. I obtained the gold elsewhere, and the diamond from a friend in Mexico City. If Euphemia should not like these, I can have others sent up."

"What will you do when Effie and I are married?"

"I will go back with Quandaris to Mexico for a few months. I will sell the mine, and Quandaris and I will laugh at how we searched for and avoided each other."

"And you will not leave until after our marriage?"

"Of course not."

"And when you leave Mexico, what?"

"Quandaris will go study for the priesthood, and I will return here and try to help you, provided I may keep my same jacal."

"Could I suggest something?"

"Shoot."

"As long as you continue to advise Senora Hernandez, why don't you see if she will take the poor people beyond the camp for her empty jacals? It is called Poor Town there, and was settled by the peons who came from the brush to help bring Effie and Senora Hernandez here. It would help them, and her."

"I will ask her," my father said.

Effie and I were married at the Shrine of Violetta, but for me it was a day of utter torment. Everything, in spite of the careful preparations, had gone wrong.

The wedding would be formal in the Spanish tradition, or as formal as we could make it in Los Alamos. It would in part be secretive, with arrangements made by Miguel and Meander to have horses ready in Meander's hut at dark, so Effie and I might escape the wedding party for our honeymoon, and avoid the chivaree which we knew would follow during the night, for our white and Mexican friends would be there from miles around.

Effie and I had discussed our honeymoon, whether to take the passenger cars at Sanderson and go to San Antonio or El Paso. But there would be the long ride to Sanderson, with my uncle's shoot-'em-up and other uproarious cowhands making life miserable, and I was certain there would be plenty of peons and senoras participating in the revelry on a lesser scale.

"Our cave!" Effie said suddenly. "Who would think of our being there?"

So Miguel and Meander had stocked the cave for us, leaving the supplies under the watchful eye of Astabo, and we would have a ride in the darkness when we left Los Alamos. We had told our plans to my father and the senora, and they enjoyed the conspiracy as much as we.

"How long will you be gone?" my father asked.

"We will come back on the morning of the tenth day."

"Then I will wait and leave for Mexico after I see you again."

On the day of the wedding, the ceremony was set for four o'clock, but my troubles began earlier than that. The dress for the men—my special friends—was to be formal, which meant a black suit bought at Alpine or Sanderson. Some suits fit, and some didn't. Dr. Smedley's ancient cutaway looked well, and Luis Peinado's and Meander's and Guillermo's suits bad; those of my father and Uncle Mike were good; Tomas was handsome in his train suit; that of A. B. Champion, my lawyer, was perfect, but Sheriff Haymaker and Karl Steuben from Pack and Tote might have found better clothiers.

The wagons and carriages of our guests had come from fifty to seventy-five miles away on desert trails, and some good people had camped out on the way. The ranchers had their high boots shined; the women were big-bonneted and long-skirted. Each wagon was filled with progeny of all ages.

A gracious Minnie Barr had come—the heroine of Pack and Tote—wearing a black sack dress and a wide-brimmed hat which flopped up on one side and down on the other, surmounted by a nest of ostrich feathers.

Upon their arrival, the women went first to the genteel rooms of the hacienda; the men went for a snort at a bar set up in Pedro's old hut.

The first trouble of the day came from Miguel, my celluloid collar and black tie already getting tighter by the minute. I was sent for at the crack of dawn, when the wagons and guests were arriving, to come to the Street of the Whistling Bones. Already the village was being decorated, bright paper flowers everywhere, red streamers and colored rope blowing tail-out from the top of the squeaking windmill, and white-clad, black-eyed little flower girls practicing their tossing, while singing some chant or other near the depression.

A group of disgusted cowhands I had never seen before galloped in; they took the small boxes they carried to the springhouse. They left immediately, without even going to Pedro's bar for a drink.

I entered Miguel's hut. He stood in his black suit, fierce and awesome with his upturned waxed mustachios. "I have never worn a black suit," he said, "and I do not know what to do with this off-leg which keeps flopping. Should I cut it off, as I do with my work pants, or what?"

"Maudine or Teresa would double it back and sew it for you. Leave it on; you will look distinctive."

"Then you will carry my pants to them?"

"Yes, Don Miguel, give me your britches. It will be a pleasure to carry them through the streets of Los Alamos on my wedding day."

At noon the barbecue pits were opened, but I still had not seen Effie; she was in the hacienda with her mother; tradition, I thought. Then, while I tried to eat a bite surrounded by my gentlemen in black, a despairing clang sounded from the padre's church bell, then the entire scaffolding collapsed. I had meant to fix that thing for a month, but had never gotten around to it. The frantic little priest leaped and twisted his hands together.

"Very well, padre. Don't worry. Take off your coats, gentlemen."

Within an hour the scaffolding had been repaired and the bell rang again, although our work had been hampered by Father Dore's geese; one child of Uncle Mike's had opened the gate, and we had worked in a flurry of feathers, leaping this way and that as all the children in Los Alamos chased the geese. Then the geese chased the shrieking children.

One child was caught by a honking old gander while trying to escape beneath a barbed wire fence. A barb caught his dress and lifted it up. A fair target, the gamboling gander thought.

The frantic child ran to his mother in the plaza. "Gootie peck it! Gootie peck it!"

"What?" the mother asked above his screaming.

In full view of the uproarious plaza, the child bent, and pulling his dress above his pink, diaperless, and wounded bottom, pointed backward and cried again, "Gootie peck it! Gootie peck it!"

Haymaker's antipathy was explained to the guests, and just in time for more trouble.

The upper bolts of the windmill snapped, and the vane stopped

264

turning. Only a trickle of water came from the low spout. And with all these mouths craving liquid!

Karl Steuben had some old bolts in the back of his wagon. Off came our coats again, and Karl and his blowing beard and I climbed for water. At last we had a flange in place, and bolted it back, tearing out ground-up rope and ribbons from the clogs.

When the windmill catastrophe was over, Tomas came to me. "Senor, the people who are left at Poor Town—they, too want to be at the wedding. There will be the long line of the processional from the hacienda to the church when the senorita walks with your father. They wish to stand behind the people of Los Alamos for what you have done for them."

"Tell them yes, but they are not to bring presents."

Karl Steuben said, still heaving from his windmill climb, "It was that ribbon and rope that jammed the windmill." Just as if we hadn't known it!

It was two o'clock; I was as nervous as a cat.

During the day rancher after rancher, both Mexican and white, had tried to talk with me, but thinking of standing up with Effie at the ceremony and with all the rest which was happening, I had few words with them. One by one they dropped away, and sat with their drinks in the plaza, watching my wandering steps and laughing. Even the people of Los Alamos ignored me in my sternness and left me alone.

Maudine in a black dress came from the hacienda and spoke to Meander. He nodded, and followed her back inside. One by one my other men in black were summoned for consultation. I strode up and down the patio, left completely alone.

I needed rest; I went to my hut and stretched out on my mat; I was up in five minutes, stalking the patio again. Then a goat stampede upset the plaza.

At last my father came from the hacienda, grinning. "Tradition and getting to the church are two different matters. Some of the good ladies of the county decided that since Euphemia would be on my arm in the processional, how filled with sentiment the occasion would be if you followed with Senora Hernandez on your arm! I am afraid they have carried the day, and you will not have to wait at the church."

"Will it ever be over?" I said. "I've worn a trough two feet deep walking this patio."

"At the door of the church, I will stop with Euphemia, then your gentlemen will drop from the line and move to flank us."

Miguel came outside. He said, "I have ridden through hell with you, so I will walk with you through this."

Coley O'Reiley bent double with laughter. "You may come in now," he told me.

When I saw Effie that day for the first time, I knew the waiting had been worth it.

My father had gone down the corridor to the doorway of the ladies' apartment. Still standing there, he extended his arm inside; he moved a step backward, and there stood Effie.

She wore a lace headpiece and a fingertip veil of tulle; the floor-length gown was old lace over satin, embroidered in sequins; there was the long train. Somewhere, someone had secured a bouquet of miniature lilies of the valley, centered with an orchid. She held the bouquet closely.

At the sight of that lost flop of hair in that splendor, I was helpless. I followed my father down the long lane of visitors and flower girls in the processional to the church—the stone hut in which I was born—and for the wedding it had been decorated with white carnations.

As we marched, Senora Hernandez whispered, "My poor Colin."

"It's been a hard day," I said.

As we entered the doorway of the church, the solemn padre stood behind his altar. My gentlemen in black had gathered about, and sun-burned, weather-beaten white women and serious Mexican and white ranchers and old senoras were standing or kneeling.

And when the ceremony was over, I didn't know if I had

stood or knelt, or rode a pitching pony or a windmill. There was the tenderest of pressures on my lips, and through the clamor of well-wishers Effie and I walked back toward the hacienda.

Because some of the sentimental and deeply touched women began to weep, pressing their handkerchiefs to their eyes, the flower girl choir in its last chant began to break down and howl, and never in the history of the Big Bend or elsewhere did a wedding end with such caterwauling.

But it was a nice wedding after all, and as Effie and I walked onward as man and wife, I wished that some of our old friends could have been there with us.

We had a large table in the dining room for the traditional wedding feast, but first we must open the presents. For this we had set up smaller tables in the patio. There were presents of all descriptions—silver services, coffee sets, tea sets, a pair of pistols from Haymaker, spurs and rowels, and woven things for Effie.

My father had given us two twelve-branched candelabra, and Senora Hernandez two smaller matching ones; Miguel presented the leg bone from his hut, and Tomas an Apache sheath knife. Dr. Smedley had said, "I will give you nothing. Sooner or later you will call for me. That will be your present."

The people of Los Alamos had brought little gifts of dulces, trinkets, clay pots with our names painted and baked on, until at last the opening of gifts became more of a task than the wedding had been, and we went inside the hacienda.

Juan Garcia, a squat young Mexican rancher in a red sash, came toward me.

"Senor Garcia," I said, "I apologize for my rude treatment in not talking with you this morning."

Garcia laughed, showing his white teeth. "Senor, on the day of my marriage, I was so afraid I ran from the church. Someone looped my heels with a *pial,* and I was dragged back to the altar. Since that moment, I have never regretted my marriage. But to business. I have been chosen to represent our smaller Mexican ranchers; it is our declaration that in matters regarding decisions on range and water disputes and all the rest, we will abide by your word, so we may all live in peace."

"I would like to help, but only if all have agreed. But I do not seek this."

"They have already agreed, as I said. I do not mean to be presumptuous, but could you and your senora visit our casa someday —a fiesta?"

"With a catfish fry and a fiesta, we will assuredly visit you."

Garcia said, "Others wait to speak with you. We will talk later, and may you have every happiness."

The heavy table was now laden for the feast, but Senora Hernandez and Effie had drawn apart from the other women and stood at the wide door opening toward the patio. I had a drink of mescal with my black-clad gentlemen.

Effie left her mother and came to me; it was almost the first time we were to speak directly to each other since the ceremony. "Colin," she whispered, "two or three hours in leaving won't matter. Come look beyond the patio."

I followed her to the door and beyond the walls I saw all the faces, the patient and faithful faces of Los Alamos, and behind them the people of Poor Town.

Effie said, "Can't they move their own tables into the patio and share the feast?"

"I see," I said, "that I have chosen the proper mistress for Los Alamos."

I had expected Effie to smile, but her eyes filled with tears.

"Miguel," I called, "have the people move their tables from the adobes to the patio, even those from Poor Town. If you can, take the big table out, also."

At the end of hours of music and festivity, of marimbas and guitars and trumpets and castanets, the people joyful at their tables or dancing, Meander said, "Those two horses you got waiting in my adobe—it's hours after dark now, and they're sure making a mess of things. Now you two have got to get going."

Effie whispered, "I'll slip inside and change," and motioned to her mother.

268

"You will wear the black cape over the going-away gown?"

"Yes, dear. Meet me by Chujo's door."

In Meander's adobe the horses had indeed made a mess of things, but Maudine hugged Effie, then me. "I sho' wish you the best," she said, the baby squalling. "I do love you so."

Meander kissed Effie and extended his hand to me, his eyes serious, but at least part of his old grin remaining. "Good luck, cousin."

As we mounted our horses and left Los Alamos, the black cape flying, I said, "Effie, we're married."

"Yes, darling. Forever and ever."

Several days later in our roughing clothes, we sat on our ledge before the cave, gazing down at the lands of the Sostelos and the Herreras.

Effie said, "Colin, it's all over. The land is so peaceful."

"But it is still a hard land—as hard as three centuries ago, when the first of the old dons came. How would you like to take a trip on the *Dewdrop?*"

"And throw logs into a fire box? No, not on my honeymoon."

"About furniture for the hacienda—we could order it. But there are many good woodcarvers at Los Alamos, and I know of others. They could build a bed the way you wanted it, or a huge dining table or chairs in any style, and all from Chisos wood."

"I would like that, and to remember where each tree stood."

"Where did the flowers for the wedding come from?"

"Dr. Smedley knows a woman who keeps a greenhouse in Sanderson. He had the flowers packed in wet moss and sent down by two relays of cowhands at night, so they would remain fresh."

"I saw those cowhands. Imagine those gun-toters carrying posies across a desert at midnight. No wonder they wouldn't have a drink at Pedro's—they'll never live it down! But Doc had said he wasn't going to give anything, the old devil."

I had been looking through the padre's spyglass and handed it to Effie. "The little mesa near the piñons—what do you see there?"

"My mother and your father on their horses."

"Shall we go down to chaperone?"

"No, but I do wonder if they are serious."

"They have both had miserable lives. I would wish them every happiness."

We had spent much of our time exploring the deeper Chisos, finding new caves and echo places, and one morning when I came early from a cave, a hairy figure squatted outside.

"Astabo," I said, *"buenas dias."* I could see two glimmering eyes peering through hair.

"I saw you here yesterday. Today will be good for wandering. I know many secret places, low parks where the fantail deer play, and trickles that become small waterfalls where swallows dip in the spray, and mists where you can touch the tips of the rainbows. Would you and your senora come with me today?"

"I think we would like to go. Let me wake Effie."

I went back into the cave, and she sat up, wrapping a blanket about her bare shoulders. "Of course, we'll go," she said. "Has Astabo had breakfast yet?"

"Yes, three rattlesnakes and a horned toad."

There were other days in the mists with Astabo, and many times I looked at him and wondered. Had he known all that preceded the Battle of Pack and Tote? Who had really caused the extra guns to be placed on Luis Peinados's bar? Had Astabo even known my father would be there, or that I would be?

But one asked Astabo nothing, for there was never an answer.

In keeping with my promise to my father, on the tenth day Effie and I broke our honeymoon to return to Los Alamos. As we rode down the rocky trail from the last cave I asked Effie, "Would you like to visit your mother first?"

"Yes, it would be nice."

Senora Hernandez led us to the ornate living room. There was a strange radiance about her. Then suddenly I saw it.

"Senora, give me your left hand. Effie," I called, "come here."

Blushing, Julia Hernandez extended her hand. "Look," I said to Effie, "a diamond exactly like yours. What a master of duplicity my father is! He showed me only the one velvet box; he did not tell me about the other."

Senora Hernandez said, "Do you mind, Colin?"

I took her in my arms. "No, I am happy for both of you."

Then Effie and her mother were holding each other and weeping with happiness.

"This is no place for me," I said. "I'll go on to Los Alamos. I'll be back for Effie tomorrow."

Effie said tearfully, drawing away from her mother, "But why? Are you deserting me already?"

I kissed her gently. "You and your mother will want to talk, and I want some man-to-man talk with that father of mine."

At Los Alamos, I found my father and Quandaris seated in the plaza, their horses saddled and packed.

My father rose and said, "We thought you would be back about now. But where is Effie?"

"At Senora Hernandez's. The diamond I saw on a beautiful senora's finger there—you doublecrossed me nicely, didn't you?"

Quandaris laughed aloud, and Coley O'Reiley squirmed. Then he looked me straight in the eyes.

He said, "Colin, I could not tell you until I knew positively. But yes, I asked her to marry me. Do you mind?"

"As I told her, I do not mind. Effie and I are very happy for both of you."

"When I return from Morelos, you still promise my old hut?"

"*Si.* And after you marry?"

"We will live at the Sostelo hacienda, if that is what the senora wishes."

"It's quite a switch," I said. "Just too damn many O'Reileys on earth."

"We will stay at Mike's ranch tonight, then cross the border tomorrow."

I watched Quandaris and my father start from Los Alamos, the hunter and the hunted in their thorny chaps, riding toward the rugged line of the Chisos. Now and then, side by side, they laughed, the dust of their horses rising behind them.

How much larger the world had grown since first I came here!

I was tired, and tomorrow I would ride back to bring Effie home, but now I wanted to think. I walked down to the church and sat on the settle at the Shrine of Violetta.

The day Effie and I had talked in the misty mountains of the book she wanted me to write, and of the pearl we had found in our cave on Lost Mine Peak, she had seen things far better than I. She said that I had always known a certain thing, but that I did not know I knew, and that the thought and reality would come later.

And Effie had known all along.

Perhaps from all the centuries of war and hatred, there had lurked a greater treasure in the Chisos after all, and it seemed that somehow, someway, we would always be there together in the mists.

Father Dore waddled after his geese, and I smiled.

# ABOUT THE AUTHOR

John H. Culp, whose grandfather was member of the Frontier Battalion of Texas Rangers, under the immediate command of Jeff Maltby, Lieutenant Ledbetter, and Ed Seay, heard many of the incidents of his stories at his grandfather's knee. Born in Meridian, Mississippi, Mr. Culp has worked on ranches in both Texas and Oklahoma; and his varied experiences include teaching school, running a music shop, and serving in the Air Corps during World War II. His earlier novels, *The Bright Feathers, A Whistle in the Wind* and *Timothy Baines,* were hailed by readers and critics alike. The author makes his home in Shawnee, Oklahoma.

11 02